WHAT
DRA

And she had trolls. Marcia stared at the wall behind Borphis. Trolls! Or gnomes—whatever. She had never even had roaches. She looked furtively from side to side, moving only her eyes. There were no little creatures in sight. No pixies; no fairies with insect wings. Everything was, for the moment, perfectly normal. Just her and a demon from Hell, eating doughnuts.

Ace Books by J. Calvin Pierce

THE DOOR TO AMBERMERE
THE SORCERESS OF AMBERMERE
THE WIZARD OF AMBERMERE

THE WIZARD OF AMBERMERE

J. CALVIN PIERCE

ACE BOOKS, NEW YORK

This book is an Ace original edition,
and has never been previously published.

THE WIZARD OF AMBERMERE

An Ace Book/published by arrangement with
the author

PRINTING HISTORY
Ace edition/October 1993

ISBN: 0-441-01959-5

ACE®
Ace Books are published by The Berkley Publishing Group,
200 Madison Avenue, New York, NY 10016.
ACE and the "A" design
are trademarks belonging to Charter Communications, Inc.

PRINTED IN THE UNITED STATES OF AMERICA

10 9 8 7 6 5 4 3 2 1

I want to thank my agent, James Allen, for providing advice and encouragement, and my editor at Ace, Peter Heck, for his skillful work on the three Ambermere novels.

PROLOGUE

Ulda sat with her eyes closed. She had sat thus for a long time, her attention caught at first by the same tiny riddle she had noticed in the past. Within her realm lay a secret. Some elusive fold in the mantling darkness that blanketed her domain concealed a mystery. She had meant, this time, to track it to its source; to exert herself and root it out. Then she noticed a more pressing matter.

The sea. Long dormant, little more than a vast stagnant pond—now it was suddenly *alive*. She could hear it stirring, lapping at the muddy shore, encroaching slowly to dampen dust long dry. She let her memory drift back to an earlier age. Then, yellow water had reached from the edges of the plain on one side to the peaks and cliffs on the other. Long-oared ships had skated on the swells like giant insects. Gales had disturbed the sullen air and sent foaming surf to batter at the shores. But through the slow course of time, she had herself seen the waters recede, seen the swampy bottom dry and harden, crack and turn to fine yellow dust. And now, out of season, this dead sea began to rise.

She meditated long on the subtle turning of the waters until her reverie was interrupted by an unexpected disturbance. She dropped her thoughts of the sea and cast her vision far outward. Here was a burst of raw force, jarring in its unrestrained intensity. It took her some moments to trace her way back along the echoes of the shock, and yet some more to extend her sight to that distant place.

She found only a gorgle, a desert hunter, now a twisted corpse on a rock-strewn byway, broken like a victim of a stone-wight or a dreen. But that blast had come from no such, nor from a demon lord, nor yet from any Middle-Regions mage who might be wandering there. The heavy force she had felt, though naive, had come from a different order of power.

Who had intruded here? Who stalked the Lower Regions? When she felt the power being exercised again, this time with more control, Ulda moved her distant eye and found the source of the disturbance.

It was an interloper from the Middle Regions, a woman, attended, unaccountably, by a demon of the plain and pursued by an entire clan of gorgles. So many, so stupid; next to a gorgle, the dullest troll would seem a creature of lively intelligence. Had they been capable of understanding anything more complicated than hunger, the gorgles would have been running the other way.

Yet the interloper was not using her power to attack, but to withdraw. The crone strained to see past the woman's aura to the source of her strength. As the intruder was enveloped by the bordering mists, Ulda saw the glimmer of a ring. She caught her breath and strained to hold the vision to the very boundaries of the Middle Regions, but the view faded and she was left to observe the antics of the bewildered gorgles.

Still there was something amiss. The sorceress was gone, the demon with her, and there yet remained the feeling of imbalance, intrusion. She continued to search, looking for the source of her disquiet, but she could find nothing. After some time, she stopped her careful probing and cast the net of her perceptions wider. She would be patient. She would wait, and she would watch.

Borphis was elevated in his chair by a stack of phone books. "Pizza, huh? It's great. As far as I'm concerned, we can have this every day." A clump of cheese and sausage fell from the overburdened slab he held. He caught it deftly without taking his eyes from his hostess. "You know what would be good on this? Mushrooms." He washed down the rescued morsel with a swallow of wine. "Along with the sausage, I mean. The sausage is important."

Marcia nodded distractedly. The pizza was almost as big as the little demon, yet it seemed likely that, except for the two slices she had accounted for, he would eat the whole thing. She sipped at her wine. *Home.* She was safe at home. She hadn't been mauled, ripped, chewed, and digested by the gorgle. Her mutilated corpse was not disfiguring the landscape of the Lower Regions. She was in her apartment. Her library book was on the lampstand beside her chair. She was back in the world of credit cards and telephones.

It had been quite a week. Eight days ago the biggest problem in her life, aside from tedium, had been a stubborn spreadsheet at the office. Since then, things had been more lively.

First, she had been initiated, sort of, into a mysterious sorority of enchantresses. Then, on her very first assignment she had accidentally followed a mysterious old man out of one parallel world and into another, where enough bizarre things happened to her that being attacked by vampires, though it had held her attention at the time, now seemed nothing more than a minor incident.

She wondered what had happened to the old man. She was supposed to be keeping her eye on him. Instead, she was slouched in a chair drinking perhaps a little more wine than she should, while her charge wandered somewhere in the yellow wastes she had just escaped. At least she assumed that's where he was.

Marcia got up and went to stare out the window. Tomorrow she would have to locate the Sisterhood. She choked on her wine at the thought of checking in the Yellow Pages under Virgin Warriors. But she was being silly, she realized, beginning to laugh aloud. The listing would be Warriors, Virgin.

CHAPTER

·1·

It seemed he was always hungry. He remembered a feast. Wine rich and strong. Meat singed in a blazing fire. Maidens with flesh bare, their plump feet soundless on pale tiles. But no—that was not the feast. No logs smoked there, no hot fat dripped and pooled on that immaculate floor. That was some other place, a place lost in the tangle of his memory.

The feast. It was an ox, or else a pig, he wasn't sure. Wine from a cask, spilled like dark blood on a floor of stone. Jeweled goblets. The woman, just one, with long dark hair. No maiden. They had tipped the meat into the fire. The smoke had billowed, filled the chimney, hung like clouds in the rafters. Stung the eyes. They had smeared the altar with fat, stained it with wine. The priests were angry, shouting. Afraid.

The old man laughed. It had been cold there. It had snowed, and then the sky had cleared. He remembered the stars, like holes in the black night, hints of a burning heaven beyond.

Here it was warm. There were no stars, no night. No day. The rhythm here was long, the pulse infrequent. He turned his gaze to the yellow dirt at his feet. What had he forgotten? About the rats? And the little ones, the frail blood-drinkers? They were like the last pale flowers bending in an autumn wind. Weak. Dying.

He began to walk, rolling from side to side like a mariner. He

4

whistled. Some old tune he had heard somewhere. The sound died quickly in the yellow air. He clapped his hands together. Smiled to hear the melody in this place. There were words, he knew, that went with this tune, but they would not come to him.

The giant couldn't hear the piper. When was that? Was this the piper's tune? He listened to his own music, cheerful as it died by his ear. The piper, too, had been dead, and his song had been a sad one. A dirge for the Wendeling kings, upright in their tombs of stone.

He saw the torches in the wall. The cat, the giant. The woman with the ring. His daughter—something about his daughter. Why had she called him Father?

He sniffed the air. It stank, but not of flesh. No cook fire burned nearby. The giant was of Wendeling blood. They had dined at inns on fowl and pots of wine.

In the distance, through the yellow air, beyond the strolling pillars of mist, he could make out the far edge of the sea, now a dry basin, a desert, but with pools of yellow water gathering, cracks and fissures oozing, deep holes bubbling. The old man cackled, rubbed his palms together. He must whistle a chantey, then. A nautical air.

He looked up again into the yellow murk. Would hulls float overhead, casting watery shadows below? How high above this dust would they be suspended? When had he first thought of this? Dust and spiders. How soon would this be bottom mud, and what things would lurk here then?

Off to one side was a pool. As he passed, something disturbed the deepest water at the center. He heard a heavy splash, watched the water wrinkle and heave. He chuckled and went on, taking up the same old tune.

It was much later when he saw the fire, in the distance among a pile of rocks. He left the path and followed the wavering flames, the gouts of tarry smoke. What were they cooking, these hooded pilgrims bunched around their meager blaze? Something bony, and with little savor. A thing to toss in the soup, not roast on a spit like a prize ewe. A little hopping thing with stringy flesh, or something cold and fishy with smooth tough spotted skin.

When he got close, he hailed them. The hoods all turned and

peered as he approached. It was a dark company. They bickered over the meat they shared, drank noisily from the stoppered skin of wine he offered. This was no feast with fragrant smoke to rise to heaven. No drops of wine were scattered for the gods. When he did so, wetting their stingy fire with his libation, they hissed and drew back, turning their hoods from side to side in agitated consultation. The old man laughed, and passed the skin around again.

The last man spoke with a voice that sounded like glass breaking. "It does not lighten," he said, handing the wineskin to the old man.

The old man drank deeply before answering. "An ocean of wine," he replied, replacing the stopper.

When the meat was gone, the bones, picked clean, and cracked and sucked, were added to the dying fire. The old man sent the bulging wineskin around one final time, then tucked it under his arm and lay himself down among the rocks at a distance from the company.

The others, all but one, put their hoods together and whispered by the fire. The old man heard their voices as murmurous clicks and hisses, strangely comforting, as he drifted into sleep.

They talked on, keeping their voices low, but gesturing sharply with thin knobby hands like birds' feet that poked from the folds of their garments. Finally the one who had spoken last to the old man silenced the others with an angry gesture.

"We cannot agree," he said.

The others nodded, bending their hoods in unison. They turned to the silent one who sat apart.

"And so we must ask Mother." He stood. "If we kill him will the wine fail?"

Another spoke. "Or turn to blood?"

"Or run bitter, like blackroot sap?"

"Children!" hissed another. "If you shrink from killing, you must give up theft. We will dig for worms, and feast on maggot stew." He turned toward the place where the old man lay sleeping. "If you must fear, fear a living mage. One that may pursue you, and come upon you you know not when, or with what powers."

The silent one spoke without raising her hood, as though she addressed the dirt at her feet.

"He sleeps. Lift the wineskin from him gently. If he wakes, kill him."

For a moment, there was silence. Then all but she rose. Together they drifted slowly, quietly to the place where the old man slept.

CHAPTER
·2·

The inn stood high on a craggy pass, at the place where the sea road and the mountain road crossed. It seemed almost a part of the mountain itself, built of massive blocks of gray stone that looked as though they had erupted from the toes of rock that supported them. From the balconies and deep windows of the broad rear wall could be seen a dizzying view of the sea below. From the front of the inn, the mountain filled the eye, and seemed to lean over the roof as though it might at any moment fall upon it and crush it.

In fact, the inn had stood for years beyond the reach of memory, growing slowly larger and more misshapen as the whim or fancy of successive proprietors dictated additions and alterations. Somewhere beneath the accretions of the ages was the original structure, a sensible building of two stories, adequate for the shelter of such men and their beasts as had journeyed that way in times long past.

Now the original form was lost, the classical purity of line obscured by dormers and cupolas; here a mansard, there a tower in the mode of the Valley People. Inside were blind passageways, and staircases that ended at blank walls, as well as a maze of corridors that had ramified beyond the power of human mapmaking.

It was a widely held belief that at some time in the past, the inn had begun to build its own additions, growing like a living thing—a coiling monster of the ocean depths, or one of the giant snow-trolls said to prowl the icy wastes above the tree line. In the dead of night, lodgers often heard mysterious noises—the sounds of rocks being chipped to shape, then raised and fitted to cap an arch, or rolled to a place in some extending wall. Winches squealed, beams were wedged with heavy mallets, and many a traveler left his bed more tired than he had entered it.

The rain had begun at dusk, whipped on by a wind that grew stronger as the night deepened. Nonetheless, the three travelers who arrived well after dark entered the common room with coats scarcely dampened. The landlord had seen mountain men many times before, and paid little heed to the great hulking fellow who had to mind his head at the lintels. And the dark-haired boy was of no great interest, but for the graceful way he moved, rather like old Fillip in his youth, when he was known through all the towns for his dancing, long years before his joints had swelled and lamed him.

It must be the third man who was the magician. Little he was, and old, and dressed in fine clothes of close weave and marvelous colors. And some mage he must be, to keep dry on such a night. Might even be a wizard, but for the fact that wizards don't announce themselves. A wizard would come in drenched and shivering, more like, just to keep his secrets. Or would know to stay at home on such a night.

The landlord had many empty rooms. Travelers were not plentiful in winter. Back in the distant mountain kingdoms, the snow would not break till spring; in the lands below, the favored path of winter travel was the sea, where evidence of the season was rain, and winds that were often cool but rarely cold.

The three guests settled themselves near the fire and called for supper, but not until the giant had questioned him most particularly about the preparation of the meat pies, and given him to understand that they wanted his best wine, and were willing to pay for it.

"I'll call them strange, for certain," he told his wife after he had cleared their table and seen them to their rooms. "The boy scarcely ate—just some meat from the pie, didn't touch the turnips—and had no more than three little sips of the wine, that black red from way the back of the cellar. The oldster, he ate like a princess—tiny bites, and always dabbing at his mouth with the cloth. Then the giant, I thought he'd be good for three pies and a half a peck of turnips at least, but he ate like it was his second supper, then complimented us on the pies, he did, though he ate just one. He did all right by the wine, but it took him forever, holding it up to the candle, and sniffing at it like a pig hunting mushrooms."

His wife looked up from her kneading trough. "Let them pay, and I don't care if they grease their hair with the gravy and put the turnips in their ears. What bed did you give them? With that hill man, they'll need a big one."

"No, they each have one. They're in three rooms, and up top, for the old one to have windows."

"Well, lords and ladies, husband! Three rooms, and you're worried over their table manners." She began to count on her fingers. "The good wine, you say?"

"Yes, but while you're figuring, don't forget what I told you about how their coats weren't wet from the weather when they came in. There's magic with them for certain, so watch your fiddling."

"It's not fiddling," she murmured without looking up from her counting. "Anyway, if they're too grand for one bed, they're too grand to miss a few pennies."

At midnight the house was silent, but for the rain that still fell, and a faint tapping, in some distant corridor, that sounded like a mallet nudging a chisel or driving a wedge. A traveler passing in the dark might have missed the inn entirely, back from the road wrapped in black shadows, except that at one window, high beneath the dripping eaves, there flickered the faint light of a single candle.

Alexander sat just at the edge of the candle's wavering glow. The logs in the fireplace were smoldering beneath a layer of ash, and radiated a comforting warmth that cheered the corner, if not the entire room. He was still and silent. He might have been a corpse propped up in a chair, though the delicate pastels of his silk shirt and ascot were anything but funereal.

A log snapped and settled in the fireplace. A flame rose for a moment, sending shadows to dance along the walls and floor. A very attentive listener might have heard a small answering noise, like an echo, from the shadows at the far side of the room. Alexander raised his eyes from the floor and watched the rain against the window. Outside, the night was filled with the noises of the weather; inside, he sat in an island of peace and silence.

He smiled faintly, almost imperceptibly. Although he was in a world where time was measured by the sun and the seasons, yet the minutes ticked away just the same. He raised his hand to brush back a wisp of gray hair and leaned forward in the chair.

"You must come into the light where I can see you," he said. His voice was thin and whispery.

The room was silent.

"Come. Don't make me impatient. You've had enough time."

Again he was answered by silence. He turned his head slowly and stared into the shadows at the opposite end of the room.

"Not your house." The voice was rough, and pitched low.

Alexander shook his head. "No. Not my house."

There was a rustling sound from the shadows. "Something wrong. The stones . . . something . . ."

"I know. It's very odd. I'll come back someday, I think, to investigate." Alexander looked up at the ceiling.

"No. Your house is good. You belong there."

A dark form moved in the corner. It raised up and floated along the wall. Alexander watched as a man almost as tall as Breksin, but impossibly thin, drifted around the bed and slowly approached. He was pale, and dressed in tightly buttoned clothes of pitch black. He moved like a person walking underwater, lifting his knees high with every languid step. The light from the candle caught his eyes. They were yellow.

Alexander rose carefully from his chair and went to the mantel. He poured from a pitcher into a pair of deep slender cups.

"They have a wine here that's almost black. Most unusual." He slowly approached the ghostly being and handed him a cup, then returned to his chair. "You may sit, you know, Fildis."

Fildis sat. He perched himself on a stool, bending like a folding knife, with his knees against his chest.

Alexander sipped from his cup. "Try the wine. I think you will find it good."

"I will not lie to you."

Alexander nodded. "Still, I wish you would drink. You always do at my house."

Fildis raised the cup to his lips. When he lowered it, his narrow smile bared teeth that were curved and sharp. "Always a gracious host," he said. "Even away from home." He turned his yellow eyes to the wine. "The spirits from your cabinet are better, though." He raised the cup again.

"There were disturbances," said Alexander. "Here, in this Region. Now they are gone. I called you to ask only one thing. No riddles this time, nor will I keep you long."

"The disturbances here are in this house. They have awakened something in the roots of the mountain."

Alexander put his cup on the floor beside his chair. "But that is simply local, like a haunting."

"Not ghosts. Mountain things."

"I understand. What I seek is something else."

Fildis looked into his cup. "I know nothing of these matters. You must ask some lord. Why do you speak to me of these things when you can summon even the great Rhastopheris?"

"Not summon. Rhastopheris I call. Sometimes he comes. But I dare not call him here, to a place not sealed."

"Well, I am only Fildis, and must come when summoned, but I know little of the Middle Regions."

"But what of your place? What of the Lower Regions?"

Fildis turned and watched the rain at the window. He emptied the cup. Alexander rose silently from his chair and brought the pitcher from the mantel. Fildis held his cup as Alexander poured, then sipped again.

"Pools of water gather in the desert. Deep holes bubble. My lord's castle looks out now on a *pond*." Fildis curled his lips. "Soon we will be an island." The yellow eyes sought Alexander's. "Some say it was the old man."

Alexander looked sharply at his guest. When he spoke, his voice was even softer than before. "Tell me of the old man," he said.

"I know only that he passed."

"Was this a necromancer?"

Fildis smiled a toothy smile. "No. Your pardon, necromancer, but this was some Power—a potent being." He paused to sip again from his cup. "It is said that in ages past a sea filled the great valley where my lord's castle stands. Some say the sea is coming back. My lord says he will not permit it." The demon stared into the fireplace and began to laugh, softly at first, and then louder and louder, until the sound filled the room. Alexander began to raise a cautioning hand, then turned abruptly as the door from the hallway opened.

A dark-haired youth slipped in quickly and closed the door behind him. Fildis froze in mid-laugh, staring at the intruder. He tore his eyes away and turned to Alexander.

"Necromancer! I have your cup in my hand. You are pledged—"

"Be still," said Alexander without taking his eyes from the door. "You are in no danger." He rose from his chair to address the young man.

"Egri. What is your business? Why do you disturb us?"

Egri took his eyes from Fildis. "My business is to see the giant safely to Devlin, as you know. I disturb you when I hear the laughter of a demon." He looked around the room. "Is this place not bad enough? Must you raise the Lower Regions?"

"Fildis will be gone soon. I am only asking him some questions."

Egri looked from the demon to the necromancer, then turned and left without a word.

The demon stared at the door. "You know what he is?" he said. Alexander nodded and returned to his chair. "They are dangerous," Fildis continued. "He is not bound to you; you cannot control him."

Alexander smiled. "I have my powers," he whispered.

"Yes," replied the demon, "but you cannot see him as I do. If you could, you would not be so certain. I am from the Lower Regions; you are a man of these worlds. Yet you and I are more like each other than either of us is like him."

"I am sure you are right, Fildis, but I am more interested in the old man. You did not see him yourself?"

"No. I know only what I have told you. I can tell you what I believe, though."

"What is that?"

"I believe my lord will drown in his castle." The necromancer and the demon laughed quietly together.

"You see," Fildis said. "Tell me when you ever heard this Egri laugh."

When he was alone again, Alexander went to the window. The rain had stopped, the wind abated. He stared out at the night. Now what did he know? Breksin was on his way to the pirate stronghold of Devlin for reasons that didn't concern Alexander. Egri was accompanying him. As far as he could tell, their relationship to the old man was incidental and unimportant.

It was the woman, Marcia, who was the key. She had followed the old man, Father, they all called him, for lack of any other name, from another world of the Middle Regions. Though she was but a novice, she wore a ring of great power. She had only an imperfect understanding of her mission, but she was doing her best to follow the orders of her Sisterhood.

Alexander had left Marcia at an inn four days ago. They had hoped one of them would find Father. Now it seemed that Father had crossed to the Lower Regions.

And what of the desert sea? If Father was causing momentous upsets in the Lower Regions, was it not reasonable to assume that he had been the cause of the signs and portents that had brought Alexander so far from home? He thought of his house, high on a cliff above the ocean. Maybe he had come too late. He smiled. He would gladly go back home.

He pictured the climbing roses on his garden wall, his quiet rooms, the fog that so often obscured the sea below. Breksin and Marcia had both said the old man was out of his wits, that his talk had the character of delirium. And yet it seemed he possessed vast powers. Egri said nothing of him, whether because that was what he knew, or because he was willing to say no more, Alexander did not know. But if he was gone, none of it mattered. Alexander would not enter the Lower Regions just to satisfy his curiosity. The preparation required was too strenuous, and still there would be dangers.

He returned to his chair. So, he had come all this way for nothing, leaving his studies, the comforts of his refuge. Now he would have to return to Ambermere, cross from there to his own world, and then still be faced with crossing the continent. He sighed. It almost made a shortcut through the Lower Regions seem appealing. Almost.

He pulled his thoughts from quiet mornings in his garden. Before he returned, there were one or two things to be done. First, there was the matter of Marcia. Though she evidently had substantial powers of her own, she was, after all, a novice. She had been carried into this world by Father's magic. When the old man did not appear, she would wait at the country inn where Alexander had left her, so his first chore was to return to her. From there they could journey to Ambermere together and cross to their own world.

A happy thought occurred to Alexander. He had invited

Marcia to visit him someday, to look in his books for answers to some of her questions, and to meet Rhastopheris. She could come with him now. It would be interesting to have a house guest. He cherished his refuge, but it was, he realized, lonely, even gloomy sometimes. He supposed that was why he called demons to talk and play at riddles. He shook his head sadly. Just another lonely old man looking for company. Still, the idea of inviting Marcia was a good one. For the time, it seemed that she was separated from her Order anyway. A few days more—a week or so, perhaps—wouldn't make any difference.

Alexander got up and went into the dark corridor. Egri's room was next to his, a reflection, he supposed, of how little trust the youth had in necromancers. He raised his hand to knock, then thought of how Egri had entered his chamber. The door was not latched. Alexander pushed it open. Inside, the embers cast a faint glow from the fireplace. He peered into the shadows. The bed was piled with blankets and cushions, but the young man was not in it. He took a step toward the far wall, but there was only darkness and an empty chair. After seeing the demon, Egri must have gone to stand watch in Breksin's room. Alexander turned to reach for the door, then started at the sight of the young man, sitting cross-legged on the bed.

"Oh. Sorry, did I waken you?"

Egri looked at him in silence.

After a moment, Alexander went on. "I wanted to tell you I am leaving."

"Tonight?"

"Yes. If I leave now I can reach the inn by dawn."

"You have learned something of the old man, then."

Alexander nodded. He sat down in the chair. "He is gone." He peered through the darkness at the dark eyes of his host. "Back to the Lower Regions."

Egri's expression did not change. "Breksin will be disappointed. When he saw your tricks—chilling the wine, keeping us dry in the storm—he began to hope you might help him in Devlin."

"But what could I hope to do?"

"Nothing. Nor is there anything that Breksin can do. When he considers it, he will see that if things go wrong, he can hope for nothing more than revenge. With my help, he might free the prisoners from a cell, but how to escape Devlin?" Egri leaned back slowly until he rested against a pile of cushions. "What will happen, will happen."

In a few minutes, Alexander returned to his room. He put his few belongings together and made his way quietly down the stairs. As he began to open the outside door, he heard a faint sound from below, like something large and heavy being dragged through the cellars far in the back where the inn was built against the mountain. He listened for a moment, then went outside.

He stood in the entryway for a time, preparing himself, eyes open, staring sightlessly into the night. There was a momentary disturbance of the air around him as it seemed to coalesce, so that the little gray-haired man in the pastel clothing was hidden from sight. The shimmering air wavered, then moved into the night and was gone.

CHAPTER

◆3◆

On the morning after her escape from the Lower Regions, Marcia sat in her bedroom thinking about all that had happened to her in the last nine days. How to unravel the complications? She had now, it appeared, participated in so many strange events, had acquired a history of such a surrealistic complexion, that the most amazing adventures had come to seem perfectly normal, if a bit intense.

Marcia's life had not often been disturbed by intensity. She lived alone, had worked in the same office for fifteen years, and had begun to suspect that the pattern of her existence was not likely to change. Even her unusual talents, which she was inclined to view as quirks—her ability to see auras, her sensitivity to unspoken communication—had become predictable and ordinary. Auras either confirmed judgments she would have made without their help, or else reminded her of the discouraging difference between appearance and reality. As for her mind-reading skills, they were too slight to be of any use, though they occasionally caused her to suffer hurt feelings or embarrassment that someone lacking the gift would have been spared.

But embarrassment and boredom had not been her biggest troubles lately. Last night, just after she had made it back to her apartment with her mind still full of the nightmarish horrors she had escaped, she had begun to doubt her sanity. Then she discovered she had not returned alone. Borphis, once she noticed him, proved that either she was sane, her perceptions accurate, or else she was so hopelessly lost in hallucination and fantasy that there was no point in worrying about it.

She smiled and stretched lazily. This morning her head was clear, she knew exactly where she was, and the Lower Regions seemed very far away indeed. She had not forgotten her guest, nor any of the unsettling events that had occurred yesterday, but she felt herself to be solidly grounded in the moment and in this particular place. She did not fear that she would find Hell in the next room—only one small devil.

A few minutes later, Marcia, wearing a blouse and slacks, came into the living room with a cheerful smile on her face. She had been thinking that it was a pleasant novelty to have a house-guest. It was also a pleasant novelty to wake up in her own bed among her own things, but that, she had figured out, was at least partly because the trappings of her familiar life were illuminated by the drama of the past week.

The pillow and quilt were in a pile on the love seat, but Borphis was not in the living room. Marcia looked toward the kitchen. Could he be making breakfast? Did demons cook? Marcia had entertained few houseguests, and only one who had insisted on cooking. Early in Cousin Ellie's memorable visit it had become clear that she thought of herself as a sort of Caucasian Aunt Jemima. Every morning she had made stacks of "multi-grain" pancakes that had the heft of horseshoes and the consistency of something that should have been fed to animals with more than one stomach. Marcia sincerely hoped Borphis was not standing on a chair at the stove rustling up some breakfast specialty from the Lower Regions.

As she crossed the room, she noticed her purse lying open on the floor. She hurried into the kitchen. No demon. She went back to the living room and looked behind the love seat, then in every other place where a three-foot-tall gnome might hide. Were demons fond of tricks? she wondered. Was Borphis being impish? She recalled the sight of little Borphis lifting and tossing a boulder the size of a dishwasher and shuddered to think what form impishness from him might take.

Marcia went so far as to check under her bed and in her closets. She even peeked into the hamper. A one-bedroom apartment offered only so many hiding places—even for a little man three feet in height. She made one more pass through the rooms, going from one to the other in a methodical way that would not allow her to miss anything, nor permit a mischievous demon to slip past her. Once or twice she thought she saw something out of the corner of her eye, but when she looked, there was nothing there.

He was not in the apartment. Marcia opened the door and looked up and down the hallway. When the elevator chimed, she pulled herself back inside and closed her door. This was no time to run into an inquisitive neighbor. She went to the window, opened the drapes, and tried to figure out what to start worrying about first. When she happened to notice her aura in the daylight, the problem of what to worry about was solved.

Every color had changed. She looked more closely, distrusting what she saw. Last summer after she had been given the ring, her aura had changed, had taken on a cast that had exerted a subtle influence on all the colors. Now another cast had been superimposed. Sometime since she had last looked, her aura had become one that, had she seen it surrounding someone else, would have frightened her.

She sank into a chair by the window to stare at the eerie colors that clothed her, but her reverie was interrupted by the sound of the door opening. Borphis entered. He was carrying a large white paper bag.

Marcia bounced up from her chair. "Where have you been?" she asked, speaking at a pitch normally reserved for climactic moments in coloratura arias.

Borphis regarded her calmly. "I think we ought to move," he said, closing the door behind him. "I had to go five blocks just to get doughnuts." He took some bills and coins from his pocket and handed them to Marcia.

Marcia took the money without taking her eyes from the demon. "You went out?" Her disbelieving gaze shifted to the bag beside him. "For doughnuts?"

"I got hungry."

Marcia's eyes settled on him in an astonished stare. "But you're a demon. You can't . . . I mean . . ." Marcia stuttered to a halt, then started again. "How can you just walk around on the streets?"

Borphis shrugged. Marcia looked at him carefully. Actually, the only thing terribly unusual about him, besides his pallor and his yellow eyes, was his height. He didn't have horns, or obvious fangs. When she thought about it, she realized that he was by no means the strangest-looking person to be seen on the streets of the city. He would just be taken for a particularly ill-favored and oddly dressed little boy. The people at the doughnut shop probably hadn't given him a second glance.

Marcia made a pot of coffee. No matter how good the tea had been, richly aromatic and laced with cream you could float a spoon in, she had thought about black coffee every morning while she was away. She poured two cups, and carried them to the dining room. Borphis was sitting at the table, elevated in his chair by a stack of phone books with a pile of doughnuts in front of him.

"I want you to try something," she said, inserting a cup among the pastries.

Borphis glanced up from his doughnut. "Oh, coffee. Thanks."

Marcia sat down with a quiet sigh. She closed her eyes to shut out the sight of Borphis and his hoard of doughnuts. A nagging dream-image from last night floated at the edge of her consciousness. She remembered being able to *see* the relationships between her world and the others she had visited: the enchanted woods on the mountain, Arrleer, Ambermere—even the Lower Regions. She had suddenly understood the relationships in concrete terms. The places she had visited were simply occurrences, or manifestations, of a certain kind of permutation, or combination of . . . harmonic energies. . . .

Marcia opened her eyes. How quickly words could deflate an insight. Using language to explore her intuition was like trying to build a sand castle with cinder blocks.

She had just looked up from her coffee when she saw something move near the love seat. She turned quickly, but there was nothing, or nothing more than a hint of a passing shadow. So now she was jumping at shadows. It wasn't really surprising, she thought; she had a right to be a little jittery. After the things she had been through, it was a wonder she was willing to leave her bed, let alone function, although her ability to function, beyond dressing and making coffee, was only a supposition so far.

It was while she was in the kitchen pouring more coffee that she was visited by another memory from last night. She remembered opening her eyes and seeing, not the ceiling over her bed, not the shadowy forms of her bedroom furniture, but a vision of points and lines against a background of deep black that had an

impossible quality of luminescence, as though darkness, if suffi-
ciently profound, possessed a paradoxical power to radiate light.

Last night, half-asleep, she had found the vision no more trou-
bling than any dream image that might come to her in the small
hours. Now, recalling it, she recalled as well the sunrise she had
seen a few days ago. The strange old man they called Father had
touched her ring. When he did, the sun, the distant mountains,
the clouds, all had become flat and colorless, like the blueprint
of a sunrise.

She glanced up at the light fixture in the kitchen ceiling. One
of the bulbs must have burned out, she concluded. The illumination seemed suddenly pale and wavering, as though provided by
torches set in the wall. "That would be a nice touch," she
murmured as she turned the light off.

She had overfilled the cups, and was concentrating on balancing them on their saucers when she noticed the small person dis-
appearing into the hallway from her living room. Her immediate,
unreflective assumption was that it was Borphis, though the
clothes were wrong. There was no wrinkled jacket or battered
hat. For a confused moment, she tried to figure out how Borphis
could possibly possess a change of clothing, and anyway, hadn't
she made it abundantly clear that he was not free to just go wandering off whenever he happened to feel like it?

Borphis was still seated at the table. Marcia stopped abruptly,
staring, then looked back at the hallway.

"Who was that?" she said, trying not to shriek. Her thoughts
raced. Was she going to be responsible for an infestation of demons? This had to be connected with Borphis, or with their escape from the Lower Regions. Had her apartment become a
vestibule of Hell?

Borphis was swallowing a doughnut. "Looked like a cellar
troll to me, only a lot smaller. More like a biggish hearth gnome,
but," he said, glancing around the room, "you don't have a
hearth. In fact I've been wondering about—"

"A what?" Marcia was no longer concerned about her tone of
voice. She looked down at the cups she was carrying as though
she had no idea where they had come from, which at the moment
was true.

"You know," said Borphis, wiping his mouth with a napkin,
"one of those big sooty trolls that—"

"Just wait a minute," said Marcia, interrupting. She walked to the table and put the coffee down. Not a drop had been spilled. She sat, and fixed her gaze on Borphis, noticing, against her will, the abundance of powdered sugar that had fallen on his vest and jacket.

Marcia tried to focus her thoughts. "A hearth troll," she said.

"Gnome," said Borphis, looking up from his doughnut. "There's no such thing as a hearth troll."

Every once in a while Marcia found herself wishing she had been blessed with a talent for profanity. This was one of those occasions.

"Is that so?" she replied evenly.

"Sure. A good thing, too. Just think what it would be like, living around trolls. For one thing, they're kind of clumsy, and," he added fastidiously, "they're really not very clean."

"But gnomes are?"

"Yeah, they're okay." Borphis put his doughnut down and looked at Marcia quizzically. "Why are you asking me, anyway? I'm from the Lower Regions. Gnomes, trolls, elves, whatever, belong to the Middle Regions. You should know more about them than I do."

Marcia looked startled. "You mean that thing, whatever it was, belongs here?"

"I don't know." Borphis shrugged. "You sound like you never saw him before. Isn't he one of yours?"

"One of my what?" asked Marcia in a weary tone.

"You know, uh, dwellers, or whatever you call them here."

Marcia shook her head vaguely. "Probably," she said. "He's probably one of mine."

Marcia ate a doughnut slowly without tasting it. She sipped at her coffee distractedly. All the time she was away, she had been wishing for a cup of strong black coffee. Now that she was back, all she could think of was the wonderful tea she had been served at the inns and taverns. Coffee had an aroma that was bracing and enticing, but tea, she now realized, had a *fragrance*.

And she had trolls. Marcia stared at the wall behind Borphis. Trolls! Or gnomes—whatever. She had never even had roaches. She looked furtively from side to side, moving only her eyes. There were no little creatures in sight. No pixies; no fairies with insect wings. Everything was, for the moment, perfectly normal. Just her and a demon from Hell, eating doughnuts.

She choked back a rush of laughter. "What," she said, trying to look like a person talking about something perfectly sensible, "do these gnomes do, exactly?"

"The usual, I guess," said Borphis. "Steal earrings, mix up socks, stuff like that." He glanced at Marcia's ring as she reached for her coffee. "Of course, they wouldn't do that around you."

"Because of the ring?"

Borphis looked perplexed. "I'm getting confused," he said apologetically. "You walk alone through the Lower Regions, blow up the nastiest gorgle in the valley by waving your hand at her, then bring both of us here without using a Passage, and without any spells or jumping around or anything. It's pretty obvious you aren't a conjurer, so I have it figured out that you're connected with the Upper Regions, but then you act like you've never even seen a gnome before." He looked down at the table. "Do you mind if I eat this last doughnut?"

"Go right ahead." Marcia lifted her cup and drank, then scowled at it as she lowered it to the table. When she thought she saw a furtive movement by the window, she followed it with her eye. There was nothing there ... except, there was *something*—there, just by the lamp ... where she couldn't see anything. She squinted and tilted her head. It was like trying to see around a corner.

She stopped squinting and made herself relax. Since getting her ring back from Father, she had become good at concentrating. She let her thoughts fall away and drew her attention to a focus.

What she saw by the window was movement. She saw nothing move, and yet, somehow, saw the movement itself, as though a quality could be seen independent of the object that possessed it. This was of course impossible, but Marcia was doing it anyway, which she found perplexing.

Intensely conscious of her ring, and its connection to what she was seeing, she pushed at her perspective, at the visible spectrum itself, until she began to see a trace of color moving past the curtains. She skewed her vision more, making small, unconscious motions with her ring hand. The colors were becoming more substantial; she tilted her view even further, feeling the shift in the spectrum, then stopped as she became aware of how odd everything else looked.

Marcia could make out the details of her apartment—the furniture, doorways, even the curtains at the windows, but everything seemed shadowy and insubstantial. Only the auras were whole and solid, including those she hadn't expected to see. In the kitchen doorway were stripes of primary colors in the form of a person smaller than Borphis. And by the window, just in the shadow of the tall bookcase, she could see intertwined blues and greens, a pair of them, slender and fluttering like little flowers in a breeze.

Except for the auras, everything was in shadow, devoid of color. It was like looking at a faded negative from her mother's old photo album. As a child, Marcia had liked to pull the curling negatives out from behind the pictures and look at them, holding them up to the light. She remembered giggling at the tiny black smiling teeth and the halos of absent hair. Then, if you turned the shiny side away, and held the negative up to the lamp just right, you could see the image the other way around—white teeth, black hair; eyes whole, not hollow and dark.

Unlike the eyes that stared at her from across the room. Marcia peered at the shadowy form, surrounded by no aura, of an old woman dressed in a shapeless gown. Marcia thought of the ladies in her mother's album, buttoned and posed, immobilized in black and white, but did not recognize the negative image that watched her from her bedroom doorway. Not a family ghost then, she thought, with surprising calm. Mother would not approve. It would be more fitting if it were the shade of Great-grandmother Mibsey come to see that Marcia was keeping the sideboard polished.

Marcia regarded the specter with an unsympathetic eye. Enough was enough. If she was to socialize with a ghost, let it be either one that is invited, or some family member with a claim on her concern. The melancholy expression on the old woman's face was touching, in a remote and abstract way, but basically it was irrelevant. Marcia knew that she had merely to walk the streets of the city to find the living in misery. If the dead had sorrows, she could only suppose that she would learn of them soon enough.

She turned her attention to the ring. She had been using it without any knowledge of the forces involved. Now she began to have an inkling of what its powers were and the paths they followed. Banishing the ghost, for instance, would be no more difficult than sweeping a cobweb from a corner. And no more urgent.

She found she did not have to make an effort to return her perspective to its normal state. She allowed it to happen in the same way she could allow her mind to clear. It was as though she had quite literally tilted the spectrum, and had only to let it settle back into its accustomed position.

When she looked, the ghost was gone. She saw a hint of motion by the kitchen door, but no aura, nor any blues and greens by the bookcase. She glanced down at the ring, then folded her hands on her lap.

"What?" said Borphis. He looked at the half-eaten doughnut he was holding. "You said I could have it."

Marcia looked around the room. They were, to all appearances, alone.

"I beg your pardon?"

Borphis put the doughnut down. "You tell me to go right ahead, then you give me this really funny look."

"You didn't see the ghost?"

"Ghost? I thought we were talking about a doughnut." He looked around the room. "All I see is those window sprites, and that kitchen thingie . . . wait . . . no, he's gone now."

Marcia sipped her coffee and watched Borphis finish the doughnut.

"So," he said, wiping his mouth and dusting the sugar off his fingers, "what next?"

"Good question," said Marcia. She looked at the demon suspiciously. "Unless you're talking about a snack."

"Me? No, thanks. I couldn't eat another bite."

Marcia got up and went to the hall closet. Borphis sipped his coffee and watched as Marcia put on a coat.

"We going somewhere?"

Marcia looked down at the little man. "I am. Do you want to go out in this weather again?"

Borphis shrugged. "If you're from the Lower Regions, you don't get cold," he said. "We're built different than you are—a lot tighter." He set his coffee cup down out of the way and held out his arms. "Try to pick me up."

Marcia was in no mood for games, but she didn't want to be rude. She approached the little demon reluctantly and made a halfhearted attempt to lift him from the chair.

She might as well have tried to lift a piano. This little man

who came to just above her waist when wearing his hat must
have weighed at least two hundred pounds. Borphis pushed himself from the stack of phone books and landed on the floor light
as a cat. He looked smug until he remembered he had left his
coffee out of reach on Great-grandmother Mibsey's mahogany
sideboard.

To Marcia's relief, they made it down the elevator and out of
the building without running into anyone she knew. She was in
no hurry to find out what sort of lame improvisation she would
end up blurting out to introduce Borphis, who did, after all, look
a bit odd. Even the cab driver gave them a suspicious stare as he
pulled over to the curb. All the way downtown he checked them
in his mirror every few seconds. Since Marcia was a person who
had always tried to arrange her life so that she would remain inconspicuous, she was especially sensitive to this sort of inspec-
tion. Of course, she reminded herself, if the driver became too
annoying, she could always blow him up or, for all she knew,
turn him into a duck or a lobster. One thing that was quite clear
was that the ring had virtues she had not explored.

She had the taxi drop them off at the place where she had met
Annie nine days before. After taking a minute to get her bearings
she set off confidently to the nearest intersection. As they waited
for the light to change, she looked down at her little companion,
standing calmly at the curb within inches of the rush of traffic.
She recalled the denuded landscape of the Lower Regions. Rocks
and noxious vapors had provided the only scenery. She leaned
down so she could talk to Borphis without shouting.

"You don't seem very impressed," she said.

Borphis peered up at her. "Huh?"

Marcia looked around to see if anyone could hear her. "The
buildings, the cars and buses, the lights. How we got downtown.
You just rode in a"—Marcia gestured helplessly—"horseless car-
riage."

"I did?" Borphis thought for a moment. "What's sless?"

"What?" Marcia noticed a woman watching them warily out
of the corner of her eye. She looked like a middle-european
peasant in a Dracula movie. Marcia pictured a mob with torches
and pitchforks.

"Sless," Borphis repeated, raising his voice to compete with
the traffic.

"Never mind," said Marcia, darting a glance at the woman. Borphis began to protest. "We'll talk about it later," she insisted in an urgent whisper.

They crossed with the light, and walked down a less busy street. At the next corner, Marcia stopped.

"Now," she said. "About my question: I didn't see any elevators or taxicabs or electric lights when I was in the Lower Regions. But none of this seems to surprise you, or even get your attention." She looked around at the parked cars and neon signs. "Don't you have any questions? I mean, we're walking on a sidewalk. Stepping off curbs. Dodging trucks. This isn't exactly what you're used to."

Borphis scanned the neighborhood politely but without great interest. "This is all just surface," he said. "It's temporary, like fog. In a way it's almost invisible. It's like noise—you hear it, then it dies." He looked at Marcia's ring. "I know I'm not like one of you," he said, "but I can see what's real."

Marcia looked around uncertainly. "Okay," she said, "but what about doughnuts?"

"No, thanks. I'm really not hungry."

"That's not what I mean. How did you know about them? I didn't notice any doughnut stands in the Lower Regions."

"Well, for one thing, there's more to the Lower Regions than you saw, and anyway, the doughnut is an Idea."

"Huh?"

"Sort of like a universal concept."

"Doughnuts?"

"Right."

This was starting to sound very much like the kind of conversation in which it would be important to know the difference between Platonism and Neoplatonism, so Marcia decided to drop it.

They walked in silence for twenty minutes or so as Marcia tried to retrace the route she had followed with Annie last week. She had a good sense of direction, she thought, but she was not having much luck finding the house they had gone to. The blocks of brownstones she did find were nothing but rows of indistinguishable houses.

Marcia had never been fond of cold weather. She felt every little gust of wind that came their way, and couldn't convince herself that Borphis, dressed in clothes that were as inappropriate for the weather as they were unfashionable, wasn't being turned to ice. When they came to a small coffee shop with steamed-up windows, she went in gratefully.

They took seats away from the other customers, who all seemed to be acquainted and were talking about the weather. When Borphis climbed up onto the stool, the counter came almost to his chin. Behind it were trays of doughnuts displayed in glass cases. He craned his neck to look at them, then glanced up at Marcia with a puzzled expression. He looked back at the trays unenthusiastically.

"Listen, about these doughnuts. I'm not really very—"

Marcia ignored him and ordered two black coffees. The waitress gave Borphis a funny look when she put his down in front of him.

Borphis tasted the coffee and frowned up at Marcia. "We didn't come all the way down here for this, did we?"

A stiff gust of wind rattled the door. Marcia wrapped her fingers around the hot mug, grateful for old-fashioned restaurant crockery even if it could have been a bit cleaner.

"No," she said. "I'm looking for the place where my life started getting complicated."

"You're looking for a demon here, in the Middle Regions?"

Marcia looked around nervously. "What do you mean?" she asked in a soft voice.

"The one who marked you," said Borphis, looking at her cheek.

Marcia raised her hand to the little scar next to her eye. "No," she said, "that happened last summer when I got the ring. But after that, things got back to normal. No more demons." She looked around to make sure no one could hear her. "No witches, no magic. Then last week a woman with a ring like mine took me to another—place—in the Middle Regions." Marcia paused and looked into her coffee cup distractedly, as though she could see pictures there.

"We got separated and I ended up following an old man who didn't have an aura. He led me—took me, sort of—to the Lower Regions, and then I ran into you."

Marcia looked up. Borphis was staring intently at a tray of doughnuts.

"Really," said Marcia. She looked for the waitress. "I thought you weren't hungry."

When Borphis didn't answer, Marcia followed his gaze. On the third shelf from the bottom was a tray of dumpling-shaped doughnuts bursting with pastry cream. It occurred to her that she had not had much for breakfast. Maybe a doughnut and a cup of tea . . .

She saw something move, or thought she did. She leaned forward and stared harder, at the same time using her ring to make a slight tilt in the spectrum. As she watched, a three-fingered hand snaked out from behind the shelf. It hovered just above the fat little doughnuts, reaching down here and there to pinch or prod. It wavered indecisively for a moment, then plucked one from the tray and withdrew so quickly that Marcia wondered if she had imagined it. She stared at the empty spot in the ranks of the pastries for a moment, then shook her head and turned away.

"I don't know," said Borphis when they got outside. "A pastry elf, maybe? You understand, I'm guessing now."

Marcia wandered the likely neighborhoods for as long as she could stand the cold, then spent a small fortune cruising around in a taxi before giving up and having the driver take them home.

They picked up a carry-out lunch on the way, and managed to get back to Marcia's apartment without running into any neighbors. After having a luxurious bath, Marcia made a quick trip to the store. Last night, after their spectacular escape, she had called out for pizza. Tonight she would be a better hostess. Cooking was not one of her talents, but she knew she could manage steaks, baked potatoes, and salad. When she was picking out the wine, she thought suddenly of Breksin. Where were her friends now? she wondered. Were they safe? Was Breksin able to dine according to his standards?

Dinner, predictably, was a huge success. Afterwards, working on the theory that there was nothing like going all out, she served cognac. Borphis was gratifyingly impressed. "You can smell that stuff all over the room as soon as you pull the cork out," he said.

Marcia left Borphis happily absorbed in the spirits, and went to bed with her library book. She resolutely put all thoughts of adventures and other worlds out of her mind. She was, after all, basically a very down-to-earth person, despite having a demon in her living room.

She tried to get interested in the thriller, but couldn't. Espionage, betrayal, intrigue, narrow escapes—it all seemed so improbable and unrealistic. Marcia closed the book, turned out her light, and went to sleep.

CHAPTER

·4·

Lord Rand, chief adviser to King Asbrak the Fat of Ambermere, stood in the shadows at the end of a long, chilly corridor and gazed out beyond the palace walls. On the avenue there were lights at every window, smoke poured from every chimney, silhouettes played across the curtains of every tavern in sight, but no one braved the wind and icy rain, no pedestrians wet their boots in freezing puddles, or tried to tiptoe beneath the dripping eaves.

How very excellent, thought Rand. Despite the efforts of the king, the evening was not to be cluttered with foolish speculations and pointless chatter. Ambermere was famous for the mildness of its winters; the inhabitants were not accustomed to wet cold that knifed through their cloaks. Inclement weather like this would be sufficient to excuse the astrologer from attending the king.

Astrologers! It was bad enough that the king insisted on consulting Remeger on matters in which his advice could make no difference. For the king to send for him with the intention of discussing matters of state was one more of the plentiful instances demonstrating the romantic credulity of the monarch.

Asbrak's world was filled with excitement and mystery. He was convinced that secret practitioners of every occult art filled his capital and padded about on errands of deep unearthly import. Meanwhile, Asbrak's imagination populated the taverns and cafés with spies whispering the secrets of kingdoms, conversant with every intrigue, and united in labyrinthine networks of conspiracy. It left, Rand was often tempted to point out, few ordinary citizens for the innocent pursuit of mundane business—baking bread, weaving cloth, keeping inns. If everyone was sending furtive glances, slinking around corners, and lurking in shadows, then the advance of commerce must be merely incidental to the real business of the populace, occurring more or less by accident, tangled in a web of deeper purposes.

And as the king's view of the world resembled that of a boy lost in childish fantasies, so did many of his actions. Rand was sure that as soon as the weather improved, Asbrak would be rummaging in the closet of disguises he maintained for the purpose of passing unrecognized among the populace. It seemed never to occur to the king, who boasted the largest belt size in the kingdom, and whose rotund silhouette was represented on the signs of every merchant and tradesman in the city, that his unmistakable bulk could not be successfully disguised. Nor did any of his subjects ever do or say anything to disappoint his fancy. The citizens of Ambermere expected foibles from the royal family, and few generations of Asbrak's line had disappointed them. If the king imagined that he could go among his subjects with his anonymity intact, how much to be preferred was that to many of the notions to which royalty was susceptible.

Rand closed his eyes momentarily and pictured the triple-length sash and jaunty cap the king had worn on his last outing. He had watched from the very window at which he was now stationed as the king seemed almost to fill the avenue, the upper half of his body swaying gracefully above the choppy, stiff-legged awkwardness of his gait. Rand had watched until Asbrak was lost in the crowds, resolutely making his surreptitious way to the nests of intrigue he was convinced were sheltered in the waterfront taverns.

Rand shook his head and turned from the window, sending a departing glance down the empty thoroughfare. A man, bareheaded and slender, slipped from a tavern door and dashed across the cobbled way, picking his legs up high and dodging puddles, all the while holding the collar of his jacket at his throat with clenched fists, as though by doing so he could keep the rain from wetting him. When in a moment he had disappeared through the door of another tavern, the scene was so still that it seemed to deny that anyone had just that moment passed. The only movement to be seen was lamplight playing against the windows, and the rain that spilled from the eaves and ran in the gutters.

Except, Rand noted with surprise, a wavering mirage two crossings away. He watched, half turned from the window, waiting for the illusion to dissipate. Instead, the shadowy form became slowly more distinct, until it resolved itself into the figure of a pedestrian. Rand squinted through the falling rain. The person was approaching at a steady, unhurried pace, and instead of trying to keep to the lee of the buildings, was walking in the middle of the avenue, rather like a ceremonial procession, but one consisting of a single participant.

As the lonely figure on the avenue grew closer, a thoroughly unwelcome thought formed itself in the adviser's consciousness. Might this be, not some wandering fool who didn't know enough to come in out of the rain, but the astrologer, faithfully obeying the summons of the king? Rand leaned forward into the deep windowsill until his nose nearly touched the glass. Surely even Remeger would not be so foolish. No one would, excepting perhaps a philosopher, the actions of which category of citizens Rand had found to be particularly resistant to anticipation. One of Ambermere's most eminent insisted that time did not exist, a proposition Rand had often wished he could believe. No doubt another could be found who had convinced himself that rain did not exist, and who would arrive on a night like this in squishing shoes, sodden to the skin and denying he was wet.

It was with a feeling of profound relief that Rand noted successively that the pedestrian was much shorter than the astrologer, and was dressed in feminine apparel. As she drew closer, he could see that the woman was wearing only a hat and an ordinary cloak of a sort that would offer no great protection from the rain. Rand was on the point of ringing for a footman to go outside and fetch the poor creature, but as he reached for the pull, he saw her leave the avenue and enter a tavern.

Now the street was truly empty, and promised to remain so, for a gusty wind had begun to blow, and the rain was falling ever harder. No citizen of Ambermere was likely to brave such weather. Rand had in his youth lived in a climate not so temperate as that enjoyed in the lands that ringed the Great Sea. The winters of his youth had been characterized, not by the occasional chilly drizzle, but by hip-deep snow that forced all work and travel to cease. Here in Ambermere, a heavy rain achieved the same results.

Rand turned from the window and, not without a quiet sigh, set out in the direction of the king's chambers.

He found his royal employer watching the rain from a deep-silled window that overlooked a courtyard.

"You missed an excellent capon, Rand," said the king, revolving himself from the window to face his adviser. "The cooks truly outdid themselves. I hoped to see it tempt your appetite. You pick too much, you know. The body must have fuel; it cannot burn air." The king crossed the room at a sedate and dignified pace. The fact that his long robes hid his feet made it appear as though he were advancing on a trolley. "Why, even I," he said, coming to a ponderous halt, "with my strict habits of restraint, was persuaded to indulge myself a little."

"I regret that I missed it," said Rand, who didn't. Once at the king's table, one did not leave until the king had finished, and even at Asbrak's alarming rate of consumption, a brace of fat capons was not a snack that disappeared quickly. Rand had been dining with the king for more than twenty years, and had no recollection of a meal in which Asbrak had failed to detect compelling evidence that the cooks had outdone themselves, persuading him to abandon the "strict habits of restraint" that he imagined to regulate his behavior, unaware that no one else had ever been able to detect evidence of their existence.

"But you ate something, surely?" said the king, an expression of genuine concern on his face.

"I sent to the kitchen for a plate, my liege."

Asbrak's face brightened. "Then you tried the capon after all?"

Rand shook his head. "I'm afraid not, Your Majesty. Just some bread and soup."

The king seated himself laboriously in a heavily reinforced chair piled with cushions. "Really, Rand," he said when he had caught his breath, "I wonder that your flesh persists. I believe if it were not for those pastries you allow yourself with your morning tea you would simply dwindle away, until one day we realized that you hadn't been seen, and a thorough search could discover nothing more than your empty clothing piled somewhere in a drafty corner."

A sudden gust rattled the windows, and for a moment the two men watched the heavy rain flinging itself against the glass.

"Remeger will not come tonight," announced the king.

"No, Your Highness."

The king sighed. "I had hoped to learn something of the princess and her party," he said.

"Must I remind Your Majesty that Remeger is the astrologer who selected the day for the departure of the princess? Did he not inform us that every sign promised a safe and uneventful journey back to Felshalfen?"

"Rand, you are too literal minded. Besides, had they left on some less propitious tide, something worse might have happened to them."

"Very well, Your Highness, but as we already know that your daughter is being held for ransom in Devlin, what more can we hope to learn from a perusal of the heavens, however skillfully conducted?"

The king looked shocked. "But, Rand, we must find out what their situation is. We know the hour the pirates came upon them, and where. With those facts, it is possible to examine the heavenly aspects that governed the unfortunate events. I have asked Remeger to plot the fortunes of the princess, and Hilbert and the others, of course."

"So we may hope to learn from the astrologer whether the kidnaping occurred at a favorable moment?"

"Precisely," said the king. "And that will tell us, you see, if they are being treated with due respect—if they are being well fed, served the proper wines, things of that sort."

The king shifted his position in the chair and stared at the ceiling contemplatively. "And then there is the matter of Rogan. By tomorrow or the next day he should be in Devlin, among our enemies without their knowledge." The king brought his eyes back to his adviser. "And of course, we have Reffex carrying our offer to the pirate, old what's-his-name."

"Flanders, Highness. Black Jack Flanders."

"Ah, yes. Anyway, Rogan and Reffex will both be there, not to mention Breksin. You don't suppose his presence will interfere with my plans?"

"Your Highness, I am certain that what Rogan will be able to accomplish will be completely unaffected by the presence of the royal cellarmaster. And I have instructed Hebbick to watch for him."

"Ah, so that's why you insisted on sending Hebbick. I couldn't imagine what possible use he could be. Still, Breksin must be nine or ten feet tall; Hebbick won't miss him, I'm sure."

"I believe Breksin's height is closer to seven feet, Your Highness. Even so, he is too large to be overlooked."

"And you say he was a soldier?"

"In his youth, Highness."

"But then, how is it he serves us in the cellars rather than as a member of the royal guard? You know, Rand, he would be a most impressive figure on the parade ground."

"I think perhaps, Your Royal Highness, the cellarmaster's military experience did not include extensive training in the art of the parade. No doubt he is happier caring for Your Majesty's wines and cheeses. Besides which, how would Your Majesty replace him? How could we find another with his knowledge of food and drink?"

A look of genuine distress crossed the face of the monarch. "But what if some evil befalls him? Should we not dispatch someone to look after him?"

Rand refrained from pointing out that there was scarcely anyone at court who might be trusted to look after a lapdog. He simply smiled his diplomat's smile. "I believe that Breksin may be relied upon to look after himself, my liege. I am sure he will be back to us soon enough. In the meantime, his assistant seems to be managing."

"Yes, now that you mention it," said the king with a comfortable smile, "he sent us a very nice wine to accompany the capon. It had an aroma that was . . . bountiful." The king pushed himself from his chair energetically and moved to the window.

"Now, Rand," he said, looking out over the puddles in the courtyard. "If this infernal rain will ever stop, I will be able to pursue my own plans. I mean to take steps." He turned and fixed his adviser with a determined stare. "I will go into the town at the first opportunity. I have already alerted my valet. I want all my disguises to be in readiness."

"Your Majesty, I really—"

"You may not realize it, Rand, but there is an art to selecting a disguise. It takes talent. Inspiration. It is not every monarch, I can assure you, who could pass among his subjects undetected."

Rand pictured, once again, the massive form of the king draped in one of his "disguises." It sometimes occurred to Rand to wonder if the position of chief diplomat and adviser in a kingdom so pacific that the monarch could wander unprotected among the populace offered any test to his abilities. But then, if the royal daughter continued to be abducted semiannually, he would have plenty to keep him occupied.

"Rand?" The king was favoring him with a beady look.

"As I have so often remarked, Your Majesty is a master of disguise."

The king beamed, then sent a worried glance toward the storm. The wind was growing ever more insistent, howling in the eaves. "You don't suppose it's like this at sea tonight, do you?"

"It may be, Your Highness. But I would point out that the captain and his schooner have been sailing in winter weather since the reign of your father. Surely he has encountered rough seas in his day. I believe we may rely on the seaworthiness of his vessel."

CHAPTER
·5·

From time to time during his long career as a magician, it had occurred to Rogan the Obscure to ask himself why it was that there seemed never to be a spell to do the things he most deeply wished to be able to do. He wondered if the wealthy generally found riches and property to be as much a disappointment as he had found magic to be. He did not know of a spell to strengthen or otherwise improve wine—at least none within the range of his powers. That was more a wizardly sort of magic. He could wield no spell to deepen sleep or improve the amorous capacities. Those matters were in the province of witches.

Regrettable as these deficiencies were, at the moment his greatest regret was that he knew of nothing less violent than poison that would still the tongue of Count Reffex. Why, Rogan had been asking himself for days, would fate play him this trick? Surely any unexpiated sins of his were being amply punished simply by the fact that he was at sea, a helpless victim of the whim of King Asbrak the Fat of Ambermere. At any moment, the ship could do what he had been expecting it to do since the bitter moment he had made his reluctant way up the gangplank. Rogan had a remarkably clear mental image of the placid, uncaring swells of the indifferent deep closing forever over the decks he paced by day and night.

But no, drowning was not to be a harsh enough punishment

for whatever gods he had offended. He must be ushered to the dripping jaws of death by Reffex, whose conversation was unceasing, and devoted entirely to the subject of his own importance.

"Of course, the king has always relied on me." Count Reffex helped himself to another cup of Rogan's wine, careless of the drops spilled by the rolling of the ship. Rogan watched them gather and course to the edge of the table, then run over the lip and onto the tilting deck. The sea was always perfectly horizontal; the ship never was. This mystified Rogan. He knew there must be moments when the deck was level. He watched for them, but they seemed never to come.

"Aye, she rolls," was the captain's closest approach to an explanation.

Rogan watched Reffex drain his cup. He was sure there must be a poison that would produce a temporary paralysis of the organs of speech. Would Hannah the witch deal in such things? he wondered. Not that it mattered. The witch was ashore with all the other sensible people in creation.

He hadn't known that Reffex would be on the ship until the morning of their departure. "Urgent business for the Crown," the count had informed him in a stage whisper, glancing quickly at the officers and crew near enough to hear his announcement. "Of the utmost confidentiality. Matter of extreme delicacy." He had waved indifferently in the direction of a short, stout man who had followed him aboard. "You know old Hebbick, I suppose?" Rogan scowled at old Hebbick, who was younger than he. "Rand," Reffex paused grandly and allowed the name to resonate, "Rand insisted that I have someone to serve as an assistant. Of course, in this sort of business I prefer to work on my own, but still, the judgment of the chief adviser to the king is not to be ignored. As I said to His Majesty—when we were conferring in private—best to let old Rand have his way."

Rogan did what he had been doing for five days—stared at the expanse of water and wished he were back in his tower where he belonged. He was a palace magician, not a traveling wizard or mage to break the chains of captives and spirit them out of their dungeons.

Not that Rogan supposed the royal hostages were actually chained, or imprisoned in some gloomy cavern with damp walls and scuttling rats. Undoubtedly the princess and her consort were safe and dry in pleasant surroundings that did not dip and sway, sipping chilled wines and waiting for their ransom to arrive.

Travel on the high seas had proved to be as terrifying as Rogan had expected. What he had not expected was that it was at the same time tremendously boring. Even without the aggravation of the unendurable Reffex, the voyage would have probed the extreme reaches of tedium. An odd quality, Rogan thought, to be found in surroundings that bore such a heavy tint of terror.

The hour of the evening meal eventually arrived. Rogan chewed his way through the ship's biscuit with an air of relentless determination and ever-growing feelings of resentment against his sovereign employer. He pictured the table at the palace. Asbrak the Fat would doubtless be working his way through his third helping of roast goose or boar or whatever succulent meat perfumed the great dining room. The long table would be littered with great split loaves fresh from the hearth, and trays of steaming yams and other winter vegetables would be replenished as they were emptied by the enthusiastic diners. It was only the endless pitchers of wine that Rogan had no cause to regret; he had seen to it that his own supply was carted to the quay the night before his departure, and had personally watched the ewers being loaded onto the ship.

Rogan scowled at the meat, ostensibly lamb, lying on his platter in a pool of congealing gravy. It was tough and stringy and broadcast, Rogan thought, the unmistakable whiff of goat. Not a young one, either. Old, and boiled since breakfast. Until this voyage, it had never occurred to Rogan that he might be, by some standards of judgment, a gourmet. Meals he generally considered an interruption. He ate but one a day, when he put in his obligatory appearance at Asbrak's table. Otherwise, he had found that for a man of his many years and spare figure, a supply of wine throughout the morning and afternoon was sufficient to sustain him.

When dinner was over, Rogan, having no place better to go, went onto the deck. The ship was rocking less than usual; the sea looked like dark glass under the cloudy sky. Rogan acknowledged grudgingly to himself that if the ocean had its terrors, it had its beauties as well. If he ever got back to the peace and safety of his tower in the palace at Ambermere, there might, he supposed, come a time when he would recall his ocean voyage with more gratifying emotions than sheer relief.

Rogan was drawn from his thoughts by the snap of the sails overhead. He was alarmed by every noise the ship made, convinced that any of them might well be heralding his doom. In this case, however, all that was being announced was the awakening of the wind. Rogan peered at the rolling sea apprehensively. A drop of water struck his cheek, followed by another on his forehead. The sudden breeze was warm, and smelled of rain.

"As if there's not enough water," he muttered.

The ship began to roll more heavily. Rogan gripped the rail and stared into the night. He tried, as he had every day since boarding the ship, to remember the feeling of standing on solid ground, of looking at a world that did not ceaselessly tilt from side to side. The tempo of the rain increased. The sun had gone down, so he sensed rather than saw the clouds rolling in low above the masts. A heavy gust of wind flung a stinging mixture of salt spray and rain into his eyes. Rogan shook his head resignedly and carefully made his way below.

Reffex envied Rogan his quarters—had grumbled about his own accommodations for the first day or two—but in fact the magician's private cabin was no more imposing or comfortable than a good-sized closet. The bed was no bed at all, but a bedroll on the bare planks of the floor. "That way you don't fall out, you see," the mate had told him.

Rogan actually disliked nights aboard ship even more than the days. He spent the hours of daylight on the foredeck, either seated in a wobbly chair that rocked with the motion of the ship or, more in keeping with his mood, pacing back and forth with numerous stops to grip at a stanchion or a bit of cable and stare mournfully over the endless expanse of the waiting sea. At night, though, his windowless cabin had all the cheer of an undulating tomb. Rogan had never been an abstemious man, but he had to drink more wine than usual after dinner to assure himself of a night of sleep rather than hours of rigid worry. He took a final sip of his favorite Ambermere red, then, still dressed, wrapped himself tightly in his mass of twisted bedclothes and drifted into an uneasy slumber.

He awakened, whether hours later or minutes, he couldn't tell, with his head ringing from a collision with the wall. The room was pitch dark, but he had the distinct impression that the floor was tilted almost perpendicular. From above on the deck, he heard the sound of shouting voices and the pounding of many feet. He was still disentangling himself from his blankets when his door opened with a crash.

"We're going down!" came a frenzied shout.

Rogan sprinted for the door, which he missed, and ran into the wall. He picked himself off the wildly tilting floor and began feeling for the exit. If Rogan had possessed a sense of direction, it would have by now deserted him. He had no way of knowing even if it was the floor or the wall he was staggering across. What if the ship had capsized? He might be blundering about on the ceiling, or whatever the nautical term was. One of the most annoying things about being on a ship was that sailors refused to call things by the perfectly sensible names that served everyone else so well. The floor was the deck; the kitchen, the galley. The ceiling, he recalled, had some name that no one would ever guess.

Rogan found the door, which was actually called some other name that he had learned, then promptly forgotten. As he made his way to the deck, he realized that he was completely calm. The plentiful noise from outside suggested that the ship was not yet submerged. For that, he was grateful. If he had to drown, he would prefer to do so in open water, and not trapped in the vessel that had carried him into this predicament.

Outside was almost as dark as his cabin had been. Rogan had the impression that it was raining heavily, but realized that it might well be spray from the churning sea. The deck was crowded with shouting sailors, busy with ropes and sprinting from place to place in the murky gloom. One ran into him, then shouted something urgent and completely incomprehensible into his face as he darted past. A prayer, perhaps, thought Rogan. The deck tilted most alarmingly under him, then, as he adjusted his posture to accommodate the change, rose beneath his feet in an entirely unexpected direction. Evidently his death was to be an entertaining one. As Rogan stumbled and fought to keep his feet, he felt a pang of longing for the solid stone walls and floors of his rooms in the tower. Who would be the next magician to occupy it, he wondered.

"Rogan! Quick!"

It was unseemly, Rogan realized, to be picky about the people one died with. The face of Count Reffex loomed out of the darkness. He seized the magician by the arm and dragged him along the swaying deck. Rogan recognized the captain as they passed him in a rush. He shouted something at them, and then disappeared into the spray and shadows. When they passed a group of men working silently at securing a furled sail, Rogan felt a surge of unexpected hope. They seemed calm enough, and intent on their task. Surely they were not laboring simply to make the ship tidy for a journey to the ocean floor. He tried to plant his feet and yank his arm from Reffex's grip.

"Here! It's just here!" shouted the nobleman, and then added a strangled cry as the bow plunged alarmingly and a sheet of seawater washed over them. Rogan felt Reffex release his arm just as his feet went out from under him. When his shoulder struck something hard, he grabbed for it and hung on.

Damn the darkness and damn the confusion, he thought. Rogan remembered that he had sort of counted on quietly drinking himself to death sometime in the distant future when he was so old that he wouldn't care, or possibly even notice. To be simply washed away in the violence of a storm at sea was personally offensive to him. Another wave swept over the deck, clutching at him as it passed. As the water drained away he heard Reffex shouting in his ear.

Rogan opened his eyes. He was holding on to the back end—what did they call it?—of one of the longboats that were lashed to the rail ahead—forward—of the sighting mast. Reffex was working feverishly with a long knife, hacking at a rope. Rogan pulled himself along the boat.

"What are you doing?" he shouted into the furious wind.

Reffex glanced up from his work. "We have to free the boat," he shouted without stopping.

As a palace magician much occupied with the sort of magic associated with ceremony and spectacle, Rogan had experience not only with all manner of gadgets and contrivances, but ropes and rigging as well.

"All you have to do is untie this knot at the back here," he said.

Reffex looked at him stupidly, then turned his gaze to the knot, all the time continuing to saw with the knife. At that moment, the bow dipped and the ship seemed to be standing on its head. When it righted, another still larger wave pushed itself past them. Reffex shook his head and clambered into the boat.

"Quick, get in," he cried, pulling Rogan bodily in after him. "Untie the knot."

Rogan began to explain in a rational shout that since the knot could be released in the blink of an eye there was no reason to untie it until the boat was needed. Reffex stared at him wildly for a second, then shouldered his way past the magician and clawed the knot loose. Rogan, meanwhile, was distracted by the sensation of rising into the sky, as if the ship were being lifted from the water by some vast aquatic giant.

At that moment, a seaman slid down a rope from somewhere in the murk above. Rogan had a quick picture of the ship sedately slipping beneath the waves, the last man to drown, a watchman perched on the highest mast. The man was hurrying down the tilting deck when he noticed them.

"What are you pair up to?" he shouted, in a manner that seemed to hold no respect for their rank.

Rogan found it was difficult to shrug while desperately gripping the sides of the longboat in anticipation of the next wave. He felt the ship begin again to descend into the trough of thundering water. The seaman stepped toward them with the unconcerned ease of a courtier crossing a dance floor.

"We have to be ready to abandon ship," cried Reffex in a wavering alto that was quickly lost in the wind and rain. He tossed aside the loose end of the rope.

The seaman stared at him with an expression of sheer incredulity. He gestured in the direction of the dipping bow. "This is nothin' but a little blow, you damn fool lubber!" The man snatched up the line Reffex had dropped and began to secure the longboat. Reffex yanked the rope from his hands. In the next instant he was himself yanked unceremoniously from his seat in the boat by the impatient seaman. Rogan watched his heels bounce over the side as the titled gentleman howled an outraged protest.

It was as the optimism of the sailor's words about the "little blow" settled comfortably into Rogan's consciousness that the ship again seemed to point directly at the bottom of the sea. The longboat, no longer tethered, began to slide along the deck, until its progress was arrested by the arrival of the largest wave that had yet come crashing over the bow. Rogan felt the longboat scrape sideways, then lift and turn in a giddy tilt as the floor of water washed it, and him, over the side. He had one final view of the bounding schooner he had unwillingly vacated, before a mountain of black water rose and blotted it from view.

CHAPTER
·6·

Breksin looked down the road that tumbled across the rocky landscape to the sea. It was only midday and already he could see the city far in the distance. He might hope to reach it today. If not, by morning for certain. Now that he was traveling alone, he felt he could cover a lot of ground in a hurry. Not that his companions had slowed him down. Even old Alexander had kept up quite well, and Egri never seemed to be exerting himself, but flowed across the ground with an unconscious ease that was a pleasure to watch. Of course, he was very strong for his size. He had carried Marcia on a long, hilly road the night she had been injured, and never even breathed hard.

But now he had no companions. Old Alexander had left in the middle of the night. When he had learned of it he had been concerned, but Egri had assured him that Alexander had nothing to fear from anything he might meet on the highway.

Breksin had not been convinced. "Only think what we found in our path that night."

Egri had smiled. "I have not forgotten."

"Yet still you say he is safe alone at night."

"Beyond doubt."

Breksin had looked up from his breakfast and laid his knife by his plate. "I know he has some tricks—chilling wine, keeping us dry—but you speak of him as though he were a wizard."

Egri gave a derisive laugh. "He is no wizard, this Alexander. He is more than that." He raised his hand as though in a gesture of caution. "Do not ask what. You will not like the answer."

Then Egri too had left, and would say only that he might join him in Devlin.

Breksin strode down the steep road with the ease of the mountain born. How would Marcia—*Miss* Marcia, he corrected himself—have fared on such a path? She had been a good hiker, but he remembered cradling her in his arms and carrying her down the rocky hillside when they had to get out of a storm. Egri could have matched his pace, but Marcia and Alexander would have been left behind.

And it was best, no doubt, that he was again a solitary traveler. He had never meant to arrive in Devlin with a party. If things turned bad and there was work for him to do there, it would be work that was best done alone.

His life had been a solitary one, had become so on a single day now nearly twenty years in the past.

Present yourself to us, for our mercy. So had read his uncle's note, affixed to the door of his father's hall with a jeweled dagger. Inside, the walls and floors, the rafters, all were stained with the blood of his family. His uncle, now king on the death of his older brother, summoned him.

The young prince, at his full growth and as tall and bulky as any fighter in the mountain clans, did not have to consider long his uncle's offer. His birthright stolen, with no roof, and only ghosts for comrades in arms, he could see but one choice. His only hope was that his treacherous relative meant not to kill him out of hand, but would let him prove his loyalty to the new-made king.

He took the note, and the dagger, and presented himself to his kinsman. He listened meekly to talk of regrets, necessity. There was to be a new order. He pledged his honor to his sovereign lord, drank from his cup. His uncle, cheeks flushed with wine and bloody guilt, had cried, "Now what may we not hope to accomplish, when we can effect a reconciliation like this?"

Late that night, when wariness had faded from the glances of the men at arms, he walked on a high balcony with his uncle and his eldest cousin, now heir, to see what portents might be read in the stars on a night of such promise.

The new king's cry was piteous when he saw his brave son

lifted like a helpless infant and thrown from the balcony to die broken on the rocks below; in the next instant he gagged on the jeweled dagger in his throat.

The first guard through the door, aghast and staring, was struck down by a blow from the waiting giant's fist. Breksin snatched the hammer from the soldier's belt and stormed the royal hall like a furious army. He left a trail of corpses and staggered from the door with a splintered lance wedged in his ribs.

When he had recovered from his wounds, sheltered in a hermit's cave, and had his strength again, he knew that honor bade him go back, gather a force of clansmen, and crush the life from every cousin he could find. His duty was to wash the blood from his father's hall, and establish there a line that would endure forever.

So it was that on a day in early spring, he took the lowland road, and left the mountains never to return.

And now his hammer was in his belt again. The diplomats would negotiate the freedom of the hostages, that was a certainty, he thought. The ransom would be paid, and the royal party would go on to Felshalfen. He would return to his duties in Asbrak's cellars, and his closet would once again hide his bloody battle-hammer. But if things went amiss, as things had a way of doing, then it might be that he could be of service.

Indeed, had the captives been only the royal couple, Asbrak's daughter Iris and her husband, Hilbert the Silent of Felshalfen, Breksin would at this moment be in his cellars, seeing to the cheeses and selecting wines for the royal table. But with the prince and princess, the pirates had taken another couple, Daniel, a newcomer who had found great favor with the king, and Modesty, now the Lady Modesty, whom Breksin had known since she was a child.

Not only was she the niece of his great friend Renzel, votaress of the goddess Elyziana, or Elyssana, as they called her in Ambermere, but Modesty herself, even when she blossomed into beauty that in many would harden to pride, even when she came to live at the palace as the pampered favorite of the princess, had found time to come to him often and while away an afternoon with cards and comfortable talk.

Breksin's huge hand strayed to touch the hammer at his belt. May the gods pity the pirate at whose hands this woman came to harm! For half his life, Breksin had been a peaceful man, but he knew all too well, remembered all too clearly, the practices of bloody violence. There was a way to step beyond yourself. . . .

He pulled himself from these thoughts. His memory was amply furnished with bloody scenes of the past. He had no need to imagine new ones.

At the far turning of the road, where it dropped below a rocky shelf, a small animal appeared. Breksin squinted through the afternoon sun. As it came closer, he stopped. It moved like a cat, effortlessly flowing across the ground.

Was he to inherit another cat? For the first part of his journey, a little black wanderer had kept him company, surprising him by showing up day after day. He had last seen it when they had visited the mysterious cave Father had found. It had picked a good time to abandon him, for it was that night the little horrors had attacked them.

As the cat came closer, Breksin slipped his pack from his shoulder and let it drop to the ground. He stepped forward.

"Kitsey?" The cat trotted up to him and meowed, then ducked out from under his hand as he had always done when Breksin tried to pet him. "By the Daughters, it is the faithful kitsey." The giant dropped to his haunches to have a closer look. There was no question about it. After—he counted on his fingers—an absence of six days, his original companion had turned up again.

"But you're ahead of me." Breksin thought of the ground he had covered since last seeing the cat. "You must be a magician," he said.

He peered more closely at the cat. What had Egri said about Alexander? He was not a wizard, but "something more." They had met Alexander at the inn a few hours after he had last seen the cat. There were stories of mages who could take the shape of animals, and witches, too, were said to have as "familiars" demons—or was it spirits, or ghosts—that looked like ordinary cats or owls or wolves.

The kitsey slunk past him and began to nose at his pack. Breksin laughed.

"That's sausage you smell. Too spicy for you, I fear. But I've some cheese I'll share, once we've covered some distance." He picked up the pack and slung it on his shoulder. A moment later he felt a tug as the cat leapt easily from the path and settled itself on the pack. Breksin pictured Alexander, a whispering oldster dressed in colored silks that would have better adorned a lady of pleasure. He chuckled and glanced over at the cat perched securely on his shoulder. His smile faded and was followed by a thoughtful frown as he looked once more at his passenger. He studied the little black cat for a long moment, then laughed again and set off down the road.

CHAPTER

· 7 ·

"A wine factor?" Had he not been conversing with his sovereign monarch, the expression on Rand's face might have been mistaken for one of polite boredom.

"Exactly." The king turned his profile to the unusually wide mirror set in his wardrobe door. "Not a broker, you see. It is in the details that a disguise is tested." He waved a didactic finger in the air. "This is what you fail to appreciate. You imagine that I need only don a cloak and clap a bonnet on my head to go among the populace."

Rand, who was quite certain he had never offered, or even held, an opinion on any aspect of the art of disguise, did not protest. Having learned that it was impossible to dissuade the king from these occasional forays, he wished only that Asbrak would leave, so that he might the sooner return.

"I fear the subtleties elude me, Your Majesty."

"Indeed," said the king, studying the effect of a corner of pink lace kerchief that hung as if by accident from a vest pocket hemmed in blue silk. He turned to his chief adviser.

"That's just it, you see. Subtleties, niceties." A little man who had been completely hidden from view darted from behind the king and reached up to tug lightly at the royal lapels. The king peered over him. "If ever you are to be disguised, Rand, you must come to me. I," said the king with a flourishing gesture, "shall act as your valet."

"Your Majesty is too kind."

After he had seen the king to the garden door, Rand stationed himself at a window that overlooked the avenue. The gutters were still damp from the storm of the night before, and the lingering rain of the morning, but the skies had cleared during the afternoon, and a warm breeze had blown in from the sea. Rand reached his vantage point in time to see the king perform his caricature of slipping furtively from the gate to join the pedestrians on the avenue. Before he was lost to sight among the evening crowds and flickering lamps, Asbrak passed beneath the signs of numerous shops and taverns, all decorated with the undisguisable royal silhouette.

Rand heaved a sigh, as he had so often done when standing at that window. All Ambermere seemed to be abroad tonight. The labors of the day over, citizens were free to sit in taverns and discuss the kidnaping of the Princess Iris and her husband, Hilbert the Silent of Felshalfen. It must be pleasant, Rand supposed, to sip wine and talk of momentous events. He turned from the window and set off briskly down the hall. He, on the other hand, was expected to do something about them.

He mounted a flight of narrow stone stairs and entered an upper corridor. In fact, he thought, he might as well drink and talk. For the time he had done all that he could do. Asbrak conceived diplomacy and statecraft entirely in terms of masterstrokes and intrigue. Rand was not at liberty to be so naive. The king was gleefully anticipating the secret arrival in Devlin of Rogan the Obscure. He was convinced his functionary possessed deep magical resources that he could use to confound their adversaries. This, coupled with the intelligence he expected to gather in his anonymous nocturnal prowlings, he believed would prove decisive—but only in some vague and never-specified way.

For Rand's part, he supposed that one could hope that the unexpected arrival of Rogan in the pirate capital might precipitate a sudden critical shortage in the fortress city's stores of wine. The magician would certainly have nothing but drink to occupy his time. Count Reffex, meanwhile, would be conducting irrelevant negotiations for the exchange of hostages and ransom. Ransom, unfortunately, could not be at the bottom of these troubles.

Black Jack Flanders had not broken long-standing agreements and risked arousing the Nine Kingdoms merely to make an incremental addition to his hoard of wealth.

Rand had left the selection of the emissary to the king, knowing the business was of no significance whatever. He himself, however, had appointed the count's assistant, the quiet and retiring Hebbick, a courtier of no rank or consequence. Had he been of such station as to warrant an epithet, he might have appropriately been styled Hebbick the Unnoticed. A faint smile moved the diplomat's lips for just an instant, then vanished without a trace.

Then there was the cellar master. His apprentice had reported that as soon as Breksin heard of the kidnaping, he strapped on his hammer and set out for Devlin. Rand knew of no further military action that the kingdom could possibly be expected to undertake. Ambermere of course had an army, one that had cultivated a certain niggling exactitude in the obscure niceties of parade-ground drill. Rand was himself willing to concede that they had brought to a state of mature perfection the art of polishing dull swords to a blinding gloss, and could flourish them harmlessly with unsurpassed virtuosity.

In the person of Breksin, the only bona fide soldier in the service of Asbrak the Fat had already deployed himself. Though it would not have occurred to him to ask the giant to go, Rand was confident there would be no harm in it. Breksin would conduct himself with good sense. And it was always possible that a situation might develop in which a seven-foot berserker with a battle hammer would prove a useful tool of diplomacy.

Rand stopped at a narrow door set deep in the stone wall. It opened onto a tunnel-like stair that rose steeply to a landing where a single fat candle guttered in a niche. A door at the top opened onto a sheltered rooftop garden. Rand listened for a moment to the pulsing murmur that floated on the night air, then stepped through and closed the door behind him.

It had been many years since Asbrak the Fat had found it possible to walk from his palace to the quays without stopping for rest and refreshment. On this night he got scarcely past the first crossing before he found it necessary to stop, not for rest, but because he suddenly realized that he was hungry. Perhaps, he thought, his appetite had been aroused in anticipation of the long

walk to the waterfront taverns that were his goal. Or it might be
that he had simply been more than usually abstemious at dinner.
He was quite sure he had eaten very little of the goose he had
been served, and that he had neglected to do justice to the wine,
though it had possessed a velvety richness that had melded
gracefully with the dark succulence of the fowl. Of the potatoes
stewed with garlic and cream, he had a memory of a few
bites—no more than half a plate, probably much less.

He stopped outside a tavern and composed his features. He
was acutely conscious of the need to suppress the air and posture
of royalty natural to him. It was not enough to wear the clothing
of a commoner; he must wear a mask of affable complacency
through which the fire of the kingly eye could not be seen to
penetrate.

As was his frequent practice, the king waited until he could
make an entrance in the company of others. This, he was convinced, had the effect of *diluting* the impact of his arrival in a
room, and of further distracting attention from him, lest some fugitive air of nobility draw a canny eye to a discovery of his
counterfeit.

The king lounged a few paces from the door and gazed idly at
the paving stones with an air of innocence. After a few moments,
a small, slender man that Asbrak was sure he had seen before
rounded the corner at a brisk pace. He glanced at the king, then
nodded and darted through the door. Asbrak followed. Inside, the
little man seemed to have disappeared until the king noticed him
waiting by a barrel as a maid filled a large mug with ale.

Asbrak sauntered after the man, and negotiated with the girl
for a beaker of amber beer and some bread and brined cheese
and olives. As she peeled the wet vine leaves from the cheese,
Asbrak questioned her about the man, careful to employ the ac-
cents of lisping gentility he imagined to be a characteristic of
merchants of substance, but which were in fact the peculiarity of
a certain well-known man who had become prosperous sup-
plying the royal household with preserved roe, smoked fish, and
other dainties.

"Oh, that's just my uncle Dibrick, Your . . . Honor," she said.
Asbrak raised his eyebrows, then turned to see where the man
had gone. The girl seemed, not nervous, perhaps, but somehow
distracted and suddenly clumsy at her uncomplicated tasks. The
man, meanwhile, had seated himself by a window and was ob-

serving the scene outside with his elbows on the table and his mug at his lips.

The girl tried to lead Asbrak to a large chair by the fire, but the king, ever watchful for signs of intrigue, threaded his way among the crowded tables and seated himself on a three-legged stool near the window. He was congratulating himself on placing himself so inconspicuously near the suspicious little man when the girl arrived with his food and drink.

"Oh, here, sir," she said in a loud voice. "I hoped you would sit by the fire." Asbrak raised his hand and shook his head.

"This will do," he whispered.

The maid placed his things on the table with a clatter that made the secretive monarch wince. The man she had called her uncle didn't look up, but as she left, she strayed in his direction and bumped his table with a force that almost unseated him. He began to protest, then caught sight of the king and got to his feet.

"Ah! Ha-ha," he said, shuffling his feet and tapping the tip of his nose with his forefinger. "Ha-ha," he repeated. Asbrak stared at him. He was beginning to wonder if the man possessed the power of speech when he uttered a single word.

"Dibrick," he said. He glanced behind him, as though not sure his chair would still be there, then abruptly sat down. He grimaced at Asbrak. "Roaster," he said, getting to his feet again, "of meats." He raised his hand to the brim of his hat, then began to rub his ear. "Ah," he said, turning to look at his hand as though he didn't know where it had come from. He sat down.

"Tobbruk," said the king, trying to recall where he had seen this odd fellow before. "Wine factor."

"Ha-ha," said Dibrick. He cleared his throat laboriously, then took a lengthy nip from his pot of ale.

Asbrak raised his own glass. He began to wish he had accepted the cushioned chair by the fire. When, a moment later, he remembered his previous meeting with the roaster of meats, he wished so even more. He had talked to him, or rather, listened to his incomprehensible babble, outside this very inn one night last summer. Asbrak lifted a succulent olive from his plate, then dropped it as Dibrick began once again to clear his throat.

"Ah. Ha-ha."

Asbrak raised his eyes reluctantly from his plate.

"Ha-ha-ha." Dibrick took another heroic pull. "I sit at the window," he announced.

"So you do," said the king. He had planned to say no more, but realized that he had neglected to disguise his voice. "Soooo," he lisped from the side of his mouth, "ah, that is, ah, one can certainly see things from a window."

Instead of answering, Dibrick only grinned at him brightly. After a moment, Asbrak turned his attention to his snack, dipping a slab of bread into the pool of fragrant oil at the bottom of his plate. He made a mental note to have his kitchen procure some of this grape-leaf cheese. Here was a tavern in the very shadow of the royal residence, serving a cheese of surpassing excellence that had never, he was sure, graced his own table. Asbrak looked around the room. He did not begrudge his subjects their culinary pleasures. He knew there were kingdoms where certain dishes were restricted to the use of the aristocracy, but he found such practices inexplicable. In Ambermere, the very porters and drovers were welcome to their delicacies. Asbrak only wished them not to be withheld from the palace.

This, then, was an unlooked-for benefit of his anonymous visits among the populace. He resolved to make a practice of donning his disguises more often, if only for the purpose of sampling the products of the city's kitchens. How fine it would be if he could have Breksin accompany him. The giant had more knowledge of food and drink than anyone in the kingdom, not excepting the king. At the thought of Breksin, he remembered his absence, one that might well be perilous. As this worrisome thought intruded itself, Asbrak became aware that someone was standing behind him. He placed his glass on the table and turned to see the roaster of meats positioned at his elbow like a butler at a banquet.

"Your . . . you mentioned the window." Asbrak noticed that Dibrick's head was now bare. Dibrick paced backward to his table and picked up his mug of ale. "Last night," he began, then stopped to drink, at the same time advancing toward Asbrak. He lowered the drink and dabbed at his mouth with his sleeve.

"Last night, when it was raining and blowing so, I ran from just across the way there." He pointed vaguely out the window. "Just crossing the avenue I got"—he looked down at his clothing—"good and wet, as you might say, not meaning soaked, but it was only a few steps, don't you see, and I was mighty brisk about the business, and yet I got good and wet."

Asbrak nodded absently and ceased to listen, concentrating in-

stead on the way the mature pungency of the olives united with
the youthful tang of the cheese to produce a rare effect. He
looked for the girl, meaning to call for wine. The beer was good,
but not suitable for his little feast. What it wanted was some red
from the middle slopes, not too heavy. He tried to guess what
Breksin would send from the cellars to go with this. Maybe even
some still, luscious white, long in the cask, aromatic and buttery.

A word from Dibrick caught his ear.

Asbrak turned his attention to the roaster of meats. "What did
you say about a witch?"

Dibrick favored him again with his grin. "Well, that was the
woman, don't you see?"

Asbrak nodded. "Ah," he said. He tried to look past Dibrick's
gleaming teeth. "What woman?"

"The woman in the rain."

"A witch, you say?"

"So it would seem."

"I see," said Asbrak. "And why was that, again?"

"She came walking up the middle of the avenue in the pouring
down rain, as you might say." Dibrick blinked and sipped from
his mug. "Just after I crossed from the public house."

Asbrak looked out the window, recalling the blowing rain of
the night before. "Yes?" he said. "And then?"

"And then she came in here. Walked right past me, straight as
a soldier, wearing that hat, and dry as a summer morning."
Dibrick peered into his mug. "Near lost my thirst, I did. She
wasn't even damp. A witch is all right when you need a powder
for a cough, or some such, but a man doesn't like to see magic,
unexpected, when he's, as you might say, lifting a glass."

Asbrak fixed the man with his kingly eye. "And this witch,
then. What was her name?"

"Oh, it was that Hannah, which I've never seen her, but I've
heard her name. I didn't know she was one to walk dry through
a storm, but now I've seen it with my own eyes, as you might
say, so I'll not deny it."

The king, his plate forgotten, rose from his seat. He murmured
something absently to Dibrick and put a few coins on the table
beside his beaker. Why, he asked himself as he moved through
the room at his fastest stride, had he not thought to consult a
witch? They had magical powers without doubt, and yet one was
not accustomed to thinking of them in those terms. Witches were

ladies to whom one touched by illness turned when the attentions of physicians either failed or, as was often the case, began to show signs of doing harm.

Outside the inn, he stood undecided. His impulse was to return to the palace and have Rand dispatch someone to fetch the witch. If she was a person of substantial magical resources, it was imperative that he consult her at once. Then he remembered that witches, at least those in stories, invariably lived in cottages away from other habitations, usually in a lonely woods, or on a mountain. He glanced up at the sky. He could scarcely ask a messenger to visit her after dark, assuming she could be located.

He turned again in the direction of the docks. He must continue with his original intention of visiting the taverns at the waterfront. It was there, if anywhere, that he might hope to overhear something that would be of use.

It was some time later that Asbrak found himself wearily passing through an alley not far from the docks. The damp night air carried the smell of pitch and salt, and the sound of a wine-smeared melody being sung somewhere nearby in an unsteady baritone. He had come all the way from the tavern without another stop, save for a sausage pastry he had bought from a vendor. This he had meant to eat standing, but the man had politely relinquished his bench, and then had gone so far as to fetch him a cup of hot spiced wine from another stall across the avenue. As always, Asbrak felt a glowing pride at the courtesy with which he was unfailingly treated when he walked the city streets in masquerade.

But now he had begun to feel a burning ache in his knees and ankles. He had left the lighted street for the alley in the belief that it was a shorter route to the taverns by the water. Now he was not quite sure which direction he was going. He knew only that the inhospitable backs of darkened buildings offered little cheer.

The song, which had died, rose again. It seemed to come from farther down the alley. A tavern then, or inn. Asbrak pictured a chair, perhaps cushioned, and a platter of steaming shellfish, or a chowder, rich with lumps of butter and aromatics from some sunbaked hillside. He quickened his pace. Even an alley grog shop would be a grateful haven, if only for a moment's rest.

But for the song, renewed again just as he passed, Asbrak would have missed the entrance. He stopped and peered into the darkness. Though no sign hung above the door, the music was coming from behind it. He lifted the latch and pushed. He could see no light of lamp or candle, but the song spilled into the alley.

Once inside, the king could see a dim light. He walked down a hallway almost too narrow for one his size. At the end was a short descending stair. Just as he started down, the song rose again, this time carried by a number of careless voices. At the bottom, he was confronted with a hanging tangle of loosely knotted ropes decorated with beads and shells, sailors' handiwork, as he recognized from other visits to the docks. He was at the point of pushing his way through when there was a loud clatter from the room beyond, and the song dissolved into shouts and laughter.

"Go ahead, break another one! Finnie don't care."

"Don't worry, the rats'll drink it."

At the mention of rats, Asbrak looked around nervously, trying to see into the corners. He hesitated for a moment. Clearly he had come in the back door. Still he hoped to slip into the room unnoticed. He leaned forward, attempting to see through the curtain of ropes before committing himself.

Only shadows could be seen, and the glow of smoking lamps. There was a lull in the talk and laughter. Asbrak hoped the song would come to life again. He wondered if he might enter singing, and thereby seem merely to be another member of the company, unnoticed in the darkness and jollity. He would signal for wine and settle quietly in a corner.

But now the gathering had grown murmurous, a lazy drone of voices decorous enough for a tea party. He waited, perched on the last step, his joints aching. A few moments more, he decided, then he would simply enter as quietly as he could.

"And then there's the chickens."

Asbrak jumped at the quiet voice almost in his ear. His left foot slipped and he had to lean backward to keep from pitching headfirst through the curtain. He bent forward at the waist to keep his balance and sat down heavily on a narrow step that seemed to rise to meet him with a painful thump. At just that moment, a woman shouted something that was greeted with general laughter. Asbrak began to struggle to his feet, then was stopped by the sound of another voice.

"As loud as they say, are they?"

A second man had spoken. They were seated together at a table just on the other side of the curtain. Asbrak was, in effect, seated with them. He heard the sound of a glass being filled and realized he was very nearly in a position to reach through the hanging and steal the wine from their table. He wished he dared.

He squirmed on the step. The one he was sitting on offered but scant support for him; the one just above was pushing into his flesh in a most incommodious fashion.

"Louder. And the city just sleeps right through it like it was a lullaby. I tell you, Possick, I was with a woman the first night, and them chickens—sea hens, they call them—brought me out of bed at dawn like the muster of Hell. And there I stand—naked—trying to sort out if I'm dead or alive, and that little witch from the public house is snoring! Ladylike, you know—soft—but snoring, and cuddled in the blankets like a baby in a basket."

Asbrak was trying to adjust his position to one of less discomfort. He had heard of sea hens, but in what connection, he could not recall. Rand would probably know.

"Still," said Possick, "you're a great traveler. It's not everyone's been to Devlin." He laughed. "And bedded a pirate beauty."

"Pirate, is right," said the first man. "She got her price, she did, and counted every copper, too." The two men laughed. "Then in the morning I saw a thing as made me wonder if I was still drunk from the night before. I was up with them cursed chickens, like I told you, so I went outside to see the city in daylight, and just as I came out of the inn, a man walked by that was the image of a great lord from home, but that he was dressed plain, and was by himself, which would never be."

This got Asbrak's attention, but at that moment the song was picked up again.

Asbrak leaned forward, every ache and discomfort forgotten. These men were speaking of Devlin. And spoke on, but the raucous song made their words difficult to hear. The king inched himself forward on the step so that his rolling flesh gradually translated itself down to the next step. Now his knees were almost touching the curtain. As he strained to hear, he tried to think what lord the man could possibly be referring to.

He supposed a common sailor might consider Reffex a great lord, if he knew nothing of him, but Reffex would not be one to be about at dawn, or dress himself in modest garb, either. Be-

sides which, the count and Rogan could scarcely have arrived in
Devlin by today; this seaman must have left Devlin before they
arrived.

" . . . the king's nephew. I've seen him often enough. I was
going to say something, but he passed so brisk, he was around
the corner before I got my mouth working."

As Possick made remarks about the effects of wine and
wenches on the brain and other organs, Asbrak made a rapid in-
ventory of his nephews, a task that was greatly simplified by the
fact that he had none. His only living male relatives were a few
distaff cousins at barely calculable removes, none of whom could
have been mistaken for a great lord by a bumpkin fresh from the
hamlets, let alone a worldly salt like this one.

"You may say so, but we sweated the wine out, the little witch
and I. My head was clear. The thing was, even his hair was the
same, cut straight, not curled to fashion. And he was shaved the
same—only a mustache. I tell you, I wish now I'd run after him
and looked for his scar."

"And then," said Possick, "what?"

The answer was drowned out by the swelling song. When it
subsided, the two were discussing particulars of the little witch,
so that Asbrak soon was acquainted with details of her body and
her habits to a far more intimate degree than was seemly or
proper.

The two men talked on and on, and spoke of everything except the one subject of interest to Asbrak. Some lord had been in
Devlin. But who? Of what court? And when?

When, much later, the men rose to leave, Asbrak was sure he
would be unable to gain his feet without either crying out in
pain, or pitching forward and rolling into the room in an absurd
and undignified manner. He carefully straightened his legs, allowing the tips of his boots to stray between the strands of rope
that hid him. As soon as sensation returned to his feet, he pulled
them back and planted them on the step. Being as quiet as he
could, the king, balancing himself like an acrobat walking a
rope, slowly brought himself to an upright position.

He had barely finished congratulating himself when he noticed
that, given the shallow steps and narrow passage, he was unable
to turn around. Feeling very put-upon, the king began to slowly
ascend the stairs backwards. Having gained the corridor, he

turned, with difficulty, and made his way to the space and freedom of the alley.

Despite his hunger and thirst, Asbrak visited no other taverns, but made his way to the lonely spot where a groom waited with his horse. With the help of a mounting ladder, the king gained the saddle, and soon was on his way home.

CHAPTER

·8·

"One and one is three." Marcia was packing the satchel she had bought at the village market a few days ago.

Borphis was watching from his perch on the edge of her bed. "Oh yeah? Who says?"

"No one. It's a math thing. Any system you want to invent is okay as long as you make sure it's internally consistent."

Borphis screwed up his face and stared at the ceiling. "Oh, okay," he said after a moment. "You mean imaginary numbers." He crossed his legs and dropped back on one elbow.

Marcia's memory played a recording of her mother's voice on the subject of shoes on the bedspread. "I don't know about imaginary numbers," she said, rolling a sweater into a tight bundle, "I didn't get that far in math." She looked up at Borphis, then at the sweater. *What am I talking about?* she said to herself.

"What math? I just meant numbers that aren't real. What you were talking about is sort of like pictures of numbers, right?"

Marcia stuffed the sweater into a corner of her pack. "Pictures of numbers? I'm talking about numbers. Well, actually I'm talking about packing my bags for a trip to the Lower Regions. The only way that makes any sense at all is that it's consistent with all the other crazy things I've been doing. I mean, I should be getting ready to go back to work on Monday, checking on my dry cleaning, things like that. Instead, I'm on my way to track down a crazy old man who is wandering God knows where, and when I find him the only thing I know to do is follow him, because those were the instructions—at least I'm pretty sure they were—that I got from my . . . den mother on my second day in the Celestial Girl Scouts, which is headquartered here in a run-down part of the city, but with a rear entrance on Mount Olympus." She looked up at Borphis. "You get the picture."

The little demon rolled over on his back. Marcia couldn't refrain from glancing nervously at the bedspread to check for marks from his shoes.

"Yeah, but numbers are real."

"Huh?" Marcia could feel the blank look on her face.

"They're real things."

"Numbers?"

"Right."

Marcia straightened up and finished rolling the pair of socks she was holding. Lately it seemed that she had developed a knack, if not a genius, for getting into conversations like this.

"You mean like bricks?" she asked.

"What?"

"Numbers. Are you saying they're real things like bricks are?" Again her eyes were drawn to the bedspread. "Or shoes?"

Borphis sat up. "Sure. You mean you didn't know that?"

Marcia ignored the question. "I just have to ask you this," she said. "Would you say chance is an illusion?"

"Uh-huh." He nodded.

"And time, too?"

"Right. What's your point?"

Marcia stared at him for several seconds, then looked down at the socks she was holding. She shook her head slowly.

"I don't know." She put the socks in the pack. "Let's have lunch."

Borphis was polite about the egg salad. Marcia had always liked it, but Mother had made it better. After they ate, she cleared the table. "Do we have to take water with us?" she asked as she put their dirty dishes in the sink.

"What for?"

"To drink," she called over her shoulder. "Can we find water there?"

"Well, yes," Borphis answered unenthusiastically. "But aren't we going to pack some wine? And some cognac?" he added.

Marcia put a movie from her collection on the VCR and left Borphis curled up happily on the couch. It was clear that he saw no reason for them to go anywhere. He had mentioned that there was "more excitement" in the Lower Regions, but he seemed in no hurry to get back.

Alone in her room, Marcia finished packing, remembering to leave room for a few bottles of wine. She settled herself in Great-grandmother Mibsey's rocker and relaxed, allowing her eyes to close. After her ring was stolen, she had learned to put herself into a meditative trance. And since Father had put the small gold band back on her finger, she had found the trance much easier to get into. That was how she had been able to follow him into the Lower Regions, and more important, how she had been able to get back to her own world.

Her eyes blinked open. She looked across the room at the satchel she had packed. She wondered why it hadn't occurred to her until this moment that if she really could cross from Region to Region freely—although that was a proposition that had not yet been thoroughly tested—she should be able to commute. She could look for Father during the day, then come back for a shower and a safe and comfortable night in her own bed. She laughed aloud. Should she take weekends off? Knock off in time for "Mystery" on Thursdays?

That, of course, was the lighthearted view of the question. There was also the chance that she wouldn't be able to take herself anywhere, or that she might not be able to control the destination; or her personal favorite—that wherever she ended up, she wouldn't be able to get back.

Which brought up the question of Elyssa. Where was she? And would she come if Marcia got lost somewhere in the confusion of dimensions and worlds?

With that cheerful thought, Marcia got out of the chair. Having interrupted her meditation anyway, she decided to clean up the kitchen so she could pursue her insane strategies with a clear conscience.

Borphis was still engrossed in the movie, a vintage musical full of big-band jazz and lively dancing. Marcia waved to him as she passed through the room. The dishes she had left in the sink were not there. A quick check of the cupboard revealed that they had been washed, dried, and put away. The cutting board had been scrubbed and hung up on its hook. The counter was wiped clean.

"Wow!"

"What's wrong?" Borphis came into the kitchen. From the living room, Marcia could hear what sounded like an argument between a trumpet and a drum.

"The dishes," she said. "That's great."

"Right." Borphis looked around. "What are we talking about?"

Marcia smiled at him. "You did the dishes. I appreciate it."

"What did I do to them?"

Marcia looked around the tiny kitchen. What had Borphis stood on?

"You didn't come in here and wash the dishes and the cutting board and put everything away and wipe off the counter?" Somehow, saying it aloud made it sound silly.

"Was I supposed to? What should I stand on?"

Marcia was getting out of patience with forever wondering if she was crazy. She *knew* she hadn't done the dishes, and she refused to speculate any more about her grip on reality. If she was nuts, she'd just have to try to enjoy it.

Borphis was looking up at her. "Anyway, doesn't the kitchen thingie take care of that?"

Marcia stared into the sink. At Annie's cottage, all the chores, including cooking, had been done by invisible hands.

"Evidently he does." She wandered back into the living room. "I should have let him make the egg salad."

She retreated to her bedroom again. Maybe, she thought, too many things had been happening in too short a time. She had worn the ring since summer without experiencing any profound changes in her life, her perceptions, or how her housework got done. But since last week, everything had undergone a radical change. Her aura had become positively eerie, and now she had an elf working in her kitchen. Which made a lot of sense, when she thought about it—the kitchen was really too small for a human being.

She sat down, determined to stay in the chair until she accomplished something. If she was going to follow Father, it would be a big help to have some idea where he was. She allowed herself to drift into a quiet state and let her mind wander, putting her head back and closing her eyes.

Pale, unwholesome-looking corpses. Black cloaks in tatters. They were the size of men, nearly, but looked like furless rats. Nasty little teeth were bared as if in pain. Among the boulders were furtive movements, shadows that eased themselves forward with slow and patient secrecy.

One cloaked figure sat, a little apart, still but not fallen. Pale sharp fingertips showed from under the dark folds of the garment. The shadowed hood was turned from the corpses, looked across the cold ashes of a fire, down a rubble-strewn hill. At the bottom, a pool of water reached with dirty yellow fingers among the broken rocks. It seemed dead and still, but at its edges it pushed against the dry ground with a slow, unhurried pulse.

The hooded figure rose. It moved among the corpses, pausing once or twice, then drifted down the hill. It skirted the water and moved onto the rutted path that lay like a twisted ribbon across the plain. It moved at a pace that seemed unhurried, yet soon it was a distant shadow, black against the yellow ground.

From the garden of heavy boulders above the water, there arose a chorus of eager noises as the feeders advanced.

Marcia opened her eyes and looked around her bedroom with anxious glances. She sighed and got up from the chair. With visions of Hell fresh in her eye, her bedroom looked like Heaven.

What had she seen? Dream images, perhaps. She had looked for Father, and found instead a scene of misery and desolation. The figure had been draped and hidden, but could not be the old man she sought. She recalled the sturdy pitch and roll of Father's gait. She had walked with him for days and never seen him float like a specter as the hooded figure had.

And what of the other old man she had met? Where would Alexander be now? He had gone with Breksin hoping to find Father. Had he come back to the inn for her? Marcia began to feel uneasy.

Would he follow her to the cave? To the Lower Regions? And if he did, then what? He was only a necromancer—a mage of this world. She did not know the precise limits of his power, but he himself had told her that without the convenience of a portal he could not readily travel between Regions. She stopped to think. Actually, only Elyssa and Father were able to manage that particular trick. Present company excluded, she reminded herself. Weird.

Marcia went back to her chair. She wanted to know what was going on, and she wanted to know now. She did not try to attain a state of relaxation; her jaw was set in a determined frown. She closed her eyes and leaned forward in the rocker, her heels planted in the carpet.

After a few sterile minutes, she was forced to conclude that gritting your teeth and squeezing your eyes shut was not conducive to visions. She had seen just what anyone unequipped with a magic ring would have seen—an uninformative pattern of faint lights and shadows that doubtless had less to do with clairvoyance than with the electrochemistry of vision. She allowed herself to settle back in the chair.

She was going to have to be methodical, she decided. Perhaps if she were to shift her view of reality, as she had yesterday morning when she saw the ghost and the sprites, she would have more luck. She tried to recall the feeling of tilting the spectrum, of shifting her perspective.

Nothing happened. For all the good it was doing her at the moment, her magic ring might as well have been a wedding band. She got to her feet, hoping that a little constructive pacing might help her to concentrate.

In the living room, Borphis was propped against the window-sill, gazing down at the traffic. "Where is everyone going?" he asked without turning around.

Marcia glanced at the clock on the mantel. "This is sort of the early warm-up for rush hour," she replied.

Borphis looked at her with a smile. "I like that," he said. "Rush hour." He turned back to the window. "Is it some kind of contest?"

"Not exactly," she said, going into the kitchen. She stopped and stared at the steaming carafe on the counter. "You made coffee?" she called.

"Sure, if you're making some."

Marcia looked around uneasily.

"That was fast," said Borphis when she put the cup down next to him. He took a sip. "This is better than what you made this morning." He raised the cup to his lips a second time. "A lot better."

"Thanks." Marcia scanned the room again before trying the coffee. Borphis followed her eyes.

"Uh-oh. I'll bet we're getting ready to leave." He glanced regretfully toward the window. "I hate to miss rush hour."

"I don't think you'll have to," said Marcia, peering into the kitchen. "I think we're staying until tomorrow morning."

"Suits me," said the demon. "Can we order pizza again?"

Marcia was still standing at the kitchen door. "You may have just done it," she said.

When she finished her coffee, Marcia went back to her bedroom and sat herself down on the rocking chair. She put her feet flat on the floor and folded her hands in her lap. This time she did not close her eyes, but stared straight ahead at the wall.

The women were naked. The room was vast and dimly lit with candles. Shadows lay like smoke on the floor of bare tiles. The bed was curtained, wide and white and empty. There were narrow windows set high in the wall. Bright blue sky filled them, but no light entered the chamber.

The women moved like dancers, aimless, rhythmic, like curtains blowing in a breeze. Their laughter was like song. Incense burned in pots of polished brass. From outside came the muted sound of chanting.

Marcia guided her vision from the scene. This was the choreography of her imagination, material for a dream intruding on her search for Father. Maybe she was trying too hard. She would let herself drift, and see where the current carried her.

When the mist came, it surprised her. She rose from the chair without willing it, moved forward as though floating above the ground. It pulled her into it, this mist. She remembered that when she left the Lower Regions, she had been afraid she might break the fragile vapor, the spell that was saving her—that if she lost her concentration it would evaporate. The fog that surrounded her now was not like that. She could see nothing but a blanket of white. In a moment, she decided, she would turn, pull away.

The air felt damp and warm. Marcia turned her head. The fog, definitely wet now, was everywhere. She wrenched her body to the side. She was only testing her powers. She didn't mean to go anywhere. She wasn't ready. She would pull back, she told herself. Rise above this sticky fog. And not be carried—she would walk. She fought to get control of her legs. She took a step, then paused and breathed deeply. She was going to remain calm. She would clear her vision—this clinging mist would go away. She would walk into the living room—she took another step—pick up the phone . . .

She smelled water. Heard it—a gentle, slapping noise. She moved ahead blindly. They could eat early tonight. Borphis was always hungry anyway. She felt water pour into her shoe. She dragged her foot back and stumbled slightly on a hard, uneven surface.

"Wait!" she called out. "I'm not . . ."

Her voice was swallowed as it left her mouth. The mist felt like wet cotton in her throat. From somewhere nearby she heard a noise, a quiet scraping sound. She raised her hands and pushed desperately at the fog that blinded her.

She could sense the water in front of her. She turned and took a careful step. The ground was rough and seemed to rise. She took another step, and then another, planting each foot carefully, holding her hands stretched in front of her. She continued, climbing a gentle slope. Once or twice she thought she heard the scraping noise following her. As the mist began to thin, she moved more quickly. She could see large angular forms, whether of rocks or buildings or something else, she couldn't tell. From somewhere ahead, she heard a sound like a distant voice calling.

She stopped and listened. She was greeted, not with silence—for the fog seemed to be filled with speech, a rustle of inarticulate whispers—but with a sense of the surrounding emptiness. A voice in her head wanted to whimper, to whine *What have I done?* She ignored it and listened behind her for the scraping sound. Hearing nothing, she went on.

In a few minutes she reached the top of the hill. She was on a wide street bounded on one side by a high, windowless wall, and on the other by a jumble of low, dark buildings. Here and there a light flickered. An occasional cry or distant shout could be heard. The mist had given way to a murky twilight in which she could make out few details, but the impression was of a shanty town.

She turned and looked back. The fog was like a sea of filthy clouds. She stared, trying to organize her perceptions. Intuitively, it seemed that somewhere down there Great-grandmother Mibsey's chair should be waiting for her. She pictured it, empty, but rocking steadily on a beach of cinders at the edge of an encroaching tide.

She turned away. She had no idea what she was going to do, but descending back into the fog was not it. A dozen steps brought her near the end of the high wall. Ahead was a wide street crossing the one she was on. She was about to leave the shadow of the wall when she heard a scratchy high-pitched noise that sounded like rats fighting in a bucket. As she watched, a long two-wheeled cart squeaked into view. It was pulled by a trudging man with a thick short neck who leaned against his burden and stared at the ground in front of his feet.

Marcia waited until he was out of sight, then stepped forward. She kept away from the looming wall, favoring the low structures on the other side of the street. She had nearly reached the corner when she heard the creak of hinges and saw light spilling from an open doorway. Just inside it, bathed in wavering lamplight, a naked couple lay entwined on a pile of ragged cloth that shifted and twisted under them. The man was short and muscular, the woman, tall and thin, but with generous breasts and ample hips. As she watched, they turned to her, licking their lips and making noises in their throats.

Marcia reeled, the image of the rat corpses slamming at her memory. These two were neither so small nor so inhuman, but the resemblance was unmistakable. The man bared his little teeth and rolled from the woman to display himself. As Marcia stared at the glistening hairless flesh, another person, standing in the shadows outside the shack, began to move in her direction.

Marcia heard a quiet laugh. She pulled her eyes from the couple and saw a smiling round face. The man said something she didn't catch, and reached toward her with a groping hand. A scent of overpowering sweetness assaulted her, catching in her throat.

"No!" She heard her own voice as though it had come from someone else. She took two quick steps backward. Her ring hand hung heavily at her side. She didn't try to raise it.

"No," she repeated. Her voice sounded weak. She stared for a moment at the man, almost near enough to touch. Beyond him the lovers were framed in the lighted doorway. For a moment, Marcia stood as though powerless to move, then she turned and walked away quickly.

The air was oppressively warm, and seemed almost too thick to inhale. As soon as she had put some distance between herself and the shack she stopped. She peered into the murky night behind her to make sure the man hadn't followed her. She saw nothing; the street was quiet.

She was at the crossing. On the far side of the street, a few pedestrians passed, but there was no one nearby. She walked forward, stepping into the larger street that crossed the one bounded by the shanties and the wall. She stood now where the man had passed pulling the cart. There was no other traffic.

She had passed the corner of the wall. It was the blind side of a dark building, massive and ugly. The front was built of heavy block, piled in clumsy detail that gave it the look of an angry face. Shutters hid the rows of windows that started one story above the street.

For a building the size of a cathedral, it had an insignificant entrance. No broad steps swept up to arched doorways, no columns or latticed balconies framed a stately portal. At the level of the street was a single slab of hewn stone, the step to a modest door that might have graced a tenement, or served as the back door of a tavern.

It hung open. From inside came a hint of glowing light. Marcia thought she heard faint music. She looked around again, wary of being taken by surprise. The only movement she saw was across the wide avenue, where quiet figures passed in the night.

This had every earmark of a dream, or nightmare. Everything seemed imbued with symbolic import. She looked down. Except her foot. What could it mean that she was burdened with a sopping shoe?

But everything else. Glistening, lustful bodies writhing in a filthy hovel, beckoning her with empty animal eyes. The threatening shadow-man, the musky stench. Her shrinking weakness, her retreat.

Then there was the ominous wall, the hulking church-mansion, the shuttered windows, blind. The open door. The empty avenue, the passersby, remote and silent.

Again she turned in a watchful pirouette. What was this place she had come to? She did not bother to pinch herself. She was not dreaming, much as she might wish to be. She was wide awake, and had carelessly, foolishly brought herself here. This was worse by far than her other predicaments, because it was so completely pointless. When she had followed the strange old man who had no aura, she had had some semblance of a rationale; watching Father was her . . . assignment. When she had pursued him again to regain her ring, she was walking paths she had walked before, and for a clear and pressing reason. And when she had followed Father into the Lower Regions, and had found herself lost and alone, she at least could say why she was there.

And now she was back, she suddenly realized. She sniffed the heavy air, recognizing the stench of the Lower Regions. The day before yesterday she had escaped. Now she had brought herself back by meddling with powers she did not understand and could not control. Powers, she reminded herself, that she possessed only because Father had stolen her ring and worn it for a few days. The ring that she had been told most particularly was never to be removed. Perhaps once the ring had been taken from her, she should not have dared wear it again. It had, almost, been wearing her since she had retrieved it.

She raised her hand and gazed at the ring. If she took it off, would she still be here? She pictured herself removing it from her finger and flinging it into the darkness, then shuddered, clutching the ring to her breast. If she was lost in the Lower Regions, her ring—and she felt it to be hers despite her misadventures—was her only connection to her own place, her own life. And it was her connection to Elyssa. Would she come, this enchantress—or goddess, or mega-witch—and make everything all right? Or was Father here, somewhere?

The street she had climbed, between the wall and the shacks, terminated at the avenue. It was nothing more, it seemed, than a way leading to the water, whether river, lake, ocean. Or mud puddle, for all she knew. She hoped it was not the way back to her apartment, because she could not imagine passing by those hovels again, let alone braving whatever might be waiting in the fog.

After assuring herself there was no one, or nothing, nearby, she moved into the darker shadows by the building. She kept clear of the door, stationing herself several yards away from it.

She brushed her ring with the tips of her fingers and made a conscious effort to compose herself, to concentrate. Surely, she thought, she could bring this excursion under control. Given another few moments of peace, and just a little bit of luck, she could be back home in time to send out for pizza.

CHAPTER

· 9 ·

Marcia stared into the middle distance, trying to bring her thoughts to a single focus. She closed her eyes. It was a matter of visualizing clearly, of releasing the power of the ring. Then home would lie just a few steps away.

The heat and damp distracted her. She closed her mind to them. She would walk through the bordering haze and leave this dreadful place. She struggled to bring herself to the sense of elevation that was required. Her scalp was wet with perspiration; her sock felt like warm mud. As she fought to exclude her surroundings, she heard a whispered hissing sound.

Her eyes snapped open. She saw no transitory mist, no sign of magical boundaries. Moving not at all, she looked toward the crossing. There, just passing the corner of the wall, were three figures. She could see them with surprising clarity, as though they were actors on a stage, surrounded by theatrical darkness, but picked out by subtle hidden lights.

The shortest was the man she had seen with the woman, dressed now in baggy pantaloons, a blouse with a high collar that came past his ears, and a wide-brimmed hat pulled down low above his eyes. One hand was at his belt, the other he rested on the woman's hip, his arm around her waist.

She was attired in a single clinging garment, light in color and nearly transparent. A long filmy scarf bound her head, circled her neck, and fell over her shoulders. She was barefoot.

The third in the party was between the other two in height, dressed in clothes that were dark and nondescript. His cheeks were ruddy, his face animated by an eager smile. As the others walked into the avenue, he stopped and turned from side to side. His glance passed over Marcia, standing motionless in the shadows. When he stepped forward to join them, she silently released her pent-in breath.

The three stopped. As Marcia watched them, she heard again the sound of faint music, a little louder than before. Must be a convention, she thought flippantly, then froze as the group on the avenue turned in her direction. The man's face was still lit by the smile. The couple merely stared ahead, the light reflecting from their little eyes.

Marcia remained motionless for the space of two rapid heartbeats, then moved with quick steps to the doorway. With one last look at the advancing trio, she went inside and pulled the door closed behind her.

The latch dropped and engaged. She looked to see if there was something she could fasten, a bolt to slam into place. There was nothing but the flimsy brass fixture. She caught a whiff of the sweet unwholesome odor that had enveloped her outside the shack. She turned away from the door, expecting at any second to hear the click of the latch.

She was in a hallway. What illumination there was came from the other end. With a final backward glance, she walked quickly toward the light, trying to make as little noise as possible. Her wet shoe rubbed at her heel and made sucking sounds with every step.

At the end of the hall she turned, half expecting to see the smiling man and the rat couple catching up to her. The gloomy passageway behind her was empty. She stood at the crossing of another hallway, wider and lighted by lamps placed on narrow tables. The music was louder now, and she could hear a steady pulse of low-pitched bumps, as if someone in a far-off room were pounding monotonously on a wall or floor.

She began walking toward the music. By the time she reached the end of the hallway, it sounded like a weekend party upstairs at the dorm. Except for the music. It was loud and insistent, and with a driving propulsive rhythm, but was from the era of the oldest films in her collection. There was a trumpet, and she was quite certain she could hear a clarinet mingling its squeal with the fragile crashing of a hammered cymbal.

Marcia hesitated and looked back. The corridor was empty. At this end there was no place to go but up a flight of stairs, and despite the cheerful sounds from above, she had no desire to join the party. She began to retrace her steps, slowing down cautiously as she approached the place where the two corridors met. She took a deep breath and gathered herself for a rush past the other hallway.

When Marcia heard her name, she didn't scream. The sound she made was more like a shriek. The voice had come from behind her. She whirled to face it. At the end of the hall, just at the bottom of the stairway, was a man wearing evening clothes.

He called to her again. "We're down here. Come on. Where have you been?" He took a step in her direction. Marcia looked over her shoulder quickly, then back. The man was standing with his hands at his sides, smiling at her. Who could know her name? Who could transport her in this way? This almost had to have some connection with the Sisterhood. She looked behind her again, then began to walk toward him.

"The band is great," he said as she reached him. He turned and started up the stairs.

"Wait," said Marcia. Her heart was pounding. She couldn't tell if it was from relief or terror. "Who are you?"

He smiled. Marcia tried to remember where she had seen him. He seemed to stand out, to be more real, somehow, than his surroundings. The sensation was like that of unexpectedly seeing someone famous in the flesh.

"I'm Victor." He started up the stairs again. When she didn't follow, he turned and beckoned.

"Come on up. You have to meet everyone. The whole gang." Marcia looked at her clothing, squirmed her foot in her wet shoe, and followed hesitantly. On the landing at the top of the stairs, Victor stopped with his hand on a doorknob. The music was louder here, but the song that was being played was slow and soft. Marcia could imagine multicolored light being reflected from a rotating sphere.

"You can check your ring with the girl." He opened the door.

The floor was crowded with dancers. From across the room a pretty girl kissed the air with pouting lips and sent a wink in

Marcia's direction. Victor had gone ahead and stood with his back to her.

"I can take your ring for you, hon." The girl was seated in a booth. She was chewing gum.

Marcia just looked at her, feeling awkward and out of place. All the women were wearing shimmery clothes that glittered. She looked down at her feet. There was a dark spot on the floor under her wet shoe.

"She's completely reliable."

Marcia jerked her head up. Victor was beside her. He was very handsome, she thought. About fifty, wavy hair with a touch of gray at the temples. Distinguished, her mother would have said. Sophisticated.

"Huh?"

"Jeannine." He nodded in the direction of the check girl. "She'll take good care of it."

"Oh, I—" Marcia stammered.

"You bet! I'll make you a ticket." Jeannine began to rummage in a box behind the counter.

A pair of women in short black dresses squeezed between Marcia and Jeannine. Their heads were together. Marcia heard, "I don't care, he's a drip," pronounced in clipped businesslike tones as they passed.

"Okay; here you are." Jeannine was holding a beige ticket out for her. Marcia stared at it.

"Ring check," said Jeannine.

Victor appeared at her side. "Ready?" he asked.

"I can't take my ring off."

"Is it stuck?"

Marcia stepped back. She wished she could have a moment to think. "No, but Elyssa said—"

Victor shook his head and laughed softly. "Oh, her," he said, rolling his eyes and cocking his wrist in a way that gave him an air of charming vulnerability. "She's a pip. She drives everyone nuts with that stuff. You'll get used to it." He peered at Marcia's puzzled frown. "Oh, don't get me wrong. She's swell, it's just . . . you know. . . ." He gave her a patient smile. "No one wears a ring here. You should have been told."

Marcia hesitated, then grasped her ring and began to pull on it, at the same time looking nervously around the crowded noisy room. No one ever told her anything. It would be a relief, she thought, to take the ring off for a while, to put aside her burden. She imagined the feeling of the thin band slipping over her knuckle. She looked down at her finger, uncomfortably conscious of the fact that she was making Victor wait.

Remove it for no one but me. That is what Elyssa had told her when she put the ring on her finger. And Marcia had obeyed. She had not given the ring to Father; he had taken it from her. And when he returned it, he had put it back on her finger himself.

Marcia raised her eyes to Victor and favored him with a cold smile as she extended her hand. "Want to take it off for me?" She had not meant to sound harsh and mocking, but found she didn't care.

Victor took a quick step away from her. "Forget it," he said. "It's not important. We'll take care of it later."

He started off through the crowd. "Come on, I want you to meet the gang." Marcia looked back toward the door, then followed, favoring her wet foot.

The band began playing to an urgent, pounding beat. The bass drum looked big enough to be used in a marching band. The little drummer was almost hidden behind it. From the floor, Marcia could see only his head, and the blur of drumsticks flailing at a cymbal suspended by a string.

The musicians all were black; the dancers who crowded the floor were white. Marcia stopped and looked around. She felt as though she had wandered onto a film set. What would happen, she wondered, if she shouted *Cut!*

In fact, what would happen if she said or did anything? It was pointless to say that something strange was going on, as that was now her permanent situation, but this particular strangeness was different from what she had been getting used to. She looked back at the bandstand. There was something decidedly odd about the band.

"Say hey!" It was the girl who had winked at her.

Marcia wondered if she was getting punchy. Yielding to an irrepressible temptation, she said, "Twenty-three skidoo."

The girl grinned. "I'm Suzy."

"Lulu," said Marcia, holding out her hand.

Suzy took a step backwards and giggled, fluttering her hand in front of her face. "I thought you were Marcia," she said. She bent forward at the waist and stared into Marcia's face. She had very pretty eyes.

Marcia wondered if she had finally lost her reason. "Marcia's on vacation," she said. "I'm filling in for her." She took a step toward Suzy. "Actually," she whispered, "she died."

Marcia noticed that the music had begun to sound very strange. The frantic tempo of the drumming remained the same, but the other instruments began to sound as though they were being played at random, like noisemakers at a party.

The dancers were still cavorting with the same vacuous enthusiasm. They looked, Marcia thought, a lot like puppets being jerked around on invisible wires. She scanned the room. One or two people waved to her gaily. Marcia ignored them.

Evidently she wasn't meant to examine things too closely here. The music filled the background nicely, was tuneful and lively. But when she focused on it, it started to show signs of disintegration. It was as though the instruments were providing noises that her brain would turn into music. She wondered about the dancers, the snatches of conversation. Was it all just gibbering and jumping that she was then organizing into a semblance of integration and coherence?

And the stuff about the ring. It annoyed her that it was no more subtle than it was, and that, with the *real* Marcia, it could work anyway. It was simply a matter of getting to the central core of weakness. There was no denying the urge she had felt to hand her ring over to Jeannine—to do what Victor had told her, to be accommodating, and hope that no one would notice her inappropriate clothing, her waterlogged shoe.

Suzy was still looking at her expectantly, her pretty eyes wide and friendly. Marcia looked down at her slippers. They were the same deep red as her lipstick.

Marcia had seen a lot of old movies. She leaned back, cocked her head to one side and tried to sound like a soprano Humphrey Bogart.

"The trouble with you, sweetheart, is both your shoes are dry." She executed a few dance steps she had learned as a child from the old man across the hall, then sang the punch line from his almost favorite song.

"Lulu's back in town!"

Victor appeared at her elbow. "Having a good time?"

"You bet!" Marcia sang out. The band ended their song with a crash, then immediately launched into something slow and bluesy. "Suzy is, uh, swell." Victor was staring at her. Marcia went on. "With it," she said with exaggerated gaiety. "You know—*hep.*"

Victor smiled at her uncertainly.

"What's the matter, honey?" she said. "Aren't we going to meet the gang?"

His smile disappeared. "Of course," he said.

Marcia followed him to a table where four women were seated. He gestured to one of the empty chairs, but did not take the other one. He looked pained.

"I don't think Marcia likes her party," he said, then left.

Marcia looked at her companions. If you don't know the rules, she thought, you make up your own. The worst thing is to let the game play you.

"Lulu," she said.

The chair directly opposite Marcia was empty. The woman seated next to it was wearing a jacket with wide lapels shaped like the feathers on an arrow. With her fingertips she slowly pushed a crystal goblet in Marcia's direction.

Marcia glanced at it. "Lulu doesn't drink," she said. Where, she wondered, was this anger coming from? She could feel, faintly, like the memory of a caress, the demon's scar next to her eye.

The woman seated to her left leaned forward. "Marcia," she began.

Marcia shook her head vigorously, imagining her boring straight brown hair as a mass of bouncing auburn curls. "Marcia drank," she said. "In fact, she was a lush." She smiled at all of them. "That's how she died."

"Marcia, we are your sisters."

Marcia looked around the table at the four women. "Charmed," she said. "Listen, I have to go order a pizza." She started to get up, though not with any clear idea of where she would go.

The woman with the lapels rose quickly. "The Sisterhood commands it!" she spat. "Remove your ring and share the ritual glass with us!"

Marcia dropped back into her chair. The woman sat down with studied grace. She smiled thinly and held out her hand.

"Now," she said. "First the ring must—"

"Jesus, Mary, and Joseph!" said Marcia, almost shouting the

names. The Ultimate. Mother had permitted herself this blasphemy precisely twice in all the years Marcia had lived at home.

The woman jerked back in her chair. The first woman leaned across the table and touched the stem of the glass.

"Really, Marcia, you're overwrought," she said softly. "Never mind the ring for now. Just take a drink."

Marcia sat up straight and bent her head over the glass like a person saying grace. The woman waited silently. Finally, she took the glass and lifted it. She looked up, holding the drink at eye level. Her posture and attitude were those of someone about to propose a toast.

"You know, I think you're right. I am feeling a little overwrought." She smiled shyly and met the eyes of each woman in turn. "But I thought I explained." She raised her hand higher. When she spoke again it was in a voice not much above a whisper. "Lulu doesn't drink," she said, and smashed the goblet to the table.

Lulu would not jump away from the table, Marcia had decided. Anyway, Lulu was just wearing some old casual things that Marcia didn't care about, and one of Lulu's shoes was already wet. She had pictured these sisters of hers squealing and recoiling from the drops and shattering glass, but none of them moved. The woman across from her was bleeding from a tiny cut below her lip. She glared at Marcia silently. Marcia winked at her.

Victor shouldered his way through the dancers. Behind him was a person Marcia couldn't see, except for a flowing dress with a crowded floral pattern in yellows and faded reds. Marcia watched as Victor produced a napkin and wiped the table clean. The unbroken stem of the goblet was swept onto the floor and bounced out of sight among the feet of the oblivious jitterbugs.

The woman was old, and wore heavy makeup that seemed to accentuate the loops of wrinkles hanging under her eyes, the creases in her forehead, the long emptiness of her hollow cheeks. Victor helped her into the remaining chair, opposite Marcia. The woman's body was hidden by the shapeless garment she wore, but as she fussed herself into a comfortable position, it seemed too large for her long neck and narrow face.

Marcia watched with a trace of Lulu's smart-ass smile still on her lips. In the few minutes she had known Lulu, she had grown quite fond of her, besides which, Lulu was certainly handling this situation better than Marcia would be able to. When Lulu turned in the direction of the bandstand and shouted in a brassy voice, she felt like an observer.

"Hey, Sambo!"

Marcia cringed. She sincerely believed that racial epithets were ugly, violent, and only escaped being inexcusable because ignorance was not always voluntary.

"Stop the music. Can't you see the old dame's trying to concentrate?"

Marcia gasped. Lulu was being *rude*.

No one would ever guess you grew up in a tenement.

Marcia had never thought of it as a tenement. It was just inexpensive. A little run down.

And as far as what's shocking, trust me, you're no judge. You purse your lips when someone says "flaunt" for "flout."

Mother pursed her lips, but I don't, Marcia thought, pursing her lips.

I'm not even going to mention "ekksettra."

Marcia shook her head. Another form of insanity. An argument with an alter ego.

The band had stopped. The trumpet player was grinning at her, bobbing his head up and down and rolling his eyes. A similar image of a black man being ritually obsequious had distressed and embarrassed her when she saw it in an old movie, and she had been alone in her apartment at the time. Now everyone in the room was looking at her.

Marcia focused on Victor. His face was contorted with a snarl of anger. Both his charm and his good looks had vanished. He spoke between clenched teeth.

"Be silent, you vile bitch!"

Marcia stared blankly at him. You're on, Lulu, she thought resignedly.

"Hey, Victor."

He glared at her. She hadn't noticed before the dark circles around his eyes. It made him look . . . ominous.

"Go piss up a rope."

Lulu smiled sweetly.

So did Marcia. She had been secretly waiting for an occasion to say that terrible thing ever since a day thirty years ago when she had heard an older girl in the neighborhood use it to silence a blustering boyfriend.

It worked again. Victor uttered a few strangled noises, but no
words. Marcia didn't know a great deal about vulgarities, but she
had always suspected that an adequate retort to that one could
not be improvised.

"Why do you work so hard to anger me?" The old lady raised
her eyes and gazed across the table. Her aura was thin, and
seemed to melt into the ambient light. Marcia realized that there
was no visible source for the room's illumination, just a general-
ized glow. She, or Lulu, looked unconcernedly around the room.
Now that the dancers had stopped, there seemed fewer of them.
When the music was going, the dancers all in motion, she would
have guessed there were twenty-five or thirty couples. There
seemed now to be only a few people on the floor, all staring at
her. And the auras, as much as she could see of them, all appeared to be the same, a rudimentary arrangement of simple
hues.

The women at the table—her sisters—had individual auras,
more complex ones that had a quality of fluidity. Victor's was
like that as well. It might have been composed of flame. This
was outside Marcia's experience, and strangely unsettling. She
found herself thinking that this might be a good time for Lulu to
keep her mouth shut.

The old woman continued to watch her, not staring, but gazing
mildly at her like someone examining a curiosity.

Marcia's panicky thought, when she found herself alone with
the old woman in a cramped room lit by a single candle, was that
Lulu had been left behind. There had been no sensation of passing time or change of place. They had been in the dance hall surrounded by a silent crowd. Now they were seated at a small
table. The candle stood in no holder or saucer, but was stuck to
the rough planks of the table by its own melting wax.

"Lulu is right about the ring, of course." The old woman
glanced toward a slithering sound in the shadows by the wall.
"Do you keep pets?" she asked in a tone of polite conversation.

Marcia stared silently. Only with Elyssa had she experienced
something like this seamless transition. And even then it had
been necessary for them to join hands. This old woman had not
touched her, or even made a gesture, and yet in a sliver of time
during which Marcia had not blinked, they had been translated
from the dance hall to this place.

"The ring? Lulu?"

"I am not ready to take it from you by force. Not yet. Nor should I have to. It is mine." The woman made a weary gesture. She looked tired and old. "Simple fairness—"

Marcia interrupted. "I'm sorry, you're wrong. This is Elyssa's ring."

For a moment, the old lady was still. Marcia wondered if she had been heard.

The woman said, "Are you so sure?" in a tired voice. "Are you even certain it is the ring you think it is? You take it off, just for a moment, and I will show you how it has been changed." She looked up at Marcia. The skin around her eyes seemed to droop. "The Sisterhood has rules—laws to govern the rings. You have an obligation to let me look at it if the ownership is questioned." She extended a wrinkled hand, palm up, across the table.

Marcia felt confused. Far too many things had happened in far too short a time. She knew this was the ring Elyssa gave her. But she also knew that it had been changed, and that it had changed her aura in disturbing ways. As always, there were many questions and no answers. She looked at the old woman's outstretched hand. It looked passive, almost dead, illuminated only by the watery light of the candle, waiting for the ring.

"You must think I'm nuts." Lulu always sounded cheerful, Marcia noted. Cheerful and calm.

The woman drew her hand back. "All right," she said in a tired, patient voice. "Just take it off. I will tell you what to look for."

Marcia didn't take her eyes from the ring when she answered. "I am not permitted to take it off."

"You weren't supposed to," said the woman after a silence. "But you did. Another wore the ring you call yours, changed it. Of course, change is the law. Even the sea changes: rises in one age, falls in another; steals kingdoms from their rulers and deeds them to swimming things. And if the sea may change its boundaries, you and I may change a rule. Especially one that has been broken already and no longer matters. Take off the ring. I will show you something that will surprise you."

"I will not remove the ring."

There was a moment of utter stillness. In the dim light, Marcia thought she saw a gathering of shadow behind the woman. It seemed almost as though she were growing larger. Marcia watched with mounting apprehension. The silence stretched on.

In a single violent motion, the old lady erupted from the table with a howl of rage. She sprang backward like a gigantic cat, then hurled herself forward and gripped the edge of the table. Her stringy white hair framed her head in the candle's glow. In the uncertain light, her teeth looked impossibly numerous, and sharp.

"It is mine!" she shrieked, flinging foamy spittle from her lips with every word. With a movement too quick to see, she clamped Marcia's forearm in a painful grasp and yanked her to her feet. Her furious scream was almost unintelligible.

"I'll dine on you, and lick your blood from that ring!"

Marcia's sudden fear was overtaken by a reflexive surge of anger. For an instant, she was intensely conscious of her ring and aware, as well, of the demon's mark, and even of the scars on her shoulder. She felt a tremor of heavy force shake her. When the woman immediately dropped her arm and cried out again, Marcia couldn't tell if it was in rage or pain. She watched her pace back and forth like a bear in a cage, just beyond the light of the candle. The woman moaned, or perhaps was muttering or complaining to herself. Marcia was in a situation beyond the guidance of both etiquette and common sense. She dropped silently back into her chair, waiting for whatever might come next. Her arm was numb.

When she took her seat, the woman looked tired and feeble again.

"Now, this ring . . ." She placed next to the candle a worked gold band set with a large green stone. She took her hand from it as though with reluctance and raised her eyes to meet Marcia's. Her voice was conversational and just a bit tremulous. ". . . is a rare wonder. It has a virtue you will appreciate."

Marcia felt glued to her seat. She met the old woman's eyes with difficulty and did not speak.

"When we exchange, and you put it on, it will take you back to your home. After that, it will have no properties but its worth in trade, which is great, as you will find." She dropped her arm onto the table and shifted the ring a little away from the candle. She released it slowly and sat back in her chair.

"Now," she continued, "take your ring off and put it next to mine." She pushed herself back from the table. "When you put mine on, you will be back in your own place."

Marcia peered across the table. From somewhere outside came the sound of a high-pitched call. She raised her ring hand and looked down at the thin circle of gold on her finger. When she raised her other arm, she felt a sharp pain. She took a long, slow breath and reached for her ring, then put her hands together and looked up.

"No."

Marcia had expected the woman to fly into another rage. Instead, she remained completely still, moving only her eyes, first to the ring on the table, then to Marcia.

"Tziann will not come here."

Feeling like an idiot, Marcia uttered a polite, "I'm sorry?" What, she wondered, were the conventions of discourse with a monster? This old hag had threatened to make a meal of her, and Marcia was talking to her as though she were her hostess at a garden party.

"The one you serve."

Marcia began to answer, then stopped and leaned forward. The old woman's aura was more defined when she was out of the light. In the dance hall, Marcia had seen only a feeble emanation that was swallowed in the surrounding light. Now, in deep shadows, the aura radiated a suffocating murk of evil hues that seemed to extend to the limits of the room. Marcia had to resist an impulse to hold her breath.

"Elyssa?" she said.

The woman smiled. Marcia made an unsuccessful effort not to look at her teeth, then was startled to notice that they were neither sharper nor more numerous than her own. The smile turned to quiet laughter.

"A pretty name," she laughed. "Is she pretty for you, this Elyssa? Is her appearance pleasing?"

Marcia nodded. In fact, the most noticeable thing about Elyssa, besides her impossible aura, was her eyes, which were deep and cold and somehow wild. It was because of her eyes that Elyssa's presence was disturbing, even frightening. More frightening, yet, than this frightening hag, which was a comfort, Marcia supposed. If Elyssa would only come, how gladly would she welcome the sight of those cold, wild eyes.

"And who has marked you, marred your pretty skin?"

Marcia wondered if she should refuse to speak. Was there some trickery in this quiet talk? She thought back to the night last summer in the alley. Elyssa had called the monster by name.

"Rassadder? Balder-something?' she said. "And some other names, I think."

The old woman nodded. "Yes," she said, "one of our petty kings." She pulled her chair closer to the table. "So it is his scar you wear, then? You stood before him, bore the weight of his malice? Was it worth it?"

"What?"

"The strength you gained. Was it worth—?" The old woman glanced at Marcia's arm, then looked away quickly. She seemed to frown before baring her teeth in a gruesome smile again. Marcia took her eyes from her hostess long enough to look at her forearm. On the underside, just by the bone, were four purple bruises. Three of them were bleeding. More scars, she supposed. She was pretty sure there were veterans of gang wars who bore fewer permanent marks of violence than she did. She had the demon's mark next to her eye, the traces left by the punctures in her shoulder, and now these wounds.

The dancers were gone. Only Victor and the four women remained. Marcia looked around for Suzy. She was absent, as was the fearsome hag. Again there had been no sensation attendant to the change of place, though the chair she sat in, and the table before her, were different from the ones in the hut.

Had she imagined the old woman, the table with the candle? She turned her arm over. Beneath the tatters of her sleeve, the blood still flowed from her bruises.

She looked up at Victor and the women. All of them were staring at her injuries. She addressed them in Lulu's voice.

"Some bouncer."

Victor took one step away as the four women got up slowly from the table. Marcia just watched them wearily. She wondered what time it was. When Victor spoke, it was in a hushed voice.

"She is too—"

He was interrupted by a woman who had not spoken before. "She has sent her back, that is all. Just wait."

Victor took another backward step. "But, her arm, she—"

"Where is the dreen?" The old woman, still dressed in her flowered gown, was walking across the empty dance floor.

Marcia found her gaze wandering to the bandstand. The bass drum was all that was left of the band. Above it, the suspended cymbal still moved slightly, like an expiring pendulum. *Dreen?* she thought. She brought her eyes back to the old woman. There was something different about her. She was walking very slowly, and looked somehow larger than she had before.

"I am here," said a voice from the shadows. Suzy's flapper outfit was in disarray, as if she just spent twenty minutes in the backseat of someone's flivver. Marcia wondered how she could have missed her aura before. She didn't remember noticing it at all, and yet it was not one that could easily be ignored. And the way she was moving was different. Before, Marcia had seen Suzy perform antique dance steps with the frenzied grace appropriate to them. Now her gait was brisk and purposeful.

The ache in Marcia's arm was icy cold. Pain reached from her shoulder to her fingertips. With effort, she pulled her attention from it and forced herself to concentrate on the old woman and her allies. She got up slowly from her chair.

The old woman's stare seemed to bore into her. "I tell you, Tziann will not come here, will not challenge me." She gestured to the others. Suzy came to stand at her side. "Look around you at the power you think to defy." Suzy took something from the woman's hand and began to walk toward the table. Marcia stepped around her chair and backed away, glancing quickly over her shoulder to check behind her. Suzy's eyes, still pretty, but hard, caught hers. She opened her hand to display the ring the old woman had offered Marcia before. She placed it in the center of the table, then stepped away.

Marcia fought to keep her concentration. The pain in her arm had the dull insistence of a toothache. It was becoming difficult to push it away.

"I offer you this ring one time more," said the old woman.

Marcia straightened her back. She wanted to put aside the pain in her arm, to forget it until a more convenient occasion, and yet it seemed to clamor for her attention. On the other side of the table, her enemies were ranged against her. As she watched, they took one step forward, moving in unison like a chorus line or drill team.

She tried to think about her options. There was, of course, the option of trading rings, but one and one had to continue adding up to three, and yielding didn't fit the pattern. Then there was the matter of her ancestry. Had her straits not been so dire, she might have smiled. Here she was, proving to be a Mibsey woman after all. Stiff-necked and stubborn to the end.

She brushed her thoughts and theories aside. There were, in fact, no options. There was only one thing to be done. As she stepped toward the table, she realized she had to let the pain go. This was no time to divide her energies, such as they were.

She stumbled at her second step, hesitated, then moved on. From the other side of the table, the old woman smiled a very ugly smile. Marcia bent her injured arm and raised it to her chest. The pain seemed more manageable now than when she had tried so hard to manage it. It seemed almost to buoy her, as though pain itself could be a source of strength.

Marcia had stopped hoping that Elyssa would come to rescue her. She was on her own, just as Annie had said. There was no one to rely on but Marcia. She would do what Marcia could.

She stopped at the table, looked down at the ring. She raised her eyes to the old woman.

"What is your name?" she said, listening to her voice crack. She felt very tired.

"Remove your ring and exchange it for mine."

"I will take nothing without the name," said Marcia wearily, not knowing why she cared, but feeling it was important to win this one concession.

The old woman stared at her carefully, still with the smile on her lips. She turned to Suzy.

"Take back the ring."

Suzy was a few paces from the table. At her first step, Marcia raised her ring hand from her side.

"Do not come nearer." Marcia's voice was low and dry.

The old woman shifted her weight. "You are ignorant," she called. "You cannot stand before a dreen." Victor and the four women laughed. The sound was intimate, almost friendly. Marcia waited for them to stop.

"Give me your name."

The old woman didn't answer, but waved Suzy toward the table.

"I will not have you any closer to me," said Marcia.

"Step back then, Lulu," said the flapper. The quick look she sent to Marcia was somber, almost sad.

Marcia crowded closer to the table. Suzy took half a step toward her, then looked back at the old woman. There was a long silence. Marcia felt light. The pain was gone from her arm. She wondered if she was going to faint.

"Ulda." The hag's voice was flat.

Marcia put her hand on the table. She wondered how much more effort she could put forth. She tipped the table over and kicked it aside. Suzy moved backward out of the way.

Marcia gathered her ring hand into a fist. She had no more ideas and no more patience. Whatever strength, whatever force she had, she would use. She concentrated her thoughts on the ring, trying to put all her energy there. She felt weightless. She raised her eyes and stared at the old woman. "Ulda!" she cried in a hoarse shout, and began to advance across the floor.

She stumbled and looked around her in surprise. She was back in the place where Ulda had attacked her. The candle still burned in its place on the table. The dancing shadows barely reached the walls of the small room. She was alone. The room was as it had been, but for Ulda's absence. She went to the wall and made a careful circuit of the chamber. The floor seemed to be of packed dirt, the ceiling was low, and there were no windows. In the corner furthest from the table she found a wooden door. She put her hand on the latch, then let it go again. She would take advantage of this respite to gather her thoughts.

She sat down in the chair she had occupied before, as grateful for the rest as if she had spent hours on her feet. Yet she had not been here for long. She had no watch, but guessed it was probably now about the middle of rush hour.

Still plenty of time, she thought, to order a pizza with double sausage. She wondered when Borphis would miss her. If she could manage to get back soon, he'd still be at the window watching the traffic.

And she might get back. Ulda and the others were afraid of her, or of her ring. If she had been more sensible and less aggressive, if she had yielded, or tried to avoid conflict, where would she be now? According to Ulda, safe at home. Marcia shook her head sadly. She was picturing the mutilated corpse of a naive apprentice sorceress. She had learned a valuable lesson tonight. Now she had to try to live long enough to benefit from it.

It took less than an hour to establish that she could not at the moment escape this place by means of magic. She tried repeatedly to reach a state of displacement, abstraction, but the only vision she saw was of her physical surroundings—the only mysterious shadows, the ones that cloaked the room she sat in.

Her arm had begun to hurt again. When she had been injured last week, her puncture wounds had made her ill, despite the protecting power of the ring and the ministrations of the village witch. Now she had been wounded again, and there was no witch to treat her with herbs and potions.

She rose wearily from the table. The room was warm and damp, but Marcia felt hot and dry. She suspected she looked like the consumptive heroine of a tragic opera. That was certainly the way she felt as she shuffled unsteadily to the door.

It opened on protesting hinges to a sight she had not expected. The floor of dirt and blank walls had led her to believe she was in a cellar, perhaps a dungeon. She had thought to find a stairway, or corridors of dripping stone patrolled by rats and spiders.

The light outside was the same as before, but the mist was heavier. Marcia stepped out and closed the door behind her. She peered through the vaporous atmosphere that clothed the landscape of shacks and rubble. She took a few careful paces and looked back at the shapeless hovel she had emerged from. It was the twin of the one the rat people had occupied. All around her were others, only a few yards apart, dark and silent.

She guessed she must be somewhere in the slum she had passed earlier. She saw no sign of any structure larger than the huts around her. The large building with the great blind wall was nowhere to be seen.

There was a stirring nearby. Marcia turned in time to see something big launch itself from one of the neighboring roofs and flap heavily into the mist. From behind her came another sound. She whirled, but saw nothing. Here and there in the distance were lights. She recalled the rat people and their open door.

Marcia felt dizzy. Making sure she wouldn't lose track of where she was, she made her way around two shacks built close together, staying clear of the deepest shadows. Ahead there seemed to be a narrow lane. She oriented herself again. The vile little shanty she had crept from a moment before was now her only refuge. It would not do to lose it. She studied its ramshackle contours carefully before turning again to the lane. Thinking she might get a better view of her surroundings, she started toward it, but before she had taken her second step, she was halted by a familiar noise.

It was the quiet scraping sound she had heard in the fog when she had first arrived. As she listened, her breath in her throat, it stopped, then started again. It was close, and getting closer. Being exquisitely careful to make not the slightest sound, Marcia moved into the deeper shadows by a leaning wall of scrap wood and rotting cloth.

The man looked gray, like an image in a black-and-white photograph. His clothing was scant and made up of rags. He was tall and muscular. His expression was vacant. His eyes were fixed; unmoving as his head swayed from side to side. He dragged a large sack by a rope. It looked heavy.

Marcia watched him pass. She waited until the sound of the sack had faded into the distance, then retraced her steps to her—as she approached, she tried to think what to call it— bungalow, cottage, cabin, hut, shack, shanty. She thought of the rat people. Whore's crib? *Hi, I'm your new neighbor.* What a place for a virgin warrior.

By the time she got inside, she felt almost too weak to cross the room. She collapsed onto the chair and put her head down on her arms. Her skin was hot. She could smell the blood drying on her bruises. She would rest for a few minutes, she decided, then figure out what to do next.

CHAPTER
◆ 10 ◆

At dawn the Devlin sea hens boiled from the cliffs and screamed the morning into being like a waiting army that strikes at first light. In the town the bakers and others whose business it was to be about at such an hour left their pillows and their dreams, but the other citizens slept on, no more disturbed by the familiar chorus than a slumbering sexton is by the peal of tower bells. It was only away from home that Devlin hands were early risers, drawn grouchy from their beds by a peaceful sunrise.

Devlin had no wharves or docks; seagoing vessels were piloted through the protecting reefs and anchored well out from the strand in calm deep water. Instead of inns and taverns where the sea met the land, the drawn-up boats and drying nets of fishermen dominated the waterfront. Next came their dwellings, from huts and shanties of castoff planks to sturdy cottages of stone and painted timbers. Behind them in Fish-Head Alley were the salt shops and smokehouses where the catch not used fresh was prepared for laying by.

Then came the town itself, sprawled out between the forbidding cliffs and the sea. There were tall buildings and squat, broad buildings and narrow, buildings that faced each other, buildings that stood shoulder to shoulder and faced the sea, buildings with their backs to one another, buildings angled toward a neighbor—the architecture of Devlin had as many attitudes and postures as the shoppers in a crowded market square. It looked like a town put up by careless children working in the dark.

On the tenth morning after he had left Ambermere, Breksin entered the city of Devlin by way of the narrow, winding road from the mountain passes. He had risen early and was already on the skirts of the last hill as the sea hens passed. On his back was a satchel, on his shoulder, a small black cat, and hanging from his belt was a heavy battle hammer, old and covered with faded stains.

He had no difficulty locating the fortress residence of Black Jack Flanders, the preeminent criminal in this city of thieves. It sat on the knuckles of the Devlin cliffs, four stories of hewn stone. It looked like the castle of a petty prince and sat apart from its neighbors, bordered on the front and sides by a small park of gnarled seaside trees and unkempt hedges.

With the help of a baker's boy on whom he bestowed enough pennies to make a week's wage, Breksin found a quiet, respectable inn, meaning one in which the common room furniture did not have to be put back together every morning. Even pirates, it seemed, grew with advancing years to relish a quiet cup after dinner, and cards or dice unaccompanied by knives and cudgels.

He spent the day getting used to the city, and more importantly, letting the city get used to him. If there was no hope that one so large could be inconspicuous, at least he could become a common sight—an exotic, perhaps, but not a rarity. His hammer he left with his other belongings at the inn and ambled through the lanes and alleys, just another giant with a black cat perched next to his ear.

After stowing his gear, he took a late breakfast in the company of bleary-eyed tars in a waterfront dive, where he concocted a punch of raw eggs and cooked wine, to which he added spices from a pouch he carried. This steaming brew he offered around with the assurance that it would cure those who could keep it down, and make a noticeable improvement in the condition of those who could not. It worked well enough that a number of the sufferers spoke of little else during the day, and numerous schemes were proposed for getting the packet of spices away from him, either by fraud or outright violence.

At midday, he repaired to a cobbled lane where every window had been shuttered till noon. There he enjoyed a fine lunch among a crowd of newly awakened whores. As a son of the high mountain clans, Breksin was an incurable prude, but he tried to enjoy the luscious beauty of the women in spite of their lewd talk and scanty garments, and though he could not bring himself to pronounce the shameful words they used so freely, he left them with the promise that they would "see more of him" on some night very soon. He blushed when he had to lift the faithful kitsey from the ample bosom where he had draped himself. His blush deepened at the parting words whispered in his ear by the girl, who was easily young enough to be his daughter.

By evening he and the cat had seen most of Devlin, and Breksin had spoken to a number of merchants, tradesmen, and artisans, but nowhere did he hear any talk of the royal hostages. An Ambermere ship had stopped yesterday, but only long enough to put a small party ashore. That seemed odd, but he supposed the diplomats had a well-established protocol for the exchange of hostages and ransom. He also learned that Black Jack Flanders had returned to the city four or five days ago, and that he had been seen very little since then, having kept to his house more than was his custom.

"He's a great one for the taverns, is the cap'n. The taverns and the ladies both," a wine merchant had told him.

"They're all divils," the man's wife added sourly.

"Who, the . . . freebooters?" Breksin asked. He had learned that the word *pirate* was considered unacceptably blunt in Devlin. The woman narrowed her eyes and looked up at him.

"Men," she said.

After visiting a number of taverns, Breksin was inclined to agree with her. Had he not known better, he would have begun to imagine that it was possible to tell honest men from thieves simply by looking at them. It was certainly undeniable that the majority of the men gathered in the taverns were as scurrilous a bunch of villains as might have been readily assembled this side of Hell. Still, he exerted himself to play the part of a sociable stranger, losing at cards more than he won and buying the odd round of wine without giving the impression of tempting affluence.

Despite his cautious efforts, he heard nothing of ransom or hostages, even though he had met more than one of the pirates who sailed under Jack Flanders. But even the oafish "Jummy Griggs, fresh back with the cap'n," who was almost too drunk to sit in a chair, breathed no word of the prize they had taken, beyond praising "those Ambermere wines" with passionate incoherence. It was evident that the sailors' proverbial love of gossip was not shared by those who sailed with Black Jack Flanders.

Still, he went doggedly from tavern to tavern, hoping he would learn something of use. Breksin was a better gambler than anyone he played with. He had always been an avid card player, sometimes even allowing himself to be lured to the tables where the aristocratic gamesters of Ambermere trifled away their days. If he could manage to avoid Reffex and his annoying cronies, it was sometimes possible to pass a pleasant evening there. The court's ranking duchess, for instance, though it distressed Breksin to see her indulge her inexplicable fancy for adulterating excellent wines with honey and mint, was a canny old bird with a card memory that was simply astonishing. Even Daniel had been impressed with her.

It was from Daniel that Breksin had learned, not so much new things about cards and wagers, as how the individual elements he had deduced over the years fit into a pattern. Not only had the knowledge been gratifying for its own sake, but the resulting increase in his prowess had made him positively unwelcome in the circle of the great Count Reffex. But now Daniel was a prisoner, locked away somewhere in this metropolis of thieves.

Breksin gave up his seat at the card table. He had given up, as well, any thought of hearing news of the captives. He would visit the scandalous girls again tomorrow—buy them another meal. It might well be that gossip not retailed in the taverns had been whispered on a whore's pillow.

Breksin did not need much information. He wanted to know where the prisoners were being kept, and under what guard. He had reason to hope that in their stronghold, the pirates would be careless. If they were, then a single man, given skill and determination, might free the prisoners in the event that diplomacy failed and the situation became desperate.

But diplomacy, augmented by gold, would not fail, he was nearly certain. His other, more practical concern was for the remainder of the journey. In the many years Breksin had lived at the court of Asbrak the Fat, he had completely ignored the laughable military with their parades and polished buttons. But when the royal journey was continued, it was his firm intention, despite his inbred horror of travel by water, to be a part of the guard that accompanied it. And if they were challenged again, he himself would direct the defense, and even the Ambermere laggards *would* fight. He frowned. It was hardly more than a fortnight ago that he had stood on the Ambermere quays to see the royal party off. The merchantman had carried a force of armed men sufficient to repel even a pair of the small, fast pirate ships, let alone the single vessel that had taken them.

He made his way back to his lodgings by way of the busiest streets, greeting those he had met during the day. By tomorrow, he thought, there would not be a soul in Devlin who had not seen the giant or at least heard of him. After breakfast, he would minister again to the sufferers in the taverns, and again make a great mystery of the spices he added to the concoction, although he had ground them according to a witches' formula that was no secret in Ambermere.

It shouldn't take long for Captain Flanders to hear of the giant and his cure. Breksin hoped that it might be as soon as tomorrow that he would be invited to the house of the pirate who must, if his reputation was deserved, have frequent need of such a medicine.

He made a detour through the street where the girls worked. Here the way was not so well lighted. Instead of the glow of lamps, the air was filled with the music of plucked strings and flutes. Beyond the last houses of joy, the street was given over to more respectable, less profitable enterprises, all of which were shut for the night. From these dark windows came no songs or soft laughter.

Breksin slowed his pace. On the pretext of tugging at his boot, he sent a quick sidewise glance behind him. At the next corner he turned away from his destination and back toward the sea. At the next turning, he crossed the empty street, continuing to an unpaved lane that ran behind a row of houses. There he picked up his pace. At the next street he turned away from the sea again, walked more slowly to the nearest corner, turned, walked a few paces, then stopped and stood silently in the shadow of a leafless tree. As he was reaching for the cat, it dropped from his shoulder and faded into the darkness.

Though many walked the streets of Devlin armed with great bare knives in their belts, or carried cutlasses into breakfast, Breksin thought such behavior affected and childish, besides being stupidly provocative. He would not prowl the city with weapons on his belt. On the other hand, the character of the city and many of its inhabitants urged prudence. Accordingly, he had purchased a heavy staff of seasoned hardwood that he used as a walking stick. As he stood behind the tree, he shifted his grip to the point of balance and held it ready.

He heard a furtive step at the corner; then came a silent pause, followed by the sound of a hurried stride. As the man strode past him, the giant stepped from under the tree and laid his staff lightly on the man's shoulder.

"Turn slowly," he commanded in a deep voice that was no less terrifying for being soft.

Instead, the man yelped like a spaniel. In ducking away from the staff, he tripped over his own feet and collapsed backwards, waving his hands in front of him.

Breksin peered down. "Reffex?" he rumbled. "By the gods, man, I might have murdered you!" Reffex got up slowly, brushing his clothing and looking at the ground.

"Damnable cobbles," he muttered, still on one knee. His voice quavered. "They tripped me up. That was a maneuver, you see." He got to his feet. "Roll away from the enemy, then come back with force. Element of surprise. Principle of combat—very important in the—"

"Reffex!" Breksin lowered his voice. "Count Reffex . . . Your Grace. Why in the name of the Blessed Daughters were you following me?"

The count stepped closer to Breksin. "We must speak confidentially. Also, I think I bruised my wrist when I . . . was maneuvering. Perhaps a glass of wine, though it's wretched what they serve here."

Breksin stared over the nobleman's head into the darkness for a moment. "I'm stopping at an inn where the wine is not wretched. We'll go there."

As Reffex fell into step beside him, he said, "Mind those cobbles."

The count seemed positively astonished at the public room of Breksin's inn. There were a few affable arguments in progress over cards, but the fiddlers could be heard above the voices and there was no sign of blood or broken furniture.

"I must say," he murmured in a tone of injured dignity and envy, "Captain Flanders might have put us here. Our inn is entirely overrun by ruffians."

"You are with the envoy?"

Count Reffex drew himself up in his chair. "I *am* the envoy." Had the count been a mind reader, the look of surprise this announcement produced on the giant's face would have given him no delight.

The tables around them were unoccupied. Still, Breksin lowered his voice when he spoke again. "Rand has sent you here?"

"Not Rand," said Reffex. He paused before continuing with an air of drama. "I have been sent by . . . the king."

Breksin thought for a moment, then nodded. "I see," he said. "And what of Modesty . . . I mean, the princess and her party?"

Reffex leaned across the table. "That's why I was following you," he said. He looked ruefully at his bruises. "Of course, you are a friend, so I meant you no harm. If I had been following an enemy, I would have struck with—"

"But what of the royal party?"

"What? Oh, they're fine. They aren't forced to lodge with scoundrels and ruffians. You know, there's no sleeping at my inn until nearly—"

"Where are they?"

Reffex gave him a blank look. "Why, everywhere. In the hallways, falling down the stairs—"

"The royal party, you . . . Your Grace."

"Oh. In the pirate's house. They have rooms on the top floor, a view of the city and the harbor, maids to serve them, plenty of—"

"You saw them, then?"

"Yes, of course. But not until today, and just Daniel. He was very surprised to see me there, I can tell you," said Reffex with a complacent smirk. "Of course, I am not one to dwell on my accomplishments. I am content to go on quietly. My king knows I am available in time of need. You may not be aware, for instance, that the position I occupy at the royal table is of my own choosing. Only a word to His Majesty and I might sit . . . well, I'll just say, much higher." Reffex raised his eyebrows and adjusted his smirk. "Much. Let's leave it at that."

Breksin was willing. "You said you were following me because of the royal party?"

"Yes. Well, because of the strange way things are going. Black Jack Flanders seems to have no interest in the king's offer. He keeps putting me off. I must say, it's very trying for one of my rank to be treated like a messenger. And now that I have no assistant, I am left to perform every slight chore for myself."

Breksin looked skeptical. "But, you landed with a party, I heard."

"Three seamen," Reffex said with a scowl. "Common fellows. No help at all." He shook his head. "We shall see when we are back at court. It's nothing short of mutiny. Old Hebbick, sent to assist me, set me down in this place to make my own way, and ordered—ordered, I tell you—the ship on to Felshalfen." The count took a long pull at his wine. "And the captain obeyed him. Hebbick. A man of no distinction at all. I will tell you, things have not gone right since the night Rogan was lost."

"Lost?" said Breksin. "Lost where?"

"At sea. Didn't I mention it? Washed overboard in a storm."

"Are you sure?"

"Of course I'm sure. I was there. No great stroke of luck in that; some oaf of a seaman tried to blame me." Reffex raised his chin and fixed Breksin with an outraged stare. "I was only trying to calm him, but he must have loosened the ropes, because the wave lifted the boat right over the side. Things were very confused. This sailor, you see, didn't—"

"He was in a boat, then?" Breksin asked. "He may have been washed ashore."

Reffex said, "Well, yes, that's what the captain says, but I would think we've heard the last of Rogan the Obscure. A great pity, of course, but he was old, after all. Lived many years." The fiddlers struck up a lively tune. Reffex looked around the peaceful room, then turned a mournful eye to Breksin. "Do you know if they have a vacancy here?"

While the count arranged for lodging and for the transfer of his belongings, Breksin thought about the royal magician, comforting himself by reasoning that the gods, though known to be capricious, could not conceivably have had Reffex at their mercy on a stormy sea and then chosen to drown someone else instead.

Reffex returned to the table with a fresh pitcher of wine. He was out of sorts because the landlord, when acquainted with his rank and title, had been insufficiently obsequious.

"Insisted that I pay in advance," said the count. "Only imagine. I am cousin to a duke. Thrice removed," he added grandly, as though that genealogical detail contributed to the dignity of the connection.

With as much patience as he could muster, Breksin pursued the topic of why the count had followed him.

"Well, you can see," said Reffex indignantly, "my authority is being flouted by underlings, so when I saw a functionary of the court, I naturally assumed it had something to do with me, and since no ships have called since the one that brought me, that was a great mystery in itself." He stopped and squinted at the giant. "I still don't know who it was that sent you."

"I am here by chance, Your Grace. The wine trade," he added to make his lie more plausible.

"In Devlin? I assumed all their wine was stolen."

"Not all of it. Some they purchase," Breksin replied, knowing but not caring that he had lapsed into truth.

"But," objected Reffex, "should we supply them with wine while they hold the princess? It seems almost dishonorable, somehow." He pursed his lips. "I suppose it's quite a profitable market? If we don't sell to them, someone else is sure to."

Breksin stared at Reffex. Surely, he thought, Rogan was not at the bottom of the sea. "Yes," he said absently. "But I have finished my business, now. I think, Your Grace, that you should appoint me your assistant."

Reffex looked startled. "But you are a . . . that is, there are protocols, the matter of diplomatic standing."

"Well, of course, if you don't need help—"

"No, no," Reffex said hastily. "You're quite right. And unlike many in high positions, I have always been open to suggestions from those in stations of subordinacy. When I next wait on the great pirate, you shall be with me." Count Reffex favored Breksin, son of a line of kings that extended back to days lost in legend, with a look of generous condescension. "Actually, I'm sure I can pass you off as a soldier—even an officer. And if the conversation should take a military turn, I will keep you from making a fool of yourself. Just you follow my lead and we will make an impressive pair."

Breksin raised his glass by way of reply. When it occurred to Reffex to ask how he knew he was being followed, Breksin made up a lie about the marvelous alertness of his cat, and then used the pet as an excuse for leaving the count.

"Wouldn't do to have the faithful kitsey spending the night out of doors," he said as he rose from his chair. He dropped a few coins on the table and bid the aristocrat good night, promising to be at his disposal the next day.

Outside, the streets were quiet. Breksin walked for an hour or more, keeping to the parts of the city not frequented by carousers. He needed quiet so that he could sort out his worries.

He thought first of Rogan the Obscure. The magician, though advanced in years, had been unchanged for so long that the question of his death had never entered Breksin's mind. Surely, he thought, a magician in a boat would be able to come up with some spell to keep afloat on a stormy ocean. There was every reason to hope that even now, Rogan was sitting somewhere, perhaps a seaside tavern, drinking local wine and dreaming of the cellars at Ambermere. Breksin vowed to invite the magician to his keg room for a private tasting as soon as they were both safe at home.

The great question, though, was the matter of the prisoners and their ransom. Rand would never have entrusted Reffex with a mission of any importance. Both he and Rogan must have come on the whim of the king. Hebbick, on the other hand, was clearly Rand's man. And if Hebbick had changed his plans and gone to Felshalfen, that meant the center of the trouble was located there, and not in the pirate stronghold. This could only mean that the question was not one of simple, honest piracy, but of politics. That made it all the more important for him to learn all he could of the prisoners' situation.

CHAPTER

· 11 ·

"I should say you will not! You'll not breakfast on wine while I have the care of you."

Rogan looked at the plate of biscuits and bacon with an expression not far removed from horror.

"But I have a delicate stomach," he explained querulously.

"I shouldn't wonder," said the woman. "I think you may count yourself lucky you have a stomach at all, the way you use it. A diet of pure vinegar, you might as well say, with a piece of bread at bedtime."

"Oh, your wine is not so bad as all that," said the magician. "And I ate those potatoes last night. And the chop."

"Well, this bacon's from the same pig, so you're already acquainted."

Rogan adjusted himself on his pillows. "And what," he asked as he adjusted the tray on his lap, "does one drink with such a meal?"

"The tea's brewing, Your Lordship." The woman curtseyed and disappeared through the door.

Rogan sighed. He picked up a biscuit and nibbled at it. Although this was only his second day in Edorra's care, he knew she would give him no peace until he ate at least part of the food she had served him. He had already heard her "What do you suppose I cooked that for?" more than enough. It was simpler to make a show of eating. At least the food was good. Even one accustomed to the luxuries of Asbrak's kitchen could not fault Edorra's culinary efforts. This biscuit, for instance. Rogan turned it over in his hand like a connoisseur. If it were any lighter, it would float up off the platter. What would Asbrak say, as he started on a second dozen? *Under ordinary circumstances I wouldn't, but as these are so very excellent, I believe I will permit myself another.*

A boy entered carrying a tray with a teapot, a pitcher of cream, and a wide-brimmed mug with two handles. He put his burden carefully on a table next to the bed, and seated himself in a wooden chair.

Rogan gave him a sidelong look.

"Auntie says I'm to sit with you. She says you're to make the food disappear in the, uh, *customary* way, and not by magic." He grinned. "Could you really make it disappear?"

"Well, ah, yes, I suppose. Not really my line, you see."

The boy looked disappointed.

Rogan looked at him, then back to the tray on his lap. "There is a spell for hiding . . . now, how does that go?"

"Hiding?"

"Of course. Technically, it's hiding. When something disappears, it doesn't cease to exist, you know."

"What's technically?"

"It's very simple, it's . . . Here, shouldn't you be pouring me some tea?" The magician began to mutter to himself.

"Yes, sir." The boy filled the mug three-quarters full with the steaming fragrant tea, then topped it off with cream almost too thick to leave the pitcher.

"Where's the spoon?" he said, feeling behind the teapot.

"Lose something?" said Rogan.

"The spoon. It was on the tray."

"Evidently you are mistaken." Rogan muttered briefly again and made a few economical gestures with his free hand. The boy looked at him uneasily.

There was a clink and a splash. The boy stared at the cup, then slowly drew the spoon from it.

Rogan cackled. "Neatly done, if I do say so myself. I could still make my way in a carnival if need be." He looked at the gawking boy. "You don't seem to have much to say."

"Teach me how to do that."

Rogan looked smug. "Teach you, indeed. It would take an apprentice years to learn to do that." He smirked and spoke in the sententious manner so delightful to children. "Particularly the skill displayed in getting the spoon in the cup"—he raised his forefinger like a schoolmaster preparing to elucidate—"on the first try."

"I could do it! I could do it if I knew the words."

"Indeed, and do you—what is your name again, lad?"

"Chardric, but everyone calls me Rickey. Sir."

"And how old is Chardric?"

"Eleven. I was eleven a long time ago."

Rogan picked up the tea mug and sipped, then looked at it as though he had forgotten what he was drinking.

"And you want me to teach you the spell for hiding?"

Rickey nodded eagerly. "For what you did with the spoon, yes sir."

"Very well," said Rogan. "You must bring me some things."

Rickey sprang to his feet.

"I need something to write on." The magician peered at the boy. "You do read? I am not going to teach this to you word by word."

"I read. Auntie taught me." He began to leave the room.

"Wait," called Rogan. "That's not all. I need a flask. A flask with a stopper."

"For writing?"

"Never mind. Just you bring it." Rickey was nearly out the door when Rogan called him back with a gesture. "Quietly, mind. These things must be done discreetly."

In about the time it took to eat a biscuit, the boy was back. He delivered the items he had collected to the magician.

"Now," said Rogan, putting the writing implements aside and handing the flask back to Rickey, "whilst I indite the spell, you just run to the pantry and fill this with—you know the dark wine we had last night?"

"Auntie's best."

Rogan nodded with a smile. "That will do."

Rickey hesitated at the door. "What's 'indite'?"

Rogan looked up with the quill suspended over the ink pot. "Why, to write, of course, boy."

"Then why don't you just say 'write'?"

"Not fancy enough," said Rogan, dipping the pen.

"Is that why you said 'whilst'?"

"Precisely. Go fetch the wine."

Later, Rogan was awakened when Edorra entered the room. Although she was a pleasant-enough-looking woman, he had not been able to accustom himself to her scale. She was as tall as any man, had heavy, strong-looking limbs, and was as broad at the shoulder as at the hips. She was not without grace, and a sort of vast femininity, but her appearance was daunting, especially to a man freshly wakened from a nap.

"Not more food?"

"Nothing that will cause you harm. Just some chowder."

"Fish?"

Edorra did not reply, but fixed him with a somber stare.

Rogan sat up and leaned against a stack of pillows. "All right," he sighed. He plied his reluctant spoon under the supervision of his hostess.

"I will admit," he remarked after a number of bites, "that if one must eat at such an hour, he could find a worse cook. In fact"—he raised his eyes to her—"if you kept an inn at the capital, I believe the king would forsake his table for yours."

"It's only simple food," she replied.

"Well," he said with a melancholy glance at the tray, "it's true there is no wine."

Edorra stared at him. "You don't say you would take wine with soup, Master? Do they dine thus at the great king's table?"

"No, not exactly, no. But I just thought—"

"I should hope not." She showed a faint smile. "I do have a fruit wine to go with your fresh cheese. That's for after you've finished your soup." She peered down at Rogan. "Shall I fetch it now?"

Rogan nodded and raised his spoon to his lips.

"Then you won't"—she bent over and reached beneath the pillows to retrieve the hidden flask—"be needing this."

Each time he woke up, Rogan the Obscure had to remember that he was not in his apartments at Ambermere, not aboard ship, or tossed from wave to wave in the longboat, nor sleeping under it with wet sand in his teeth as he had been when Chardric found him. He could still smell the sea, and hear it, but he was dry and warm in Edorra's cottage.

The afternoon shadows were long when Rogan was awakened by the sound of voices in the next room.

"He is a castaway, Dilmur. Must he be washed ashore with his pockets full of silver?"

"Then I," the heavy masculine voice lingered on the pronoun, drawing it out in a self-important whine, "I am to have nothing from this?"

Edorra's voice was low and matter-of-fact. "You are welcome to all that comes from it."

"Ahah! As I thought. Nothing."

"Perhaps. It is costing you nothing. I see no great loss in it."

"Hah! Loss. Don't speak to me of loss, woman. I provide you with a house. Provisions. Don't speak to me of charity."

"A cottage standing empty at the ends of the earth. A half-empty root cellar. Charity, indeed. I'm surprised you can pronounce the word."

There was the sound of a chair scraping along the floor. "Well! Go back to the city, then, my fine lady, and work for your keep."

"You know the city is no place for the boy. Would you see your nephew on those streets?"

"No. I would see him prenticed out. He's old enough, now."

"You'd sell him for the pennies he'd bring. An orphan. Your brother's son."

"He must make his way as best he can. I will not maintain him in an idle life."

"An idle life? He is a child of eleven years. And he is very apt. He has learned to read."

"What?" The man's voice rose in volume and pitch. "I told you he was not to be a scholar. Your meddling will ruin him. He'll be fit for no labor."

Rogan heard the front door open.

"When he's on Jicker's boat, there'll be no words for him to read!" The door slammed.

CHAPTER
·12·

Rand peered from the window of the king's chamber to the sun-filled courtyard below. The brightness of the morning matched his mood. Against all reasonable expectations, the king had returned from his absurd errand of last night with useful intelligence. This was, in Rand's view, as great a miracle as ever he expected to witness, but the king had tired of the subject, and was indulging his penchant for pointless speculation. Rand turned from the window.

"If Your Majesty will permit me to interrupt, I believe we might profitably leave conjectures on the efficacy of witchcraft until just a little later. I think it most important that we establish with precision just what it was Your Royal Highness heard last night."

"But we have been over this, Rand. First last night, and now again this morning. I was perishing in that place. Trapped, with nothing to eat or drink." The king sipped from a jeweled goblet. "Did I tell you I had to go up the stairs backwards?"

"Indeed, Your Highness, I am satisfied the circumstances were exceedingly trying, but still we must be certain that we are in possession of all the facts."

"Facts? What facts? I have told you what I overheard."

"Ah, but the words, Highness, the words, exactly and without omission."

"I will not retail this business of the girl again."

Rand nodded. "Quite right, Your Majesty. Most unseemly. Our interest this morning is not anatomy. What we wish to inquire into is the identity of this mysterious nobleman."

"But have I not told you of the clothing, the haircut, the mustache? I mean, really, Rand, there is no— Now wait," said the king. "Did I mention the scar?"

"Ah," said Rand. "The scar." He joined his fingertips and peered between his hands to the designs on the carpet. "I am sure Your Highness would not have overlooked such an important element, but if you might repeat the details?"

"Yes, well, you must understand, the man did not see the scar, but the nobleman he referred to had one. Evidently," said the king with a cunning glance, "it was out of sight."

"Covered by clothing?"

"Perhaps," said Asbrak. "No, wait. He said he wished he had run after him to see if he had the scar. It must, therefore, be on his face."

"I believe Your Highness is correct."

The king rose slowly from his chair. "But will all this be of use?" he said. He walked to the window.

Rand stared at the king's back. "Your Highness, owing to your efforts, we have a description of the secret enemy that logic told us existed, but of whom we had no knowledge. We have gone from a position of perfect ignorance to one of illumination."

"Illumination? Isn't that a bit optimistic?"

"Not at all," replied the adviser. "It is impossible to imagine an innocent explanation for a nephew of Finster's to be in Devlin. When we know which aristocrat of Felshalfen fits this description, we shall be in a position to deliver a crushing blow to this plot."

"But no one has mentioned Felshalfen."

"Logic has mentioned Felshalfen since the day we learned of this outrage, Your Highness. And if I may remind my king of the solitary objection he had to the otherwise unexceptionable, not to say heaven-sent, suitor to his daughter? The one minor flaw in Hilbert the Silent of Felshalfen?"

"Oh, yes. The curls. The man dresses his hair like a musician in a tavern."

Rand raised a forefinger. "In the style of Felshalfen," he said.

"Of course," agreed the king.

"But the courtier in Devlin wore his hair straight."

Asbrak looked blank, then his eyes cleared. "Not curled to fashion," he said.

"Your Majesty has penetrated to the heart of the matter."

The king lifted his chin and raised his eyebrows. "Why yes, I believe I have." He clapped his hands together briskly. "But your assistance, Rand, was most helpful. Most helpful."

"Your Majesty is too kind." Rand turned again to the window. "If I might be excused, Highness. There are one or two details I must look into."

"But it is almost time for tea," said Asbrak.

"Yes, Your Highness, but necessity beckons."

"And the matter of the witch. I consider this of the highest importance, Rand."

"Of course, Majesty, but not, perhaps, so very pressing at this moment."

The king frowned. "Oh, very well," he said. "But I'd like to see you back here for some nourishment. I won't have you wasting away." Rand bowed and strode from the room. "The pastry tray will be here when you return," called the king as the heels and coattails of his adviser passed from sight.

Upon his return, Rand did indeed find the pastry tray awaiting him, though in a sadly depleted state.

"You know, Rand," said the king, brushing crumbs from his mouth with a lace napkin, "I believe our bakers are as gifted as any that might be found in the Nine Kingdoms. I am ordinarily quite indifferent to pastries . . . tarts, crumpets"—the royal eye scanned the tray—"muffins, buns, turnovers, puffs"—he lifted a cloth covering a basket in the corner of the tray—"creams, nut rings, ladyfingers, jamlets." Asbrak leaned forward in his chair. "Hmmm, what's this?" he said, lifting a triangle of sugar-glazed dough. He nibbled at it thoughtfully. "Anyway, I was waiting until you returned before I rang for more tea."

Rand tugged at the bell-pull. The king gestured in the direction of the table where the remains of his "camp breakfast"—the cheeses and cold meats of his customary midmorning snack—lay on a platter.

"The boy can take that with him, too."

The tea arrived. Asbrak waved Rand off. "I shall pour," he said, rising ponderously. "You have been in constant motion

since dawn. Well, anyway, since I've been up. I will see you
seated, with your cup in your hand. I," said the monarch grandly,
"will make you up a platter and bring it to you. You need do
nothing but chew and swallow." The king took a small plate of
beaten silver and deftly erected on it a pile of pastries that stayed
in place in defiance of a number of well-known principles of engineering. He placed it on a table by his adviser, then returned to
his own chair.

"Now," he wheezed, as he recovered from his giddy plunge
into the cushions, "we must arrange the work of the day. I want
to send for this witch, and— By the way, what do you think of
the fellow's story—about her walking dry in the rainstorm?"

Rand was attempting to remove a muffin from his plate without precipitating an avalanche of crumpets and buns.

"Your Highness, although I say it with deep regret, I must
confess I find the story to be completely credible."

The king looked disappointed. "Really, Rand, you always—"
He looked more closely at his adviser. "You say completely
credible? That means you believe it."

"In a word," replied the older man.

The king beamed. "Rand, you surprise me. Next you will be
consulting Remeger."

"The astrologer? That is not likely, Highness. My skepticism
remains unshaken. My opinion in the case of the witch is influenced by the fact that I saw her myself."

"You? In a tavern?" An expression of puzzlement settled itself
on the face of the king. "Were you in disguise?"

"I was here, my liege, at a window that overlooks the avenue.
I saw the woman, and although I could not say if she was wet
or dry, her actions and attitude accord very well with the tale told
by the roaster of meats, unreliable witness though he is."

"You know him, then?"

"By repute, Your Majesty. Breksin informs me that despite his
intemperance, he is unsurpassed at his trade."

"I am glad to hear it. The man is so erratic and incoherent, I
don't know what other line of work he might aptly pursue."
Asbrak paused and stared abstractedly at the ceiling. "Poetry,
perhaps.

"In any event," he went on, "you and I must interview this
witch."

"That, I fear, is a pleasure I am going to be deprived of, Majesty. With your permission, I plan to sail with the tide."

The king thought for a moment, then shook his head. "Your metaphor eludes me, Rand. What tide are you talking about? The tide of Fate? Justice? Fortune? The vast eternal ebb and flow of, oh, whatever that song says?" Asbrak pursed his lips. "Odd for that to be sung in the taverns, when you think about it."

"I was referring to the actual tide, my liege."

The king shifted on his cushions and assumed an attitude.

> " 'The sky above, the helm alee,
>   The vast, damp pulse of the ocean sea.' "

He held his pose for a moment, then settled back in his chair. "Does it strike you our poets used to be better than that?" he asked with a frown.

"Indeed, Your Highness, much better, and there were fewer of them."

"That's right," said the king. "There were. We should take steps."

"Steps?"

"To reduce the number of poets. What would you suggest?"

"Short of dealing with them as Your Majesty's ancestor Melbrak is said to have dealt with an overabundance of lawyers, I see no ready answer."

Asbrak shuddered. "I take your point," he said. "Let's get back to the tides. Why were we discussing them again?"

"We were discussing my departure for Felshalfen."

Asbrak had not shot up from a chair in a generation, nor did he now, but he rose as quickly as he could.

"Why in the name of the several deities would you want to go to Felshalfen? Surely we can dispatch a messenger."

"I believe if Your Majesty will but consider the gravity of the situation, you will agree that I must be the one to go. I must be there to direct our operatives."

"Our what? Do we have operatives? What are they, exactly?"

"Spies, Your Majesty."

The king stared at his chief adviser. "We have spies at the court of Finster the Munificent? Our closest ally? Our kingdoms are united by blood." He crossed his arms and blinked at Rand. "How is it I know nothing of this? I am the king, after all."

Rand managed to get out of his chair without upsetting his plate of pastries. "That is why you know nothing of it, Highness. It is but one of an overwhelming mass of burdensome details, and a sensitive and inconvenient detail at that. If you were to concern yourself with such trivial matters, you would scarcely have time for the business of ruling the kingdom."

Asbrak sank into his chair. "Still," he said, "spies at the court of a friend."

"That is precisely where they are most needed, Your Highness."

"Practically a member of the family," continued the king.

"Majesty, every drop of blood that unites Felshalfen and Ambermere is currently in the custody of Black Jack Flanders in Devlin."

The king sighed and closed his eyes for a moment. "Very well," he said. "How soon must you leave?"

"I will leave you at once, my liege, and sail just after noon."

"But our interview with the witch," protested Asbrak.

"My assistant will know of her whereabouts by now. He will summon her at Your Majesty's pleasure." Rand bowed to the king. "I will of course report for any final instructions before I go to the quays." He turned and left the room.

Asbrak's eye fell on Rand's plate. "Your muffins," he called hopelessly.

Rand was back before the tea was cold. The king was lifting a pastry from the plate he had made up for his adviser.

"Ah, good," he said. "I don't like to see you begin a trip on an empty stomach." Asbrak looked at Rand's feet. "Rand, I think you must be better shod than that if you are to go to sea. Don't you need a well-greased boot? Something that comes above your ankles and will shed water?" He began to raise the pastry to his mouth, then stopped. "Is that something for me to sign?"

Rand unrolled a tightly scrolled vellum. "No, Your Majesty, it is a message from Hebbick that has arrived in time to save me a troublesome journey."

The king put down the pastry. "But Hebbick is with Reffex," he protested. "In Devlin. He couldn't have arrived more than a day ago. There has been no time for a message to reach us."

"You are quite right, my liege, but this message was dispatched from the ship three days ago—the day before the storm."

"Does Rogan have such powers?" exclaimed the king. "To send a message from the middle of the ocean?"

"I sincerely doubt it, Your Highness. As it happens, this message was received only a short time ago at the dovecot."

"The what?"

"The dovecot, Highness. It's where Your Majesty's messenger pigeons are housed. On the roof."

The king began to speak, then shook his head and then motioned for his adviser to continue.

"On the strength of something he learned from a crewman, Hebbick has gone on to Felshalfen. He may be there by now. Once he receives the information Your Majesty gathered last night, he will take the appropriate steps, assuming he has not unraveled the plot already."

The king looked bewildered. "Old Hebbick?" he said. "I thought you sent him to assist Reffex in his embassy. Is Reffex directing his actions?"

Rand saw no need to offer his private opinion—that Count Reffex could not be trusted to superintend the emptying of a chamber pot. "No, Your Highness. The count will have been put ashore in Devlin to carry out your instructions. Hebbick will be acting without the benefit of his guidance."

The king sent a speculative look in the direction of his adviser. "So now that Hebbick is in Felshalfen, there is no longer any need for your presence." He tugged gently at his beard in a thoughtful manner. After a brief silence he said, "No, it is impossible. I cannot imagine old Hebbick as a master spy."

Rand gave a slight nod accompanied by the merest hint of a smile. "Precisely, Highness. Precisely."

CHAPTER

·13·

It took Alexander two days to trace Marcia to the cave of the giants. As he climbed the massive stairs, he recalled that Marcia had said the place was haunted. Alexander smiled. What more congenial surroundings for a necromancer? The dead, as he had been instructed so many years ago, were the buttress of his trade.

Inside, torches burned in the wall. He stepped quickly across the floor of stone, freshly swept, just as Marcia had described it. Moments passed as he gazed at the upright caskets. This was a place to which he must return. What talk he would have with these ancient giants! But for now, he had more pressing matters to pursue. He listened in the silence, waiting for the drone of pipes. He need make no calling, wake no sleeping king to ask his questions. A watchman trod these reaches, and piped an endless dirge.

When he heard the distant melody, he followed the sound to a wall of blasted rock. He stood silently for a time, listening as the eerie tune grew louder. Finally he spoke. He did not raise his voice above his customary whisper, but it carried in the cave, and echoed from the walls of stone.

"Come! Do not make me call you, bind you to my summons. I only seek one who passed here."

For a moment the piping went on, pursuing an evolution of solemn melodic intricacies that slowly descended to a drone.

Then followed some moments of silence. Alexander waited patiently, then turned to watch as the torches were extinguished one by one.

Now the chamber was filled with silence and darkness. All sense of space was canceled, the air became an oppressive weight. For a short while the silence was absolute, then was broken by a quiet sigh.

"I am long in these practices," came Alexander's patient whisper. "You cannot terrify me, only weary me. And then," he went on in a voice even softer than before, "when I waken these kings, will they thank you that their rest is broken?"

One by one the torches lit. When the last one burned, a giant stood before the necromancer. He spoke without bow or greeting. The dead do not observe the niceties.

"Two passed. Which do you seek?"

"The woman. Was the other an old man?"

When the giant laughed, Alexander looked up at him sharply. The mirthless noise bounced from the chamber walls.

"An old man? Yes."

"They were together?"

"No. The woman followed."

Alexander let his glance travel up the wall they stood in front of. "And to what place?"

"The place? I can conduct you there, necromancer, if you dare to go."

"The Lower Regions, then?" Alexander fixed the ghost with his gaze. "You are sure the woman went there too, and not some other place?"

"I am sure. She passed me, crossing on the path he took."

"And you will put me on that same path?"

"The same. But I will not bring you back."

Alexander smiled sadly to himself and nodded. Now when would he reach his refuge above the ocean? When entertain the young enchantress? When see the roses climb his garden wall?

He looked around the cavern at the tombs, the torches burning on the wall. He took one pace forward.

"I am ready."

Alexander surveyed the bilious landscape, not certain how to proceed. His trips to the Lower Regions had been infrequent and were far in the past. Never before had he dared to penetrate the boundaries without careful preparation—the erection of a network of spells to keep him secure as he traversed the hostile ways.

Now his only refuge, if he had need of it, was to travel in the wizard's mode, multiplying the distance covered by his stride and shielding him from all but the most discerning eyes. But to travel in this fashion was to give up the ability to use the spell of tracing.

He stared into the distance where details were masked in the veil of floating mists. He had never before been in the great bare plain of the Lower Regions. When he had visited in the past, it had been to brave the streets of dark cities, or breach the walls of some fortress on a lonely moor.

He thought of those days, and the protection under which he had traveled. How would Marcia fare in this desolate place, unequipped with the knowledge and skills he had brought on his journeys? How would she survive? And if she had not, could he hope to find so much as a trace of whatever end she might have met?

To awaken the spell of tracing took almost no time at all. Her trail was at his feet as the piper had vowed it would be. He followed it for perhaps forty-five minutes, then stopped where the rutted lane topped the crest of a hill.

Ahead, the vista was one of unrelieved bleakness. He imagined Marcia trudging across those hills, facing endless miles and unknown dangers ahead. It was, he realized, almost pointless to try to find her. If she had caught up with the strange old man who possessed such great power, she might now be anywhere. If she had failed to overtake him, how much hope could there be for her?

He turned to survey the ground he had covered. What he saw reminded him of the dangers he himself faced in the hostile place. Among the yellow hillocks to his left were subtle signs of movement, quick yellow flittings against the yellow ground as seen through yellow fog. He was in no position to take risks. Whatever was coming his way was moving fast, and there was more than one. He squinted through the haze. Vermin, more likely than not, but he would not be duped by curiosity.

He drew his attention inward to himself. When, after half a minute, he had gathered his forces, he took a step, and at the same time disappeared from view.

In the cocoon of his magic he became aware of how vulnerable he had unconsciously felt himself to be. Now, moving in a silent vacuum, viewing the landscape through the comforting distortion of his spell, he felt completely secure. When he had settled into his pace, still walking but covering ground now at the rate of a dead run, he glanced over his shoulder.

Little bent things, they were. Naked and grotesque; furless monkeys with fangs and claws and empty eyes. They flowed across the way behind him like blowing leaves, then ran alongside him for a second, unconscious of his presence, before veering off to disappear among the rocks. They numbered a dozen or more. They were vermin, and possessed only their physical power, but how would Marcia deal even with a threat like them?

Alexander was anxious to cover ground, but after an hour he stopped and stripped himself of the spell. The air was acrid, the light unchanged. He cast the spell of tracing like a net. Of Marcia's trail there was no sign.

He shook his head dejectedly and gazed back along the road. He had probably covered twelve to fifteen miles at the wizard's pace. Somewhere in those tens of thousands of feet Marcia's trail had turned. Or stopped.

It took over two hours to find the place where Marcia had left the road, and then the place where all trace of her vanished. When he considered the alternatives, Alexander was grateful to be frustrated. There was, he knew, no sight he could not bear to see if the need arose, but he was glad to find no evidence of Marcia's downfall. Better what he faced now—evidence either of her disappearance, or of the failure of the tracing spell.

Not far from where he stood, the road curved toward the path he had been following. Now, at least, his purpose was clear. He would continue on the road at speed until he had gone far enough to eliminate any chance that Marcia was wandering lost and alone in these wilds. Then would be time enough to begin the tedious business of engineering his journey across the boundary of the Middle Regions.

For the next few hours, Alexander continued on the road. From time to time he stopped, on the chance he might pick up some hint of Marcia's passing. Finally he was forced to admit to himself that, traveling at four to five times the speed that Marcia could have maintained, he had come to a point farther than she could have reached. He would rest, he decided, then set about the tedious business of making his way back.

If it wasn't to be a project of truly grinding difficulty, he would have to find some reasonably level ground. Figuring in substantial changes in altitude tended to locate the chore in the realm of higher mathematics. At that point it would be easier to go on and find a Doorway.

With the arrival of that stray thought, Alexander found his spirits lifting. If a hike through Hell could not be considered a pleasure, how much less disagreeable it sounded than the dry unrewarding exercise that faced him now. In addition, the further he went, the less occasion there would ever be to wonder whether Marcia had somehow been somewhere on the road ahead.

He searched his memory for some scrap of knowledge about the geography of this part of the Lower Regions. He must be approaching the great basin—the desert proper. What had Fildis told him? Pools of water were appearing. Rumors, there were, of the rebirth of the ancient sea. This in itself, he thought with ever-rising spirits, would be a thing worth looking at. For how many millennia had that dirt been dry? Even Rhastopheris had never before seen that land with water standing on it.

He got up from the rock where he had seated himself. That was settled, then. He felt positively invigorated. He would go at least as far as the first lying pools. If they looked promising, he would venture on to lower ground. Then, once he had seen the wonder for himself, he would summon Fildis. The demon could tell him of the nearest Doorway—take him to it, probably. In a few days, he would be back at his refuge, watching in the morning as the sun awakened the flowers climbing on his garden wall.

He reached the edge of the great dry sea by what his stomach told him was suppertime. There he ate the food he had brought with him and gazed across the empty land. It had, almost, a sort of empty beauty, an analog of its complete and utter silence.

He sat on the yellow earth with his back against a rock just at the place where the road began a long descent. The mists and fogs were heavier below, evidence, he hoped, of the rising water he had come to see. How odd that this slender thread of events, this life of his, so long, so strange, should pass this point, and in passing, come to rest here in this odd place where an old, old man might sit and survey wonders not of his own world.

* * *

It was some time later that he stood on the bank of a pond that must recently have been a puddle and soon would be a lake. He had decided that he would have to make the effort to return to this place sometime soon. This was the marvel of an age, and not a thing lightly to be missed. Might he, he wondered, strike some bargain with Rhastopheris? When the arch-demon consented to make those midnight visits to Alexander's seaside refuge, the journey took him only minutes. With the proper assurances and safeguards, Alexander could go back and forth with him, skipping all the inconveniences and annoyances of days of travel.

If this pond were the birthing of a sea, how long, he wondered, would it take for yellow water to replace the yellow mists that filled the air around him? Could he hope to live so long that he might see this valley filled? Or would the wonder of an age take an age to accomplish? He was old, and expected to become much older. But even the greatest necromancer does not measure out his mortality in geologic time.

"Do I dare to eat a peach?" he murmured, smiling. He turned, and paced back from the shore until he found a comfortable rock to perch on.

Calling Fildis presented no obstacles. He was not asking the demon to cross to the Middle Regions. He was not summoning him so much as hailing him. Like shepherds calling to one another from neighboring hilltops, he thought, recalling the days of his innocent youth, so very, very far away.

He spun one light spell to assure himself that the spot was as lonely as it seemed. Any magic announces itself, makes disturbances. Alexander wanted to reveal his presence to no one but the one he called.

When every sign told him he was alone, he proceeded. The spells he used were always simple and direct, bare—skeletons of magic. They were themselves a pleasure, shorn of the complexities he had in former days been too eager to manipulate. As his understanding had deepened, he had come to appreciate the spare, the understated. In many ways, he thought, the tools he used had become to him aesthetic objects, more important in themselves than in the effects they produced. He could not hide from himself the fact that he sometimes put in motion workings that did things he had no particular wish to do, simply to indulge his pleasure in the spells themselves.

He called Fildis with a spell as simple as a shout, then left the thread of magic in place as he turned his attention back to the water. Where would he find it if he came back a month from now? A year? Ten? It seemed so long, ten years. He laughed at his own naïveté. How much empty space was there to fill? A puddle might grow to a pond in a few days. Might stretch, as this one had, until its shallow waters covered an expanse of ground. But to fill the mold left empty by an ocean. . . .

Fildis did not come.

Alexander rose and turned in a slow circle. He was alone. There were, he sensed, *things* in the water, but nothing formidable—nothing to fear. Nothing that could interrupt his magic or keep a demon away.

Though he didn't like to do it, he sent the spell again. It was soft, and subtle, this spell, meant for Fildis and no other. It wouldn't do to make a general calling here. Even the one that Fildis called lord, though of no vast powers, would be an inconvenience here, where Alexander was enveloped by no prepared spells, wound in no reticule of standing magic.

Nothing. He allowed the spell to die. Again he looked around. What could be wrong? What he was attempting was neither difficult nor complicated. For this summons to go unanswered told him that something was badly awry.

Though he disliked doing it, he quickly wrapped himself again in the wizards' spell of travel. Within its folds he was secure, but at the same time encumbered by distortions that prevented him from accurately observing the scene around him. This situation was disquieting, and probably contained hidden dangers, but it was deeply interesting as well. He moved off a little way, then stopped to survey the scene as best he could.

He soon tired of hovering like a dervish. With a last glance backward he returned to the path. He would go on as he had planned, seeking lower ground and broader spans of water. Then would be time enough to plot his way back home.

With his first step, his cloak of magic dissipated. He stumbled forward, surprised by the unaugmented speed of his step. At once he tried to reinstate the spell. Failing, he worked a quick spell of rebuff, then began to erect a web of magic, a thicket of protective spells. They hardened around him, making the yellow air dance with energy. He was not where he would choose to be, was not prepared for battle, but he could improvise a fight that would command respect.

He began to marshal his resources, then stared in disbelief as his hedge of spells collapsed and was overrun by a shadow of impervious blackness.

CHAPTER
·14·

Even as she was dreaming, Marcia knew she was locked in a hot dry sleep. Through the dull slumber and the shredding images she could smell her skin, dry and stretched. When a chill shook her, everything turned icy blue, then melted back to a suffocating pink as she sank into the warmth that rose to surround her.

Lulu didn't drink. Was that why she was so thirsty? Her ring felt heavy on her finger. She saw herself trying to raise an arm burdened with an awful weight, one far too great for her to lift. Ulda was right, she needed a lighter ring. And nicer clothes, with fringes that shook. Dancing slippers, dry and nimble, to teach her feet to be intricate.

She had not seen the rat woman clearly, not done her justice. Her small, squeezed features were fetching, even beautiful. Like a budding flower. She looked like a star from the old movies, except her hair wasn't molded into puffs of curls. It depends on how you turn your head, Marcia suddenly realized. Beauty is just a trick. She saw herself, three-quarter profile, head tilted, eyebrows raised. She felt her hips pivot in a brazen saunter. Men in shabby clothes were watching her. She was glad—proud—she wasn't some stuck-up high-priced call girl. If you're going to be a whore, it's more generous and democratic to be a cheap one.

Maybe it was all just a misunderstanding about virgin warriors. Temple prostitutes. Boxed in tight hot little rooms. Dried

123

blood and candles. The rat people would prowl with bloody lips, eyes like shiny buttons.

If she could wake and go outside, Father would bathe her head. She would catch the water with her tongue as it coursed down her face. She tried to picture the bridge where she would find him waiting.

Instead, she saw him standing ankle deep in water. His eyes looked inside her dream. Could a sad smile be demented? His lips moved, forming silent words, then he turned and walked away, splashing like a boy tramping through a mud puddle.

She was hemmed in. When would Father cure her fever? When would Elyssa come? She felt the scar next to her eye like a burning teardrop. She pushed the dream images from her, focused on the tiny pain. She seemed to be able to see it, a spot of burning brightness against a wall of black night. She willed herself to waken. This image was the candle in the darkness of the little room. She saw herself get up. Her features were stark and dramatic, lit from beneath by the candle, etched in blacks and grays. She felt apprehensive, and then was overtaken by a feeling of intense relief when she remembered she had been sent here by the president.

When she woke, it was to an oppressive silence. The pain in her arm had contracted to the area of the injury. She got up carefully, steadying herself on the table. The brief wave of dizziness that swept across her left her clear-headed and alert. When she took a few tentative steps the dizziness did not return.

She touched her forehead, her cheeks. Her skin was dry, but not hot. The chills she remembered from her dreams were absent. She was vaguely aware of being hungry. She gazed at the candle's flame and tried to collect her thoughts. After a few moments she shook her head and began to pick her way through the wavering shadows to the door.

Halfway across the room, she stopped and turned back to stare at the table. Every sense she had told her she had slept for hours—all night, she thought. Great-grandmother's rocking chair, the rat people, the dance hall, Ulda's tricks, all these things had happened last night, and now it was morning. And on the table the candle still burned.

She went back to have a closer look. The flame ducked and bowed at her approach. She bent down. The wax at the base of the candle was soft and warm. Marcia tried to force her mind to accommodate the candle's chronology. If she had slept even a fraction of the time her body said she had, the candle should be no more than a guttering stump.

The candle told her that she had slept for minutes, not hours. Her body said the opposite was true. She looked at the chair that Ulda had occupied as though expecting to find her sitting there.

Despite the testimony of the candle, she went to the door with a sense of keen anticipation. She was anxious to see what this place looked like in the light of day. When she opened it to a shadowy dusk, she blinked. She stepped outside with the eerie feeling that she had made her last foray only minutes before. If she hurried to the lane, would she see the figure of the man with the sack receding in the darkness?

Everything was the same. The air was warm and damp, just as it had been before. The same twilight cast the same shadows. Marcia advanced a few paces, careful to make no sound. She looked around, trying to penetrate the shadows with her gaze. After a half dozen steps she came to a sudden halt. Without bothering to look, she lifted her left foot and reached behind her. She ignored the pain in her arm and touched her shoe, then slid her fingers inside her sock. For a moment she balanced herself on one leg like an ibis in a pond, her smile invisible in the twilight. Her shoe and sock were dry.

She lowered her foot slowly to the ground. Never mind the candle, never mind the unchanging dusk, she had slept the night through.

"Come on, Lulu," she said, walking back to the hovel. Last night, weak and tired, she had thought of it as a refuge. Now she was grateful to be entering it for the last time.

She came back outside thinking of breakfast. She walked to the lane without any particular caution. The Lulu routine had taught her at least two things last night. It had demonstrated the general principle that just because passivity and caution came naturally to her did not mean they resulted in the best approach to every situation. And specifically, it had shown her that Ulda and the others feared her. No one had dared to confront her directly; even while she slept she had been left alone.

She tried to orient herself. If she could find the big building she would know where she was. Marcia looked around her and began to laugh silently. What would Lulu say? She consulted her

memory of old movies. Wisecracks delivered from the side of
the mouth by men and women who wore hats. *Now I know
you've flipped your lid.*

The lane was narrow. Last night she had walked on a wide
street at the edge of the . . . ghetto? At the intersection, across the
street from the dance hall—YWCA, whatever—there had been
people walking. Well, pedestrians; it didn't do to be too specific.
The Sisterhood ought to have a taxonomy handout, she thought;
a field guide with drawings of the various ogres, trolls, sprites,
elves, and other oddities a virgin warrior was likely to encounter.

Right here, right now, though, there was no one in sight. Before, she had seen an occasional light, heard distant shouts,
laughter. Now all was still. Were the shanties empty? Occupied
by sleeping rat people?

She heard a faint rustling sound and turned quickly. The shadows seemed to be empty. Her eyes wandered to the rooftops
around her. On the nearest, a heavy figure squatted. It seemed to
have the bulk of a large dog. Marcia recalled the flying
creature—she wasn't prepared to call it a bird—she had seen last
night. This thing looked like a mass of folded cloth gathered
around a hatchet beak and huge unblinking eyes.

Cousin Ellie was a bird-watcher. This would be something to
add to her list. When she had visited she sat at the window with
her binoculars hoping to spot an exotic gull or stray ocean bird.
Though Marcia had been certain people in neighboring buildings
would think she was spying, she had consented to take a look, but
almost dropped the binoculars when the magnification had
swept her out of her seventh-story window and sent her hurtling
through space. Cousin Ellie had gone to the kitchen to start
breakfast and hadn't heard Marcia's terrified gasp.

Actually, a couple of Cousin Ellie's patented two-pound pancakes wouldn't be so bad right now. Or a chili dog. Cold pizza.
As Marcia tried to make out details on the nearby roofs, she
found herself reviewing various meals she had shared with
Breksin. Visions of sausages, smoked hens, and charred rough
loaves of bread almost drove the scene before her from her mind.
How the condensation from Alexander's pitcher of iced wine had
wet the tablecloth! And that meal! Marcia could practically smell
the herbed butter that had basted the capon.

In the darkness, Marcia could make out the silhouettes of other
birds hunched on the shacks like gargoyles on a cathedral. They

had a predatory look that made Marcia want to return to her refuge, but that, she told herself firmly, would be even more insane than what she was actually going to do. She stepped into the lane and set out.

Her direction she had chosen by whim. With no sense of where she was in relation to the dance hall it didn't matter whether she went to the right or to the left. What did matter was that she get moving. The Lulu Principle dictated that she not sit around waiting for things to happen. Waiting—letting the game play you—was the Marcia Principle, and discredited. If Ulda wanted her to wait, she should have sent room service around with coffee and juice and a platter of ham, eggs, home fries, and buttered biscuits.

Her imagination provided her with a mental picture almost fattening in its intensity. Could a mirage occur after sunset? Could a mirage be eaten? Marcia stumbled and fell to one knee, catching herself with her sore arm. For a moment she stayed where she was, kneeling like a supplicant. She touched her wounds and brought her fingers away wet with blood that looked black in the dim light.

When she got up, she saw, or thought she saw, a hint of movement next to a building ahead. She took a few steps forward, then stopped and listened. Probably one of the birds. She continued walking. If she could make her way back to the avenue, she would follow the lights she had seen in the distance the night before.

She heard a metallic squeak behind her. When she whirled to face it, she felt light-headed for a moment, but ignored it. She saw nothing. The dwellings were dark and silent. Her eyes were now completely adjusted to the gloom. She could make out more detail in the shadows, could see the random patterns of the roofs against the background. Here and there the bulk of a roof bird loomed. She watched for a moment, then turned and went on.

When she had been walking for perhaps a quarter of an hour, she began to feel tired. The ache in her arm had grown more insistent. She stopped and let herself go limp. A light chill passed across her shoulder blades and seemed to slide off her back and into the surrounding warmth. She put her hand on her forehead. Despite the humid air, it was dry. It felt almost cool against her palm.

The heat seemed artificial, as though she were walking in a

huge greenhouse. Had there been plants, potted palms or something, in the dance hall? She found she couldn't remember. There had been the band, the jiggling dancers, the table with "the gang." Shouldn't there have been other tables? Marcia had an *impression* there had been, but no actual memory of any. She kept trudging along, gazing more at fugitive pictures of last night than at her present surroundings.

When she had joined the women who called themselves her sisters the dance floor had been crowded, the room alive with talk. Who had occupied the tables on either side? What had been the reaction when she dashed the drink to the table? The music had gone on; so had the dancing. Marcia stopped walking. She tried to picture in her mind the moment the crystal had shattered. She closed her eyes. She saw herself—Lulu—and her sisters. The heads and shoulders of dancers bounced just beyond the table. The atmosphere was one of noise and gaiety. Around them at the edge of the dance floor were crowds of . . . shadows.

Could it be that there had been only one table? She remembered the music, how it had seemed to *sag* when she stopped to listen. And the dancers—their shared aura, their jerky puppet motions. Just as she began to open her eyes, a final image rose in her mind. Ulda, draped in rags, towered over a wizened little man. Behind them were four sallow hags who were bent in antic postures like a quartet of arthritic monkeys. At a distance of several yards, a cloaked and hooded person stood pounding a drum monotonously with a heavy stick. Between the drummer and Ulda's group, naked rat people jumped and turned and waved their arms. Standing apart, on the other side of Ulda, was Suzy, bright and pretty in her lipstick and her red shoes.

Marcia opened her eyes and forced herself to start walking again. She was tired and hot, but mostly she was thirsty. What had the women offered her to drink last night? She had proceeded on the assumption that it was drugged or poisonous. Maybe it had been nothing more than a drink. She tried to remember if the goblet had been cool to the touch. Something, anything, cool would be welcome now.

Marcia stopped again and looked around. The scene had not changed. The lane continued, perhaps forever, between rows of nearly identical structures. It was like being lost in a development in the suburbs, except she couldn't knock at someone's door and ask for a glass of water.

In the darkness ahead Marcia saw a momentary block of light. As she was focusing on it, it vanished. She kept her eyes on the spot and started toward it. She had abandoned any idea of being cautious, or even circumspect. Her plan, such as it was, did not entail skulking around these shacks until she dropped. She was looking for a way out. If necessary, she could have Lulu stir things up a bit, but right now, Marcia was perfectly capable of looking into the matter of the light, and if Marcia ran into trouble, well, either she was strong enough to survive here, or she wasn't. Fine thing, fatalism, when you got right down to it, she thought.

She had no trouble picking out the shack where the light had come from. It sat apart from its neighbors, and light could be seen at the bottom of the door. Marcia stood in the middle of the lane. She was breathing heavily, as if she had sprinted up the slight grade that led to the solitary dwelling. Would this be another whore's crib? She hoped so; she could imagine much worse possibilities. And the rat people, after all, must drink. Putting aside the question of her resolve, she considered going on quietly, but the matter of water was becoming critical. The last thing she had had to drink was coffee in her apartment, as much as sixteen hours ago, besides which she had lost a little blood. Liquid had ceased to be a luxury.

She started to straighten up, to square her shoulders, but found it to be too much trouble. She sighed and left the lane. *Did people knock here?* she asked herself. Besides the field guide, she needed a pamphlet on etiquette and protocol. She was halfway between the lane and the door when she was stopped by a voice from behind her.

"Lulu!"

Marcia didn't bother to turn quickly. She stopped, paused, then looked back. Suzy, still dressed as she had been at the dance, stood across the lane between two shanties. She was the only spot of color to be seen. The night, the shadows, the silhouetted buildings, even Marcia's clothing seemed to present to the eye only shades of gray. Lulu looked like a hand-tinted figure in a black-and-white photo. Her matching lipstick and shoes seemed to burn in the darkness.

"Don't go in there."

Marcia noticed Suzy's voice had lost its sprightly lilt.

"What, the band's no good?"

Suzy smiled. Marcia had no idea what a dreen was, but this one was very pretty. When Suzy took a step toward her, Marcia raised her hand in warning.

"You'll have trouble there," said Suzy in a monotone that didn't go with her appearance. "And Ulda will find you if you exert your power."

"I'm having trouble everywhere."

"You are weak now."

Marcia felt the anger rising in her—the now-predictable tiny throbbing of the mark next to her eye.

"Then stop me, Suzy." She strode to the door with more confidence than she felt, and knocked briskly.

The face that greeted her seemed to fill the door. "Oh, a vissitor," it hissed. "How nice. Do step in."

Marcia took a step backward instead. She glanced over her shoulder and saw Suzy crossing the lane. Her smile had vanished; her face looked grim.

"Don't be shy," urged the voice from the door. It was high pitched to come from such a large mouth. The face drew back. It was perhaps not so large as Marcia's first startled impression had made it seem. It belonged to a man of about her own size, in appearance somewhat older, and with a rim of straight gray hair framing a bald head. Marcia took one more look at Suzy, now a dozen feet away, then stepped into the room.

The impression was that the man was wearing a mask, like some tribal dancer with a body supporting an outsize head.

"See, Mother?" he said, swinging his head in the direction of a woman who looked like his twin, and who was huddled on the floor by an open trapdoor.

Marcia thought she heard faint chittering noises. As she watched, a miniature version of the big heads poked from the opening in the floor. The woman clubbed it with her forearm before looking up.

"My, won't the children be pleased?" she crowed. She scrambled to her feet with an awkward agility that didn't fit her appearance. "Where are the hammers?"

Marcia felt uncomfortable. The woman had hardly glanced at her. She began to introduce herself, but was interrupted by the man.

"Right next to you, of course. Where would they be?" His

tone was rough. Marcia felt more uncomfortable yet. All she wanted was a glass of water. They could argue later. *Hammers?*

The man was smiling in her direction. Again Marcia began to say something. The woman put her huge head almost into the hole and shrieked. The sound seemed to continue as she bent to pick up a pair of heavy, short-handled mallets. With a final look at the hole, she joined the man, handing him one of the tools.

For the first time, the woman gave her attention to Marcia. Her look was uncomfortably personal in a very impersonal way. She stepped sideways until she was several feet from the man. They both faced Marcia with alert smiles and wide-eyed stares.

Marcia stepped back to the wall. The man was closer to the door than she was. The woman took another careful step to the side.

As though he had read her mind, the man nodded toward the hammer he held. "Makes it easier for the children," he said.

The woman nodded and spoke directly to Marcia. "The bones, you know," she said conversationally.

Marcia smiled politely. She felt grateful to the woman for acknowledging her. *Baby food.* When the woman took a step in her direction, she raised her ring hand.

"Don't come near me!" It had worked last night with the dreen.

"What's thisss?" hissed the man.

"I am stronger than you. Move away from the door." The dizziness Marcia began to feel seemed to be originating in her feet. The crude lamp hanging on the wall appeared to tip slightly. From the region of the trapdoor, the chittering sound rose again.

The woman bounded to the corner and shrieked again, then leapt back while the painful echoes were still in Marcia's ears. She moved with impossible speed, like some springing insect.

"Well, in that case . . . ," said the man. For a moment he was silent. The woman had her eyes fixed on him. Her lips were parted in a manic grin. In a blur of motion he cocked his bony arm and launched his hammer at Marcia.

It didn't rotate in the air like a knife, Marcia noted. She didn't know if that was because of the way he had thrown it, or because he was standing less then twenty feet from her. Whatever the reason, when the mallet left his grip, it came headfirst, unwavering as an arrow, straight at the middle of her face. It was, she thought, an extremely accurate throw.

She had a moment to think of the mugger in the alley last summer who had tried to hit her with his fist. Then, as now, time had seemed to slow down, to give her a chance to react.

She leaned to one side, shifting her feet beneath her, and watched the hammer punish the wall a few inches from her head. She let the weapon fall to the floor, then snatched it up, and rose to face her attackers.

The woman was jumping up and down in such a way that she only moved below the waist. Her upper body and huge head remained in one position like a hovering bird of prey. Her face was contorted with rage.

"Ours! The hammers are ours! We have the hammers! Us! Us! Give it back!" She darted toward Marcia, coming about halfway, then retreated and continued her furious dance.

The man was staring at Marcia. "She's as fast as you, Mother. Faster."

"We'll see," said the woman, settling down and sidling in the direction of the trapdoor.

"Be careful," said the man. He didn't take his eyes from his guest.

"They can help," muttered the woman.

The man contorted his mouth and called to the woman in a half-whisper. Marcia saw big blocky teeth set close together.

"Just two or three," he said.

"I know."

Marcia waited, bracing herself against the wall. As soon as the dizziness passed she was going to leave here. The woman was bent over the opening making a murmur of soft noises punctuated with short, angry cries.

When Suzy opened the door and walked in, she seemed to bring a blaze of color to the room. Although the dreen was her enemy, Marcia couldn't help feeling that the situation had improved.

The man jumped, drew in his breath noisily, and scrambled across the room to the woman's side. He pulled her roughly from the opening and screamed into it. They both turned to face the new arrival.

Suzy sent one glance in Marcia's direction, then began slowly advancing on the couple in the corner. Again the urgent noises were rising from the opening.

The man backed up until he reached the wall. The woman

dropped to a compact crouch, holding her hammer next to her ankle and flexing her knobby fist on the short handle.

"Not the children," she said grimly. "Not that."

Suzy advanced at a nonchalant stroll. Marcia closed her eyes for a second, hoping the light-headedness would leave her. At the woman's screech she opened them to see what Suzy had done.

But it was the woman who was acting. As the sound of her screech died, she launched herself at Suzy, landing on her like an attacking beast and striking at her with her hammer. Marcia watched numbly as the blows landed on the flapper's head, shoulders, her face. Even though Marcia knew that Suzy was not what she appeared, the effect was that of watching a defenseless girl being bludgeoned to death.

Marcia had taken three wobbly steps toward them before she realized that Suzy hadn't stopped. As the woman tried to spring away from her, Suzy reached out with one hand and seized her by the upper arm. The woman cried out as though she had been scalded. The hammer fell to the floor. A moment later the two women disappeared into the opening. The man had not moved. He looked at Marcia with no readable expression on his splayed-out face.

The screams had already started when Suzy pulled herself from the opening. She brushed off her dress and then looked up at Marcia with a faint smile. Her face was unmarked. Marcia's head had cleared. She took another step forward. Suzy's dress wasn't even torn.

When the dreen turned to face the man, he shrank away from her. His big, wide-set eyes were filled with tears. He looked at Marcia.

"Why did you come to usss?" His childish voice was higher now, the hiss more drawn out.

Marcia knew she had entertained more than her share of irrational thoughts and impulses lately. Still, the pity she felt for the creature who had tried to drive her face through the back of her head was perhaps the most eccentric.

Suzy was advancing on the man.

"Suzy!"

The flapper turned to Marcia. The screams from the trapdoor had subsided.

"What are you going to do?"

"Finish feeding the kids."

"Leave him."

Suzy didn't look back at the man. "Sure," she said. "Let's go." She walked to the door and stood with her hand on the latch.

Marcia almost started four or five questions, but couldn't decide which one to ask. As she joined her, Suzy opened the door.

The man called after them. "They know I'm alone. They will come for me," he said as they stepped into the night.

Suzy looked back. "Yeah, I know. Well, twenty-three skidoo," she called, and flashed her prettiest smile at Marcia.

Outside, Suzy followed a route that led them between the huts. Marcia trailed behind her and concentrated on walking. For the moment, it didn't matter where they were going. She was tired and dirty and her throat felt like she had swallowed glue. Her interests were limited to water, breakfast, and a hot shower.

After they had gone a short distance, Marcia heard a series of rapid screams faintly in the distance behind them. They rose in pitch and intensity, then were abruptly cut off. She stopped to listen, but heard nothing more.

They hadn't gone much farther when they came to the border of the shacks at a wide avenue. Marcia was sure it was the one she had been on briefly last night.

"The castle is that way," said Suzy, pointing to their left as they crossed the street. When they reached the other side, they turned to the right.

Marcia surmised that the castle was the place with the dance hall. She didn't care enough to ask. Her throat hurt. The pedestrians they passed were hidden in a murky blur. She noted without interest that there were rat people among them. Everyone seemed to be giving them wide berth, as they would a lady walking a snarling pit bull. Marcia didn't know, or care, whether it was she or Suzy they feared.

When her guide turned into an alley even darker than the avenue, Marcia followed without question. She had lost her capacity for fear, and suspicion was of no interest to her. If she was confronted with Ulda, or a dragon, or a semi-automatic rifle, she would fight if she could. She was confident that inside her was at least a small final reservoir of strength that she could call on in need.

When the dreen stopped, Marcia jerked as though she had been awakened from a deep sleep. She looked around in confusion. The alley was paved with broken stone. Thirty yards away, a light burned at the top of a pole. As she stared, Marcia saw a rat scuttle from one shadow to another.

They climbed a narrow flight of stairs. They were near the top when Marcia realized that Suzy was holding on to her arm. She opened a door and helped her through. They walked down a short hallway and passed through another door.

The lamplight hurt her eyes. The smells were strong and seemed to strike at her. A man was plucking at a musical instrument that twanged, and singing in a voice to match. *Not another dance,* a voice inside her pleaded. The room was small, and filled with tables where people—well, bipeds, Marcia thought, not bothering to look too closely—ate and drank.

They seated themselves beside a window with shutters that were partly open and Suzy called out, "Wine!" in a voice that carried.

"Water," Marcia croaked. Suzy just laughed. *You dirty, pardner?*

The wine came in a pitcher. The cups were of a soft hammered metal. Marcia was sure they weren't clean.

As she raised her cup Suzy ordered her to drink slowly, then pulled her arm back to the table before she had managed more than two or three desperate swallows. The flapper's grip was heavy and insistent. Marcia looked at her in the flickering light. A hammer had struck that face, landing with enough force to crush bone. *You cannot stand before a dreen.*

When a plate of meat pastries was brought to the table, Marcia looked at it suspiciously.

"Don't worry, Lulu, it's all stolen."

"Huh?"

"It's from the Middle Regions. It won't hurt you."

Marcia looked at the table. "Can't we get some water?"

"Now, that would hurt you."

For some reason, the wine seemed to have no effect on her other than quenching her thirst. The little meat pies were heavy and greasy, but Marcia consumed almost three of them before beginning to wonder what they might be made of. A strongly flavored, rather rubbery bacon seemed to be the chief ingredient. Napkins not being among the amenities provided, Marcia was reduced to wiping the wine and fat from her lips with her fingers, which she considered roughly the equivalent of spitting on the floor.

It was only after she had eaten her fill that she noticed the soothing, relaxing properties of the wine. She sat back in her chair and managed to ignore her more or less urgent need for a shower and a change of clothes, not to mention a toothbrush. She glanced around the room. Except for three squat little men with tiny ears, and one tall, impossibly thin man dressed like a frontier parson, the patrons did not look any more bizarre than many folks on the streets at home. The rat-people might inspire some double takes at a bus stop, she supposed. It would depend on the light.

"Well, Lulu, how do you feel?" Suzy still looked like a misplaced show girl in the drab surroundings. Everything about her—her clothing, her makeup, her complexion—was strangely colorful, with an unexpected quality of illumination, like a stained-glass window in a coal bin. She had eaten nothing, and only taken a few dainty sips of her wine. Her fire-engine lipstick remained irreproachably unsmeared.

How she felt was too complicated a question for Marcia to deal with. She leaned across the table toward Suzy and spoke softly. "What would have happened if I had given Ulda the ring?"

"Your troubles would be over." The expression on Suzy's face made her meaning clear. "It's better," she added quietly, "that you don't use her name." Suzy got to her feet. "It's time for us to go on," she said.

When they got outside, Suzy took her arm again on the steps. Marcia said, "I thought you couldn't touch me." She looked at the bruises on her arms. "*She* couldn't."

"She was stupid," Suzy said. "She should never have put her hand on you."

"She said she was going to kill me."

"As I said, she was stupid. She knew she couldn't kill you. Not while you wore the ring. Her only hope was to bully you or trick you, but she has vast powers, and is unused to considering limits. By attacking you, she weakened herself, temporarily. That's why I was able to escape her. That, and the fact that she was giving her attention to her new captive."

"You mean me?"

"No. Another one, after you. Even though she knew you would end up gaining strength from her mistake, she hoped you would stay in that hut. She was stupid, and thought I was stupid, too. I was watching. If you hadn't left on your own, I would have come for you."

"Why are you helping me?"

Suzy looked at her with a level gaze. "It is you that are helping me. Without the power of your ring, and the energy she gave up to you, I could not hope to escape her web."

Suzy led them into an alley across from the inn. It passed between broken masonry walls, tumbledown houses with dark windows, and barren little plots of ground that had the melancholy look of long-neglected gardens. They walked in silence, and all was silent around them. The alley brought them finally to a narrow covered passageway between two tall buildings. As Suzy entered ahead of her and was swallowed by the darkness, Marcia hesitated for a moment, then pushed her misgivings aside wearily, and followed.

The lane at the other end traced the contours of a hill. In one direction it rose steeply, in the other dropped quickly enough that Marcia could look down on the rooftops of buildings not far away. The lane itself was deserted, but there were lights at some windows up the hill; below the place they stood not a single candle shone.

Marcia whispered, "What else?" to herself when the dreen started down the hill. It was to be expected, she supposed, that they would seek out the most depressing route. She realized that she was already thinking of the dirty little café as an island of cheer.

"Where are we going?"

Suzy answered without taking her eyes from the ground in front of her. "To someone who can help us find the veil of the Middle Regions."

"You mean we can cross from here?"

"*You* can. How else did you come here?"

Marcia caught herself before she said Ulda's name. "She brought me."

Suzy said nothing until they came to a place where the lane turned. She stopped and shook her head. "She did not bring you. You wandered too near her. She was watching, and drew you to her."

"But I can't get away," said Marcia. "I've already tried. Nothing happens."

"Her web is strong," said Suzy. "You have the power to leave but cannot find your way. That is why we must seek help."

The hill was not so steep beyond the turning. The lane descended gently, almost level in places. When they had walked for perhaps a quarter of an hour, Marcia began to notice that the air had changed. Now it was not the heat that was oppressive so much as the weight of the air. Clots of yellow mist began to appear between houses. Marcia thought she smelled water.

When it began to rain, Suzy stopped and looked around like a person in the grip of sorcery. The drops were big, and slow. Each splashing impact seemed almost to be an individual event. Marcia saw a dozen strike the ground before one found her arm, and then another her forehead. Suzy turned in a clumsy pirouette, bright red lips stretched in an uncertain grin.

"This is not your doing?"

Marcia looked at her in pure astonishment. "What? The rain?" Another drop struck her cheek and traced a path to her chin. "I wish."

A few more drops fell, then the rain stopped. For a moment, Suzy stood with her hands out and her head tilted back, then she continued down the lane. After they had gone several paces, the air stirred briefly, the ghost of a breeze. Again Marcia caught the scent of water, as well as a faint but pervasive odor of rotting wood.

During the next minutes, the fog got thicker, now lying across their path like strips of dirty muslin. Marcia had begun to hope they didn't have much farther to go when they were forced to stop.

The dark water was like a mirage. It erased the lane and cut arbitrarily across the houses ahead that were partially submerged. Suzy stared mutely at the barrier. Again the air stirred, this time a light wind that was visible on the surface of the water. The breeze was tugging at patches of stubborn mist, teasing and curling its way erratically, blowing from first one point, then another. At some indeterminate distance beyond the fog, Marcia could see a dull rim of light, as though the water were bounded by a low, smoldering fire.

"What's that?" asked Marcia, almost too softly to be heard. It was a place that called for whispers.

"The edge of Ulda's mantle," came the low reply. "I didn't think it could be seen. But then"—Suzy waved her hand in the direction of the water—"I didn't think the water could swell like this, and rise to eat at her holdings."

"Is it a river?" asked Marcia.

"No. It is a shallow sea. It is said that in times beyond memory it was vast and deep; this is all that remains." Suzy stepped to the edge of the lapping water. "It covers the flats," she said, peering through the hazy dark. "The houses are flooded. Where will we find the little mage now?"

Marcia didn't know. "Ulda said something about rising water, an ancient sea, but I got the impression she was talking about something far away."

Suzy's answer was carried away by a sudden gust of wind. It swept over them in a rapid whisper that seemed to leave the air more still than before. A few more scattered drops of rain fell. Suzy had turned back to the water and was staring at it soberly.

Marcia breathed deeply. The air was strangely fresh, and bore a familiar scent. She was silent for a few moments, then said, "If I were home, I'd say we were about to be caught in a rainstorm."

Suzy turned to her slowly and said, "Rain does not fall here." As she spoke, the heavy drops began to fall again, pocking the surface of the water, and penetrating the mist to spatter on the lane. "As you can see," she added with a sweeping gesture and a smile.

How can she be that pretty? Marcia wondered. Suzy looked for all the world like a New York model dressed in a period outfit. She was about Marcia's height and weight, but with more graceful curves. The dreen's appearance had to be some sort of illusion, she was certain. She recalled her dream vision of Ulda and the others: the shriveled little man, the quartet of hags. In it, none of them had matched their outward appearance except Ulda, who was at least recognizable, and Suzy, who had looked exactly as she did this minute.

Suzy brushed a drop of water from her forehead. "This is some sort of working," she said. "Tell me again it is none of yours."

Marcia told her.

"Then Ulda has another enemy to deal with. That can only be good for us." She started back up the lane. "Come, we must find the little mage."

CHAPTER

·15·

The rain continued to fall. Marcia and Suzy made their way up
the hill like witches walking between raindrops, staying almost
completely dry. It was not until they had passed the turn in the
lane, and the hill got steeper, that the rain began to fall in earnest. A concentrated splash struck Marcia from behind like water
cast from a pail. One second she was relatively dry, the next her
hair and the back of her blouse were thoroughly wet.

For the space of a few dozen steps, no rain fell. Marcia and
Suzy trudged up the hill shoulder to shoulder. When she heard
the noise, Marcia stopped. Suzy walked on for a few steps, then
turned. As she had before, Marcia noted the almost luminous
quality that Suzy seemed to project; even the deep black of her
dress seemed a colorful contrast to the surrounding gloom.

From behind her, the noise grew louder. Marcia turned her
gaze down the hill. The darkness now seemed animated. All was
still except for the muted roar that approached. When the first isolated drops of rain struck her, Marcia smiled broadly and peered
into the night.

In the absence of any wind, the curtain of rain was absolutely
vertical, and approached slowly. Marcia was conscious of Suzy
standing next to her, motionless as a statue, her arms straight at
her sides. When the rain had nearly reached them it stopped. For
what seemed like a long time, they were outside the downpour.

Then suddenly they were engulfed. Marcia was conscious of the passing of time in fractions of seconds; she was aware of the progressive wetting down of her garments, was aware of the instant when she became completely soaked to the skin.

She laughed and looked at Suzy. The flapper was shaking her head and staring around her. She looked at Marcia and said something inaudible. Marcia smiled and nodded, not caring what she had missed. There was, she thought, something *good* about this unexpected storm. She tilted her head back to let the rain wash her face. After a moment, she felt a tug at her sleeve. She opened her eyes reluctantly and followed Suzy up the hill.

When they came to the covered passageway, Marcia thought they would take shelter there, but Suzy kept going. Marcia glanced at it as they walked by and thought she saw a movement in the shadows—something heavy and dark. As they passed the lighted houses farther up the hill, she caught glimpses of the inhabitants peering from windows or crowded in open doorways to stare at the rain.

By a large house at the top of the hill, a group of burly men and women dressed in tattered clothes were gathered in the shelter of an overhanging roof. As Marcia and Suzy passed, one of the men began shouting at them and gesturing wildly at the rain. When they were just abreast of him, he abandoned his refuge and came toward them at a shambling trot. It wasn't until he drew near that Marcia realized how big he was, or that his skin looked like leather, or that the teeth exposed by his open mouth were those of a beast.

In a sudden panic, and without any clear idea of what she would be able to do, she began to raise her ring, but immediately felt the weight of Suzy's restraining hand. The dreen crossed in front of her, her eyes locked on the advancing man, now perhaps ten yards from them. At the sight of her coming his way, he hesitated for a heartbeat, then bellowed something incomprehensible, and bore down on her like an offended ox.

Marcia was watching very closely, and was certain that colliding with the man had not the slightest effect on Suzy's progress. He might as well have tried to arrest the momentum of a city bus. He bounced away from her in a way that would have been comical had it not been accompanied by his scream of pain and terror. He landed on his side in the mud. Marcia noticed that one arm was bent under him at an unnatural angle. He had scarcely touched the ground before he rolled onto his back and began sculling himself out of Suzy's path with frantic thrusts of his heels.

Suzy paid him no heed. By the time she reached the house, the others had fled through the door and closed it. When Suzy reached it, she batted it aside with a single blow of her forearm. Marcia heard the clatter of ruptured planks, the squeal of ruined hinges, and watched as Suzy passed from view into the house. At the same moment, a door at the back corner crashed open and the occupants spilled out into the rain. They ignored the first man, who was trying to struggle to his feet. One of his arms dangled like an empty shirtsleeve as he slipped repeatedly on the muddy ground. When Suzy came back through the door, he howled and thrust himself across the ground in a frantic one-armed crawl.

Suzy said, "We don't like to be challenged," as she joined Marcia. She was not breathing heavily. "You must not use your ring if we have problems," she said. "If you do, Ulda will know."

They had no more problems. As they walked the streets in the downpour, what few folk they saw peering from windows or sheltering under eaves either paid them no heed or removed themselves from view. Suzy showed no interest in rest or in protection from the weather. She walked on, leading them down wide streets and narrow alleys and twisting lanes awash with mud.

Marcia followed obediently. She couldn't get any wetter, and the air and the falling rain were both warm. When she remembered how fervently she had been wishing for a shower, she laughed aloud, but the sound was lost in the noise of the weather.

Suzy did pause occasionally to go to a door, always at some small broken-down and out-of-the-way place. Some of them proved to be vacant; at others she spoke with occupants Marcia usually couldn't see. At one shack in an alley she stood on a decrepit porch and conversed with a gnarled little woman half her size for a few minutes while Marcia stood like a dunce with the rain pouring over her.

After a while it became apparent that this was no ordinary cloudburst. There was something almost mechanical in the unvarying steadiness of the rainfall. Marcia's sense of time and her state of exhaustion told her they had been walking for something over two hours, and still the rain came straight down as though drawn from an inexhaustible heavenly cistern and distributed by a gigantic shower head.

Some time well after she had decided she could not bear the walking or the rain any longer, they stopped for lunch. The tavern was small and dark and had only a few patrons. At their table in a corner, Marcia stood irresolutely behind her chair. Should she just sit down wringing wet and dripping? It seemed . . . indecorous. When she finally lowered herself gingerly into the seat, she felt certain she would never be able to get up again.

A little man with nervous lips brought steaming mugs of tea and stood twisting his hands and looking everywhere but at Suzy. The dreen glanced up at him, then turned to Marcia and said, "Well, Lulu, what do you want?"

"Hamburger, fries, and a Coke," Marcia replied, watching the water stream onto the table from her hair. She lifted the cup in both hands and held it under her nose.

Suzy said, "Bread, cheese. Wine." The man stammered something Marcia didn't catch. In a moment he was back with a platter and a stoppered jug.

Marcia, still staring at the table, began to giggle. "Maybe fajitas, and some guacamole." She put her mug of tea down heavily. "Nachos. With melted cheese and those little hot peppers."

The man was trembling as he filled her wineglass. Marcia had always been softhearted, yet his obvious fear awakened no pity in her. Instead, she found herself resisting an almost sickening urge to toy with his discomfort, to do something threatening or startling that would completely unnerve him. She looked at the pale hues of his aura, indistinct in the lamplight, and pictured him shrieking in terror and jumping away from her. When he poured for Suzy, the neck of the wine jug chattered against the rim of her glass. The noise it made sounded like a distant jackhammer, and went on until Marcia began to think it would never stop. When it did, she squeezed her eyes shut and turned her head to the wall to hide her streaming tears.

By the time she had emptied her second glass of wine, the catch in her throat was gone. She forced herself to nibble at the bread and cheese and discovered that she was hungry. When she had eaten all she wanted, she poured herself more wine.

Suzy's glass was almost full. Marcia thought of Egri. "Little Egri," she said aloud, correcting herself.

"What?"

"A friend of mine. He's sort of like you: takes little sips of wine; doesn't eat much." Suzy said nothing. "He's a familiar," said Marcia. "You know. Of a witch." She looked down into her glass. "He's really a cat. Sometimes, anyway." She stared frankly at Suzy for a moment, then dropped her eyes.

Suzy said, "It is Ulda's doing that I have this form, but it is my true form—now. I am not a shape changer."

"But you are not what you appear to be."

"No." Suzy raised her glass and drank. "Are you?"

Why was it, Marcia wondered, that lately every question was complicated? Had it always been that way, but she had just been too dull to notice? She let her eyes wander over her companion's pretty features. Suzy's hair, evidently, was naturally curly, with the result that her resemblance to a drowned cat was much less faithful than Marcia was certain her own was.

"No, I'm not," Marcia admitted, "but that woman, I mean, thing—"

"Troll."

"Okay, troll. Anyway, I saw her attack you with a hammer."

"And you were not attacked?"

"Well, yes, but . . ."

"And you had taken the other hammer." Suzy leaned forward and rested her chin in her hands. "It seems each of us was too strong for them."

Marcia thought for a moment. "What I did was just a trick, sort of. When he threw the hammer at me, time seemed to go slower while I got out of the way." Marcia dropped her voice to a whisper. "But you are *strong*. When that, uh, man—"

"Troll."

"Troll," Marcia repeated. "Anyway, when—Really? Another troll?" She took a contemplative sip of wine, then shrugged her shoulders. "They don't have much luck with you, do they?"

"No," said Suzy. "And you're right, of course. I am able to overcome threats with physical force. No mere troll can challenge me; no clumsy weapon can injure me; walls of wood or stone cannot stand against my strength. Meanwhile, all you can manage, poor dear, is to distort the fabric of space and time. I can knock down a troll, smash a door. The best you can do is defy the power of the one who rules here, who made this place, this darkness, who holds a thousand trolls—ten thousand—in the palm of her hand." Suzy took Marcia's hand and gently turned her arm to expose the bloody bruises. "Yet when that same hand dares touch you, threaten you, it is forced to withdraw in dire agony. It is only right, only natural, that you envy me my vast powers."

Marcia stared for a moment at her injured arm. "Are you saying that my power equals hers? Surpasses it?"

"No. I think that is not possible. Hers is a primary power; she has drawn it directly from the wellspring. There are few powers anywhere to equal her."

"Then what does she need with my ring?"

"You must not come to a dreen for wisdom. I can only guess. It is clear she covets the ring. It is clear that with the ring you are able to resist her." Suzy gazed at Marcia's ring. "This, then, is a thing of no ordinary potency. To interest Ulda, it must be vastly powerful. To enable you to resist her, it must come from a source as great as she, or greater. One of those from whom she is sundered."

Marcia had been staring at her ring. She looked up quickly at her companion. "Sundered? Like who, for instance?"

Suzy returned her look frankly. "This, you must know better than I. I am a simple fighter, a guard. You wear the ring, wield its power. You did not find it in the gutter. It must have been given you by one who knew you could bear its weight."

Yes, Marcia thought. That was true. Elyssa had put the ring on her finger, and when she had used it well, and had stood up to the fury of the demon, Elyssa had allowed her to keep it, said she seemed "suited to it." But she had also said that the ring was not to be removed. Yet Father—the crazy old man—had stolen it from her and worn it. And wearing it he had altered it, then put it back on her finger, but with no care or thought of her strength or capabilities. Thinking about it, Marcia began to conclude that she had only survived her encounter with Ulda through the agency of plain dumb luck.

She smiled faintly at Suzy. She had done enough chattering. She nodded as though to acknowledge the accuracy of the dreen's observation. They seemed, for the moment, to be in league, but it might be better for this armored truck in the form

of a Charleston expert to think her stronger and smarter than she
really was.

A few minutes later they left the tavern. Outside, the rain was
coming down just as before. Though she was already soaked, it
still seemed odd to Marcia to walk into a downpour. What would
people think? She shook her head as she followed Suzy from the
shelter of the door.

A quarter of an hour later the rain stopped abruptly. Suzy was
once again in conversation in the candlelight of a doorway. Just
as the door closed and Suzy stepped into the lane, the falling water, which had begun to seem permanent, ceased. One moment it
was pounding relentlessly, the next it was simply gone. The
noise of the rain swallowed itself, vanishing in a quick roar that
left other sounds defined in the sudden silence: the trickle of a
thousand tiny waterfalls and rivers, the quick splashes of Suzy's
muddy red shoes as she stepped across the lane. Marcia could
smell the quiet, the tightening heat of the air.

Suzy stopped and looked around like some inhabitant of a land
of perpetual rainfall who had never before seen a break in the
weather. She came to Marcia's side and spoke in a low voice. "I
had hoped it might be longer, this rain."

"Not me," said Marcia. "I'm wet enough."

"It occupied her, I think. The rising waters, the storm—she
has not caused these things; they are working against—" Suzy
peered toward the end of the lane. Marcia followed her eyes and
saw nothing but puddles and shadows. Without saying a word,
the dreen put her hand on Marcia's arm and began walking back
toward the doorway she had just left. She moved quickly, pulling
Marcia along. At the door, she paused, staring again into the
darkness and then turning her head slightly as though listening
for something. Marcia stood absolutely still and held her breath.
After several seconds, during which Marcia saw and heard nothing at all, Suzy lifted the latch and pushed the door open.

Inside, the smell of wet bare planks combined inharmoniously
with a chorus of other odors. The light of the single lamp seemed
dazzling after the darkness of the streets. Marcia looked around
guiltily. They hadn't *knocked*.

As if to register this breach of etiquette, six pairs of eyes
stared at them. Seated against the wall opposite the door on what
appeared to be a pile of rags was a woman. She was pale and

had curly blond hair. Her shape was pyramidic. Her head was small; her facial features seemed pinched, as though they had been forced into a space too small for them. From her chin down, her body widened—spread out—until it blended with the scraps she sat on.

Next to her, sitting on his heels with his back propped against the wall, was a small, bony man with rough black hair. The expression on his face, though static, was strangely alert. He looked like someone who has been momentarily blinded by a flashbulb. On the other side of the woman were a pair of tall, painfully slender girls with black hair and prominent eyes, a plump, shapeless boy whose stare was vacant, and a small, red, hairless dog that looked like a dyed rat.

Suzy did not say a word. Marcia smiled tentatively and fluttered her hands. A number of inane remarks suggested themselves to her. She felt like a genteel charity volunteer who has suddenly been thrust into the company of poor people.

"Suzy?" she prompted, with a fragile smile.

Suzy raised her hand for silence, then kept it raised as she listened at the door. After a moment, she dropped her hand to her side.

"What?"

Marcia smiled again and glanced pointedly toward the group on the other side of the room. She knew she was being irrational, but her mother's principles were immutable. When she crossed the threshold, she had become a guest. She could only presume the woman held up by the pile of rags was her hostess, and she had not been introduced.

The man said something that sounded like "bervull," and got to his feet. The dog whined and did a little dog-dance on its short legs, never taking its eyes from Suzy. The man was taller than Marcia would have thought. He looked vaguely like Abraham Lincoln with a very cheap haircut and no beard. He crossed the room and opened the door. The dog whined again, then rushed across the floor and vanished into the darkness. The man followed and pulled the door closed behind him.

Marcia didn't know if she had ever been in such an uncomfortable social position. Compared with this, her visit with the trolls had been a gracious event, even though their interest in her had been largely nutritional. She cast a surreptitious glance in the direction of the lady of the house. She sat unmoving, but for a slight chewing motion of her chin and lower lip, and stared straight ahead, paying no attention to her visitors. It was as though there were a television chattering and flickering in the corner.

After a dull interval that seemed like hours but wasn't, the door opened. Marcia caught a glimpse of the man as Suzy went outside. As she made haste to follow, she glanced one more time at the mute company ranged against the wall. She forced a weak smile and nodded as though in acknowledgment of hospitality offered, then was shocked to hear Lulu's unmodulated voice come sneaking past her lips.

"Thanks, it's been swell. Real swell."

After another hour or more threading their way down the darkest lanes and alleys, Suzy led her to an area that was like the one where she had first encountered the rat people. They stopped in front of a shack that was even smaller and more rickety looking than most. It was surrounded by rubble and hemmed in by its neighbors. Marcia held back. The place was claustrophobic and she had had quite enough socializing.

"How about if I just wait outside? You take all the time you want."

Suzy shook her head and beckoned. When they reached the door, she tapped lightly, like a church lady arriving for tea at the parson's cottage. Marcia pictured her earlier in the day, smashing a stout door to splinters.

The person who opened the door was hardly taller than Borphis. He was perhaps the size of an average ten-year-old, but completely bald and deeply wrinkled. He looked up at the two women silently for a few seconds, then stepped back and performed a flourishing gesture of invitation.

"Enter, good ladies, please, and grace my humble parlor. You do me high honor. High honor, indeed."

Marcia was surprised, on stepping through the door, to find herself in a hallway. The entire shack was not as large as her bedroom and had no need of an entryway—she looked down at her feet—certainly not one with a floor of dirt. She glanced at Suzy. The dreen had a smile on her face that could only be described as smug.

"This way, please, gracious ladies, if you will permit me to conduct you."

Misgivings had become a permanent feature in Marcia's state of mind. With practiced ease she suppressed them as she followed the dreen and the strange little man down the hall. At least their host talked. Perhaps he would even be able to offer them a chair.

She did not so easily suppress her feelings as she was ushered through the doorway into the "humble parlor." At first it didn't register that the room was larger than it could possibly be, given the dimensions of the shack. Her attention was entirely occupied with the polished wooden floor and the rugs that were scattered here and there. Although the room was windowless, the air was cool and fresh. Marcia stared, blinking, at the divan piled with silk cushions, at the upholstered chairs—four, it seemed, although that wasn't possible. But then, neither was wainscoting and plaster, fresh air. The aroma of steeping tea. She drew a deep breath and closed her eyes.

"Cream?"

She opened her eyes. "Please," she replied, then looked around in confusion. "What is this?" she blurted out.

"Your pardon," said the little man. "Doubtless you would like to freshen up. The facility is through that door."

Marcia proceeded like a sleepwalker. When she came back to the parlor, the little man was pouring tea for Suzy, who was wearing a long blue robe trimmed in lace.

She jerked her head in the direction of a door in the corner of the room. "You can change in there, Lulu. I laid something out for you."

The room was large and furnished as opulently as the living room. Suzy's wet clothing had been tossed carelessly onto the floor. Marcia undressed, folded her clothes, then Suzy's, before toweling herself off and putting on an elegant robe of red silk that would have looked much better on the flapper. She could not find a mirror. She hesitated at the door, imagining what her freshly toweled hair must look like. As she left the room, she found herself thinking of Albert Einstein.

Suzy looked like someone who has just spent all afternoon at a beauty parlor. She swept up to Marcia like a debutante. The little man hastened along at her elbow.

"Marcia, allow me to present the master magician, Phellep."

The little mage bowed like a courtier of *Louis XIV*. "I will

never fail to recall your gracious condescension with gratitude
and pride, my lady."

Surprisingly, Marcia was quick-witted enough to squelch
Lulu's brassy "Pleased ta meetcha," then found that all she could
think to say was "Charmed," which seemed insufficient in the
face of Phellep's euphuistic welcome.

Marcia luxuriated in the embrace of an immense armchair upholstered in a soft, supple leather. The tea bore the faint aroma
of smoke and was accompanied by a tray of plain butter cookies
that seemed to Marcia at that moment to be the most satisfying
food she had ever eaten.

So far, the conversation had been limited to talk of tea and
cookies, and a brief discussion of the weather in which Ulda's
name had been studiously avoided. Marcia was determined to
speak of more substantive matters. She thought that she had been
quite patient enough, even by her standards—meaning her
mother's—but something was bothering her, something she
couldn't define but that had the persistence of an almost-
remembered word or thought. She had the definite impression
that she was failing to notice something of importance.

She looked around the room again. There was a large mystery
there—she was sitting in a room bigger than the building it
occupied—but that was not the thing that was nagging at her.
Nor was it the clean, fresh air, or the silence. It was something
subtle. She closed her eyes and listened. A cup and saucer came
together with a small noise. The only other sound was the ticking
of the clock.

Marcia opened her eyes. She put her cup down carefully and
looked around the room. She didn't see how she had managed to
miss it. The clock was hanging on the wall next to a lamp.
Marcia peered at it as she got up from her chair, ignoring the
protests of tired muscles in her legs and back. What time was it?
she wondered, then amended her question: What time was it
here? And what time zone were they in, anyway?

The clock had a brass pendulum with an adjustable weight, an
elaborately carved wooden case, a face decorated with curlicues
in faded gold paint, and no hands.

Marcia didn't have enough energy for a fit of giggles. Instead,
she stared at the timeless clock. She recalled that a stopped clock
is absolutely accurate twice a day. She wondered what the interval of unimpeachability was of a device like this. She turned

away from the clock convinced that she had missed the point of something that was either transcendently witty or very profound.

Phellep crossed the room on silent feet. "I still have them," he said.

"I beg your pardon?"

"The hands. I still have them. I'm afraid I'm not very clever with mechanical things. I've tried to attach them more than once, but they always fall back off again. Still, it's a comforting sound, don't you think?"

The subsequent conversation about time led to questions of place, which Marcia followed, but only with difficulty.

"So we are not in . . . *her* domain at all?" She wondered if Regions would ever make sense to her.

"That is correct, dear lady. This is my little place of refuge. It lies in an intermediate area. Reaching it is a trick I stumbled onto quite by accident; I have developed it into something of a specialty."

"Then we will go from here to the Middle Regions?"

"Alas, no," said the little mage. "That is something I have not quite worked out yet. I came upon this place, in fact, while attempting to escape to the Middle Regions. I can only help you on your way."

Marcia leaned forward in her chair. "Can you come with us? If you want to escape . . ."

Phellep smiled sadly. "I am indebted to you for your gracious offer; you are most generous. But I must tarry here yet awhile. This"—he looked around his parlor—"has become my work. I want to see it through. I am rather proud, if I must admit it, of being able to continue under *her* nose. I am like a mouse hidden by the hem of her skirt. She may suspect my presence, but she cannot find me."

The mage looked up at the clock and stared at it for a moment. "Dear me," he said, slipping from his chair, "I must see to your clothing."

When he left the room, Marcia began to speak, but was interrupted by the sound of music. It seemed to be coming from within the room, a simple, slow melody being played on a lone violin, but when she looked around, Marcia could see no one. She peered into the corners. Had she, she wondered, failed to notice a stereo system as well as the clock? She glanced at Suzy, then shrugged and settled back to enjoy the entertainment.

When she woke up, she turned her eyes to the clock, and then to Suzy, who was dressed again in her flapper outfit, no longer wet and muddy, but back to its original glitter and shine. Even the red shoes were spotless and seemed to radiate a light of their own. The dreen flashed a smile and performed a tricky dance step.

"Your stuff's ready too, Lulu."

As the little mage bowed her out of the room, Marcia found herself wondering where Suzy kept her makeup. Everyone else seemed to have an unfailing repertoire of tricks. Where were hers? As she stepped out of the robe, she looked down at the thin golden ring on her finger and smiled.

When Marcia came back to the parlor wearing her own clothing, she found that the little mage had put on a different outfit as well. Before, he had been dressed in loose-fitting silk trousers, a ruffled shirt, and a tailored jacket with a velvet collar. Now he was covered in a long, hooded wrap that was overdue for a trip to the dry cleaner.

As they stepped back into the hallway, Marcia was forcibly reminded of the foul air of the Lower Regions. But why would a *place* between Regions have air at all?

At the end of the hallway, Suzy halted them with a gesture and went outside by herself. Just when Marcia had begun to think something must have gone wrong, the door opened and Suzy beckoned to them.

"Where?" she said to Phellep as he closed the door behind them.

"Any place you like, dear lady, so long as it is lonely and not too near this entrance."

"The water, then. Everyone has fled."

"That is good. She is no more likely to be there than elsewhere."

Marcia looked back and forth between her two companions. "What happens if she finds us?"

"For the two of us," the magician said, "our fates would not be enviable ones. For you, I cannot tell. It would depend on your strength and her determination. Lacking the power to destroy you, I suppose she would try to reduce you to the state of a wraith, or use the threat to mold you to her will."

It took more than an hour, by Marcia's reckoning, to get back to the rising sea. They stayed entirely to alleys and narrow passageways, and saw few others abroad except at a distance on the wider streets. On the occasions that traversing a busy way could not be avoided, they crossed separately, the dreen always first, the little mage last.

Finally they arrived at the water's edge.

As Marcia gazed somberly at the half-submerged hovels and clots of floating trash, she heard herself say, "I've always liked the seashore."

"Oh, hi there, Lulu," said Suzy, flashing her a cover-girl smile.

Lulu. Where do virgin warriors go for psychotherapy? Marcia pictured herself reclining on a leather couch. *My alter ego's getting out of hand, Doc. I mean, there I am in a parallel world, struggling against deadly sorcery, and she starts piping up with wisecracks. It's, like, damaging my credibility with all the demons and mages.*

Phellep was looking up at her with a puzzled expression. "Now," he said, glancing at Suzy, "let us commence." He walked to the very edge of the lapping water.

"What I am going to do is help you disarrange the network of *her* web. We must, of course, be circumspect, but she will not notice a small disturbance from this quiet spot, not if you are quick. It is somewhat like lifting a curtain. As soon as you are able to catch the trick of it, you must take it from me and manage it yourself. Then, while holding her force at bay, you simply exert your own and propel yourself through the veil. You must make the passage at good speed, and not walk at a ceremonial pace like an acolyte bearing a chalice. As soon as I see you on your way, I will leave, for I am exposed and must return to my refuge."

When Marcia and Suzy had arranged themselves according to Phellep's instructions, he took a position next to them and stood silently. After a silent minute, Marcia whispered, "I don't—"

"Just attend, my lady. Closely. Follow my eyes, now."

When she saw it, she wondered why she hadn't figured it out for herself. It was all part of the same fabric: the darkness, the fell vapors, Ulda's horrific web. This could all, she thought, be stripped away. Why did not the little mage simply pull it down? Still, she reasoned, she might be missing some detail. Best not to be too ambitious.

She stretched out her hand and began to advance, turning to Phellep just long enough to see him relinquish his hold and fade from her view. She felt Suzy's grip on her other hand. Remembering Phellep's urging, she moved forward briskly. Within moments, they were enveloped in the fog that veiled the Middle Regions. Marcia pictured her bedroom and, more specifically, her antique rocking chair. A few more steps, and she saw it through the mist. She had one moment of doubt—a sudden fear that she would find it, not by her bed, but by the encroaching water that Ulda had drawn her to last night. And then they were standing in her bedroom.

Marcia said, "Oh, boy."

"So to speak," added Suzy.

Marcia glanced at the clock by her bed, then went to the window and pulled back the drapes. It was evening. Eight o'clock—she stopped to think—Saturday night. She wondered if Borphis had ordered a pizza yet. There was a knock on the bedroom door. Marcia hurried past Suzy and opened it.

Borphis was smiling broadly. "Well," he said, stepping into the room, "it's about—" When he saw Suzy, he stopped talking and started backing up. The expression on his face was not an optimistic one.

From behind Marcia, Suzy called softly, "Be at peace, small one. You are safe."

"Oh, good," said Borphis without conviction. He looked up at Marcia and spoke in a soft voice.

"Do you know—?"

Suzy stepped to Marcia's side. Borphis backed through the doorway. "She knows I am a dreen."

It took several minutes for Marcia to reconcile Borphis to having a dreen on the premises. She thought she would wait for some other, more convenient occasion to mention that she did not have any idea what a dreen was.

"Have you eaten?" she asked, hoping to get off the subject of dreens without getting onto the subject of where she had been.

"No, I was waiting for you." Borphis slid off his chair with a quick glance at Suzy. "I'll call out for pizza," he said smugly. "What's the biggest one they have?"

Marcia ate more pizza than she ever had before, matched Borphis in the consumption of red wine, and then, as her little mascot began to play the part of the expansive host, joined in the round of cognac he served with a show of proprietary vanity. Marcia had been brought up in a frugal household. As she watched him pour out double portions, she wondered if she should consider stocking a brand that cost less than forty-seven dollars a fifth.

By the time the festivities had subsided, she was ready for a night's sleep in her own bed. Even the lengthy immersion in hot, sudsy water that she had promised herself could wait until morning, she decided. She began to fret about accommodations for Suzy, but her two demonic companions—she caught herself staring at them in an unexpected rush of renewed wonder—assured her that they could manage without her supervision.

She took a quick shower, brushed her teeth until her gums tingled, and then collapsed into her welcoming bed.

Marcia dreamed of soft music. A person smaller than Borphis sat propped on a pillow at the foot of her bed. He was strumming a very small guitar and singing in a voice that rang clear and bell-like, even though it was hardly louder than a whisper. She sipped cool water from a glass by her bed—one that she had not put there.

If your head is off the pillow, you are awake, she thought, confused that she could still hear the singer. She smiled at him as she let her head sink back and her eyes fall shut. She could feel the melody breathing inside her, feel the soothing harmonies of the strings, the bracing punctuation of the dissonances that arose and were resolved.

She awoke at the midpoint of the night. The glass was still on her nightstand, still full. It was decorated with a faded picture of a young man playing a guitar. She smiled to herself.

She meant to look in on her houseguests, but when she came back from the bathroom, it seemed like too much trouble. Through the drawn curtains she could hear the sound of a truck passing on the street below. As she arranged herself under the blankets she wondered why there was a pillow propped against the footboard.

Her pleasant, serenaded sleep was troubled, finally, by a dream in which she was being threatened by an invisible danger. She could see herself held prisoner in a dark place. She was dressed in colorful clothing that was not hers, yet was strangely familiar. The whole scene she viewed as though at a great distance. It was like looking down from the third balcony at a single actor on a stark, bare stage. But though the scene was remote in space, the sense of dread was intense and intimate.

CHAPTER
·16·

It was not until the second day after Edorra and Rickey had brought him from the beach that Rogan got out of bed and into his clothing. He found it very odd to dress in the things he had worn in what almost seemed another life, the one he had lived before the sea had nearly claimed him. Edorra had seen that the sand and salt water were washed from his things; even his shoes were clean and dry. Still he associated them with his maritime mishap.

Rogan had already thanked every god and goddess he could think of for the inestimable blessing of standing alive on solid ground. By some miracle, he had escaped the malice of the sea though he had been adrift in a small open boat for half the night, tossed from the tip of one enormous wave to the next. As he fastened his jacket, he ran through the list of deities again. The fact that he was quite convinced that none of them actually existed made it, he thought, all the more remarkable that they had exerted themselves in his behalf.

He sat on the edge of his bed and got himself into his shoes. It was just the early edge of morning, not at all his customary hour for arising, but two full days of rest had left him anxious to be up and about. After breakfast, he intended to take a stroll out of doors, the better to appreciate the delicious stability of solid ground. He might, he thought, even walk to the edge of the sea, if it wasn't too far, for the purpose of gloating.

Breakfast. Odd he should think of that. The woman with her relentless feeding was meddling with the settled habits of his life. Rogan cast his mind back across the decades. It was thirty years at least, he thought, since he had taken any meal other than dinner. At home, the sun was always well up in the sky by the time he left his bed. Unlike the balance of humanity, he took no refreshment upon arising beyond the merest sip of pale wine, a supply of which he kept well chilled for the purpose. As the day passed, it was his habit to fortify himself with a few modest goblets as the need arose, progressing from the light wines appropriate to the early hours of the day to the more bracing and manly beverages that enlivened his afternoons. He had found that such a regimen was perfectly adapted to the demands and rigors of a court magician's life, and enabled him to meet the challenges of his work with a zest and enthusiasm often absent in men of his advanced years.

In the two days he had known her, Edorra had been consistently good-natured, if dictatorial. This morning, it was clear that being pleasant was costing her some effort. Rogan dispatched his morning meal without protest and made haste to leave the woman to herself. He remembered the conversation he had overheard yesterday about the boy's apprenticeship, but didn't see that he could do or say anything to help. If the boy was to learn a trade, it was no more than most boys had to face. And as far as the matter of scholarship, Rogan was not prepared to say that a scholar's inky fate was necessarily better than that of a man who worked with his hands. His years at the royal court had provided him with ample opportunity to compare the life of the idle with that of folk obliged to be industrious. Rogan knew many working people who led more gratifying existences than the titled dandies who lounged around the gaming tables at Asbrak's palace.

Of course, there were occupations and then there were occupations. His own, for instance, afforded its practitioners a certain flexibility not enjoyed by, say, a porter or pastry baker. But then, magic was not a matter only of scholarship. One had to have talent—flair.

He wondered if the boy had tired of meddling with the spell. Rogan had seen him only once since he had written it out. On that occasion, Rickey had asked him a string of complicated questions that only showed he had no understanding of magic. Which of course made perfect sense. It took more than a knowledge of the words of a spell to master even the simplest of effects, let alone something on the level of hiding. Rogan had been rather surprised that he himself had managed it so handily.

The magician had not walked far from the cottage before he looked back to check his bearings. Although he was unaware that he possessed not the slightest sense of direction, he had noticed over the years that he seemed to have a talent for losing his way, even in the passageways of the palace where he had lived for over two decades. He assumed it was because his mind at some unconscious level was perpetually occupied with the deep workings of his art. Whatever the reason, it was not uncommon for him, if he had to go from one part of the palace to another, to return to the remote tower where his rooms were located so that he could make his way by a familiar route to his next destination.

The sea, quiet now, blended in with the blue-green of the morning sky so that at first Rogan did not notice it. It was only when he saw Rickey ahead among the sand and tangled weeds that he realized that what he had taken for the horizon was in fact the shoreline.

The boy was moving in stops and starts along the beach in the light-footed way children have. No doubt he was occupied with some childish fancy, his magical ambitions forgotten. It was just as well, Rogan thought. What had the boy asked him last night? Which words in the spell were the ones that had the magic? That was one question. And then another, even more irrelevant. Something about making a number of objects disappear one after the other, and then bringing them back in a different order. No wonder children accomplished so little. They were incapable of keeping their minds on the problem at hand. Rogan thought of the titled mob that populated the court of Asbrak the Fat. Maybe children were just natural aristocrats.

When Rickey saw the magician, he ran to meet him. "How far away can you be from something?" he demanded without greeting or preamble. Rogan gazed down on the boy. Rickey was staring intently at the ground. "Or could it be inside of another thing—like a house?"

Rogan had spent little time in the company of children since a very long time ago when he had been one himself. He wondered if it was possible the boy had lost his reason. His raised his eyes to the endless expanse of ocean that lay still as a pond. Had this been the raging sea that had tried to claim him? How melancholy to think that his picked bones might at this moment be lying on the ocean floor, agitated at the will of vagrant tides, the insensate remnants of a once-powerful mage. Well, fairly powerful, as palace magicians go—and not really a mage, precisely, in the strict definition of the term.

When Rogan spoke, it was in a tone of gentle sadness. "What was that again, lad?"

"When you make something disappear. How far away can you be?"

"Not too far," said Rogan in a distant tone. Really, he supposed, it was foolish to picture the bones together, arranged in the form of a body. They would be scattered, some perhaps crushed in the jaws of giant fish. He winced.

"How about a house?"

Rogan turned to the boy with an incredulous stare. "You want to make a house disappear?"

Rickey laughed. "No. Something inside a house. While you were outside." His eyes sparkled. "*Could* you make a house disappear?"

"Don't be ridiculous. Anyway, why would anyone want to make a house disappear? Magic is not a game, boy. We don't do things just because we can." Rogan's thoughts strayed to the marvelous impression the disappearance of an entire house would create. "Real magicians work their spells for serious reasons."

"Well," Rickey said with a determinedly earnest expression on his face, "what about something inside a house? You know, if you were outside and—"

Rogan cut him off with an abrupt gesture. "No, no, no. You have leapt into the realm of the theoretical, or worse yet, of artistic magic."

"What's artistic magic?"

"Magic for its own sake." Rogan shook his head decisively. "Bunch of meaningless razzle-dazzle." He fixed the boy with a stern look. "Magicians are not philosophers. We are practical men. Craftsmen."

"But it's wonderful, making things disappear, saying the magic words."

"I will tell you a secret," Rogan said. "It seems wonderful when you see it happen, but by the time you put in the years of hard work to learn to do it, a lot of the fun gets lost."

"But I—"

"And as far as magic words, they aren't, you see, magic themselves. What seems like magic is more of a knack, or a—"

Rickey raised his boyish voice in protest. "But some of the words can move things. All through the spell you wrote—indited—for me are words that are like real *things*."

Rogan was not used to being interrupted. He was not, in fact, used to conversation at all. The boy who waited on him at the palace was dull and sluggish and only became animated at mealtimes. He looked at Rickey, who seemed near to bursting with enthusiasm. Perhaps he would petition Asbrak for a servant of a more lively temperament.

"Very well, lad," he said with an indulgent smile. "The magic words of the spell I gave you are for a seventh-year apprentice, but when you master them, you be sure to tell me."

"All right. At first I—"

"But just this moment, I want you to point me back to the cottage. I feel a little chilly." Rogan sent a suspicious glance in the direction of the ocean. "Mind you don't get too close to the water, now."

CHAPTER

·17·

Marcia awoke to pale winter light at her windows. Of her dream, all that remained was a vague and easily dismissed feeling of unease. She stretched and looked around her familiar surroundings. The drapes had been pulled, the venetian blinds opened. Evidently elves and fairies were early risers.

It was not until Marcia noticed that snow was falling past her bedroom windows that she got out of bed. She slipped her feet into her slippers and padded to the window to look out.

The snow was heavy enough that she could see no more than the headlights of the few cars passing below. All detail was lost in a featureless blanket of white. Marcia's reflexive thought was of the state of her refrigerator and cupboard, but since the sprites had moved in, she supposed she didn't have to worry about supplies.

Would the sprites make pizza? And if so, how? And where? She tried to picture their kitchen, the oven they would bake in, but kept on coming up with an image of the Egyptians who operated the local pizzeria.

In the living room, Borphis was staring out the window at the snow. It was a reasonable guess that he had never seen any. For a moment, Marcia considered the possibility that he might find it unsettling, then she noticed the bag from the doughnut shop.

Suzy was sitting at the table sipping coffee. Marcia was opening her mouth to say good morning when she had an acute attack of bad conscience.

"Where did you sleep?" she asked. "Did you find the blankets? The pillows are in the linen closet."

Suzy looked the same as she always did. Even her lipstick was fresh. She raised her pretty eyes. "I don't sleep," she said quietly.

Marcia almost said "Oh, good," but caught herself. Instead she asked, "Never?"

"That's right."

Her instinct was to find something polite to say, but nothing came readily to mind. Even among all the strange, disquieting, and downright frightening things Marcia had experienced recently, the idea that Suzy was perpetually awake was especially jarring. How long had she been awake? How many years? Suzy looked like a young woman, but she wasn't, she was something called a dreen. How long did dreens live? Marcia thought of decades of unrelenting wakefulness. Centuries. Her eyes wandered to Suzy's aura. The colors were all deeply saturated, heavy tints that seemed to melt into one another and form an indistinct nimbus with shifting boundaries.

"Your vills have coffee in the kitchen. I don't think they'll bring it to the table for you while I'm here."

Borphis had slid down from the chair by the window. "I got doughnuts," he said. He glanced toward the window. "Does this happen often?"

Marcia looked at the heavy snow floating past the window. She recalled the bleak, sterile Christmas season a month ago, skies cloudy out of pure meanness; dry, cold mornings; comfortless early dusks; knifing icy winds.

"Not really," she said. *Vills?*

In the kitchen Marcia found not only coffee, but a platter of fruit, a pot of soft fresh cheese, a basket of rolls, and a wineglass full of thick, dark jam that smelled like wildflowers.

Suzy consented to nibble on a roll from Marcia's breakfast tray. Borphis wanted nothing but his pile of doughnuts. Marcia busied herself with the food that had been provided by the elves or nymphs or fairies or gnomes—whoever they were, they had found a supply of luscious ripe cherries in the middle of a January snowstorm.

She felt very good, in an indolent sort of way. Borphis was looking out the window; Suzy was sitting across from her at the table in a way that made Marcia imagine she had never really seen anyone sit still before. Her impulse was that she had an obligation to start a conversation or provide some other diversion for her guests, but the effort was just too great. For a while she just stared blankly into space, then drifted from the room without a word.

After her bath, which lasted over an hour, she got dressed. By the time she had put on slacks, a blouse and sweater, and a pair of comfortable loafers, she felt that life had almost returned to normal, putting aside the fact that there were two otherworldly beings in her living room, and her kitchen had been taken over by the Keebler elves.

She started to sit in Great-grandmother Mibsey's rocking chair, then hesitated. Finally she sat down. She refused to think of her heirlooms as snares from Hell. It was true that her great-grandmother had been a rather forbidding old lady. It was even true that the pieces of furniture that had belonged to her seemed to carry the aura of her gloomy mansion with them wherever they went. But this chair, Marcia was certain, had no connection to Ulda or the other world.

Being careful to keep thoughts of crossing Regions from her mind, she sat and tried to sort out her situation. She needed to be in touch with the Sisterhood. She didn't know where she was supposed to be, or what she was supposed to be doing, but she was sure she was not meant to be lounging around in her apartment or, for that matter, serving as an underground railroad for supernatural undocumented aliens. What would the Department of Immigration and Naturalization think?

What about the one with the lipstick? Is she a demon too?

No, no, not at all, don't worry. She's a dreen.

What's the difference?

Well, let's see . . . the demon lives on doughnuts and pizza; the dreen never sleeps, and if someone batters her with a mallet it doesn't mess up her mascara.

And that, Marcia thought with a sigh, was the extent of her knowledge.

Lunch was provided by unseen hands. Afterwards, Marcia took her guests for an outing in the snow. Suzy managed to continue looking glamorous in galoshes and an overcoat; Borphis looked slightly silly wrapped up in a short jacket of Marcia's that came to his ankles.

Suzy was no more affected by cold than Borphis was. Neither seemed to be aware of the temperature. When Marcia stopped to buy cognac, grateful for an excuse to escape the cold wind, her companions waited outside the store. She was almost able to talk herself into an adequate but not so exalted brandy, but at the last minute, she thought of Borphis and how he seemed to revel in the intense bouquet and austere refinement of the good stuff. As she took it from the shelf, she noted that the price had gone from forty-seven to fifty-one dollars.

At the checkout counter, Marcia waited for the clerk to notice her. She shook her head ruefully. She should have brought Suzy in. Looks get attention, Marcia knew, if only through hearsay.

She cleared her throat. "Excuse me," she said, making an effort to speak up.

The clerk was looking out the window, laughing. "Damned if he's not trying to pick it up." He glanced at Marcia. "Look at this kid trying to lift that truck out of the ditch."

By the time Marcia hit the door, Borphis was back on the sidewalk. Behind him, three men were standing behind a loaded pickup truck tilted steeply into an icy rut.

Marcia heard Borphis say, "It's too heavy." She sighed with relief and turned back to the store, remembering she had left her handbag on the counter. As the door closed behind her, she heard a shout and a whistle. She got back outside just in time to watch Suzy, curls bouncing, skip across the curb. One of the men said something that the others laughed at, but of which Marcia caught only the word *mama!*

Conversation fizzled as Suzy lifted the truck out of the ditch and skidded it sideways back onto the street. One profanity, uttered in a reverent baritone, hung in the cold air, but no further comments were offered.

The liquor store employees were emerging from the double glass doors like onlookers rushing to get close to the scene of an accident. Marcia pictured Suzy being interviewed on television. She stepped back into the store, strode to the counter and snatched up her handbag, and was back outside in time to hear a white-haired woman with a pencil behind her ear tell Suzy that stunts like that could damage her reproductive capacity.

"Just think what a shame," she said. "A shame."

An overweight man took a hesitant step toward the woman. "For Christ's sake!" he said in a stage whisper.

The woman faced him. "That's a nice expression to use with your mother. Very nice." She turned back to Suzy. "You see?" she said, raising her shoulders in an eloquent shrug.

Marcia found it surprisingly easy to break up the party. She bulldozed her way past the crowd and grabbed Suzy and Borphis each by the arm without slowing down. She was sure she heard the word *aliens*. As they hurried down the street, someone shouted, "Hey! Thanks a lot!"

They were nearly back to the apartment when Borphis thought to ask her if she had picked up the hooch.

"Hooch? Where did you hear that?"

Borphis looked puzzled. "In your movies," he said. "And that's what Suzy calls it."

Marcia grinned. "Well, Suzy's from—" She stopped in the middle of the sidewalk. "My movies? You used the VCR?"

"Sure. It's easy. It's just a machine."

"So's a piano," said Marcia.

"I know. Could we get one? And a harp?"

They made it through the lobby, up the elevator, and almost through Marcia's door without encountering any neighbors. Marcia had her key in the lock when Mrs. Ingram came into the hall.

"Oh, my dear, I'm happy to see you," she said. "I'd begun to think something was wrong. Have you been away?"

Marcia explained she had been out of town on business. It was the truth, she told herself.

"Not flying, I hope. I wouldn't trust an airplane. Their wings fall off."

Marcia smiled sympathetically and tried to think of a way to account for Suzy and Borphis.

"Mrs. Ingram, this is my cousin Suzy and . . . her husband, Borphis."

It occurred to Marcia that her inspiration had not been a happy one, but Mrs. Ingram seemed to take the ill-matched couple in stride.

"Oh," she exclaimed, "I'll bet it was the pancakes." She beamed down at Borphis. "That's the way to a man's heart, they say."

Marcia said, "You're thinking of Cousin Ellie. That's who made the pancakes." *Suzy lifts trucks.*

"Oh?" Mrs. Ingram sounded skeptical. "Well, you're a lucky man, Mr. Borphis." She turned back to Marcia. "Is Cousin Ellie married?"

Lulu almost managed to tell Mrs. Ingram that Cousin Ellie had been sent to prison, but Marcia intervened.

They chatted for a few minutes. Marcia noticed that Borphis sounded a little like Sam Spade, but basically he and Suzy were no more implausible than her actual relatives.

Inside her apartment, everything had been dusted and swept. There were steaming cups of hot chocolate on the coffee table. When Marcia hung up the coats, she found that her closet had been reorganized. She sat next to Borphis on the love seat sipping chocolate and tried to figure out what else was different. It was something about the quality of the light.

"My God, they washed the windows." Marcia got up to have a closer look, then checked the rest of the apartment. The bathroom sparkled. Marcia was a fastidious housekeeper, but this represented an entirely different stratum of hygiene. She stared into her sink. The rust mark, there since the day she had moved in, was gone.

If her bedroom was neat as a pin when she left it, it was now neater than a pin. Her bed, made that morning, had been made again, and by a more thorough hand. There were no little vagrant creases to be detected beneath the bedspread, no careless tucks or folds at the corners. The water glass that she had left on her nightstand had been replaced by a slender vase that held a single blood red rose.

Marcia glanced at the windows to confirm that they had been washed. The snow, which had stopped while she and her guests were out, had started again. She wondered idly how long it would have to fall before the city was reduced to paralysis. It was now two o'clock in the afternoon; by evening things could be a mess. Not that it mattered to her. The sprites seemed to be taking care of the shopping and cooking, and the only traveling she planned was of a sort not affected by road conditions.

Marcia settled herself comfortably in the rocking chair. She took a half dozen deep breaths and rested her gaze on the wall next to the window. With practiced ease she quieted her mind. It was, she had found, unnecessary and probably impossible to *empty* her mind. It was needful only to still it or, more accurately, to allow its habitual churning to subside.

She let consciousness of her corporeal being fall away until she felt weightless. Sounds, too, she rose above, stilling at last even the sound of her own breathing. She permitted herself to remain in this volitionless, carefree state for an insensibly expanding instant, her quiet mind divorced from every other thing.

She terminated her restful state with an audible breath and a subtle shift in concentration. But still she stayed within the moment. With great care and very gradually Marcia began to tilt her perceptions. She tried to see how small she could make the increments of change.

The ghost was not present today, nor were there any sprites or fairies to be seen. She pushed her perceptions further along the spectrum, observing the changes in the room. She had raised her ring from her lap, but dropped her hand. This had nothing to do with the position of the ring. There was no need to wave her hand like a conjurer. She moved her perceptions to a new point of alignment. Although she had no intention of doing so, she was confident that she was now at a place from which she could advance to the boundary of her Region.

She got up from the chair with no concern that she would somehow lose the vision she had entered. There was no instability in what she was seeing. Illusion it might be, but it was no more volatile than the set of illusions that made up her everyday reality.

At the boundaries of audibility, she heard, or perhaps imagined, the sound of a bell. Marcia glanced at the door to the living room, then paused and looked more closely. It looked wrong, somehow, as though its position had been shifted slightly. She let her eyes wander around the room. Everything, of course, appeared somewhat out of kilter, and so did the door, but more so. She was sure she was not misunderstanding the process, or failing to control it. Nothing was being changed. Only her perceptions were different. She thought about it for a moment, then opened the door. Instead of her bright living room and sparkling windows, she faced a dimly lit space bounded by narrow walls. She straightened her back and narrowed her eyes, then stepped through.

She was in a corridor. Marcia stopped and looked around in confusion. She brought her hands together and raised her ring to her chest. She felt a deep anger begin to grow inside her. If this was some trick of Ulda's, the crone was going to curse her cleverness. When Marcia had been waylaid before, she had felt lost and anxious. Now, more conscious of the power she possessed, she felt the self-contained independence of a solitary predator. "Chase a kitten, catch a panther," Marcia said with a cold smile. "Too bad."

She pulled the door closed quietly and turned away from it. Whether it would open again onto her bedroom was not a question she thought important at the moment. She would make her way. She was out of patience with interference and threats. She had her own affairs to attend to; she had no time for simulacra and tricks. She clenched her ring hand into a fist and began walking. She was not in a mood to sneak and hide; she was in a mood to hunt.

The corridor did not, however, lead to a confrontation with Ulda, but to the place Marcia had been trying to reach for days. She had only gone a short distance when she came to a spiral staircase descending into a bath of glowing light. She paused for a few moments to relish one of the few pleasant surprises she had encountered recently.

She looked back along the corridor. It was to this place that Annie had brought her almost two weeks ago. They had walked this mysterious hallway when they passed from the old brownstone to this stairway. Below would be the garden and the path to Annie's cottage.

Marcia descended the stairs and stepped into the garden with the feeling that she had never left. To her left she could just make out the near edge of the garden through the hazy light. There would be the great hedge, and beyond it, Annie's cottage.

It was there, of course, that she would go. Annie would know what to do about Borphis and Suzy, and about Father. Marcia was surprised to find that her relief was tinged with regret. Perhaps many of them had been poor ones, but she had become fond of making her own decisions. And now she had begun to see inside the power of the ring, had made a start at learning the lessons it could teach.

Still, it would be good to see Annie. She had met her less than two weeks ago, had known her for only twenty-four hours, but she thought of her as an intimate friend, truly as a sister. She thought of the sisters Ulda had tried to foist on her. That petty trick; that hall of mirrors.

She stepped still farther into the garden, breathing deeply and smiling. This was no deception, no montage of stolen images. She stopped, looked back at the stair, the flowers at her feet, the trees in the distance. What lay behind this? she wondered. Could she turn her ring just so and watch the planes shift and shuffle, see the flowers harden to glinting lines and curving boundaries?

She walked on a little, immersing herself in the scents and colors. She knelt to look more closely at a pale flower that had caught her attention. Its long petals were framed by heavy deep green leaves that looked as though they were carved from jade. From beneath one bloom, a beetle crept into view. When it stopped in a patch of light, it looked like an ornament worked in gold; its markings made a burning yellow face with two precise dark eyes and a mouth turned into a miniature frown. Marcia stared at the tiny face in wonder and imagined it was staring back. She lingered in a timeless moment that recalled those summer days of childhood where the minutes hang like hours in the sunlight.

When the beetle flew away, she continued on the path. The silence surrounded the noise of her shoes on the pebbles, the occasional snatch of song from some hidden bird. In the distance she heard the ringing sound again. A chime, she thought, for the tone was pure; it lacked the heavy resonance and brazen overtones of a bell. She followed the sound as it renewed itself against the silence.

The chime was suspended from the roof of a kiosk in the middle of a garden of fragrant orange flowers. Marcia could see a mallet of polished wood hanging on one of the uprights of the building. But who had struck the chime? The gazebo was deserted and there was no one in sight.

She was distracted for a moment from the mystery of the chime by the oddity of seeing her hand without the attending nimbus. Here, in a place where auras could not be seen, she had the same ghostly, denuded look as Father. She wondered, since he had no aura elsewhere, would his be visible here. She had thought of him as the one who had no aura, but that was unreasonable, she realized. It was much less difficult to think that his emanation was only hidden, as hers was at this moment.

She walked at the edge of the garden until she came to a path that led to the gazebo. She followed it to the kiosk through the perfume of the flowers. She was under the roof before she saw the woman.

In her great-grandmother's house had been a cabinet made of ebony polished to a high gloss. That was the skin color of the woman who stood beyond the chime. When she thought about it later, Marcia could not in honesty say whether the woman's features, color, and hair had influenced her conclusion that she was a servant whose duties included ringing the chime. The woman stood with downcast eyes. Her attitude seemed, almost, to be one of prayer. Her hands hung at her sides.

The fact that the woman wore no ring made Marcia intensely conscious of her own and of the power it conferred on her. She remembered Annie's explanation that it made the sprites nervous to be around members of the Sisterhood and their artifacts of force. Might this not be true of any who served there? She waited silently for the woman to notice her and acknowledge her presence. She didn't want to frighten her. Finally the woman raised her eyes.

"So, little sister, does our garden please you?"

Marcia tried, with no great success, to stammer a reply. She forced herself to meet the woman's eyes. They were black, and not green like Elyssa's, but that was the only difference. They held the same disturbing quality of feral intensity.

Suddenly Marcia's questions all seemed unimportant. She wondered what could have made her trespass in this garden. Why had she not simply followed the path to Annie's cottage? She tried to gather her wits. She was painfully aware that the most intelligent things she had said so far were "um" and "uh."

"Um, uh," she said again. Her eyes had now developed their own feral intensity. She managed to say, "Where is Elyssa?" realizing that it was something of a non sequitur.

"Where is my sister Elyssa?" The woman turned her hands palm up. "Not standing here with us. Elsewhere. Where chance has taken her."

Marcia found the woman's sudden unexpected smile alarming.

"Where is Junna?" she continued, still smiling. "She chances to be standing here with you."

It occasionally occurred to Marcia that the worst thing about the strange life that had overtaken her was not the hazards and inconveniences, but that she seemed forever to be at some sort of social disadvantage. Did Junna know her name? By what title, if any, was the woman to be addressed? Was Marcia supposed to bow?

"But chance," she said, "I mean, I was told . . ." This was worse than Lulu. Marcia straightened up and raised her eyes to meet Junna's. "My name is Marcia," she said.

"I know. You were of the Sisterhood." Junna seated herself on a bench and invited Marcia to join her. "Chance? An illusion," she said, as Marcia perched next to her uncomfortably. "Of course. Chance. Time. Nonetheless, here we are." She reached out and took Marcia's hand, raising it to gaze at her ring. After what seemed a long time, she turned her arm to expose the bruises that Ulda had left there.

"And these marks? What chance brought these to you?"

Marcia felt uncomfortable. The smile was no longer on Junna's face. "Ulda—" she began.

"Uldum? You were in the dark city?"

Marcia nodded. Junna covered the bruises with her hand and closed her eyes. After a moment, she began to laugh. She withdrew her hand and got up from the bench. Marcia stood up with her.

Junna walked across the kiosk, then turned and came back to where Marcia stood. "Where is Elyssa, indeed," she said. She looked down at Marcia's ring. "Who has put this on your finger?"

Marcia said, "Elyssa—"

"No. Tziann did not do this. Who has worn this ring, that you visit Uldum? And came out? Were you there alone?"

"Well, there is the dreen."

Junna sent her a sharp look. "A dreen? Do you know what a dreen is?"

"No, not exactly, but there's one in my apartment." Junna was staring at her. She did not look pleased. "And a demon," Marcia added.

Junna was silent for a moment. Marcia noticed that the soreness had left her arm. She glanced down at it. The bruises were gone. All that remained were three small scars.

"Tell me," said Junna, sitting back down on the bench, "how these things have happened." She waved Marcia to the bench. "Start with the matter of the ring."

Marcia related all that had happened to her since she had

started following the old man. Father's theft of the ring. How she had pursued him, first until he returned the ring, then into the Lower Regions.

"And this one you call Father, he put the ring on your finger himself?"

"Yes. He was going to hand it back, but it didn't seem right to me. I don't know why."

Junna's lips formed a faint smile. As Marcia went on with her story, she interrupted to ask about Borphis, and then about Suzy, but otherwise remained quiet.

"And that's all," Marcia said when she had finished. "Oh, except I have sprites now." When Junna raised her eyebrows, she went on. "Servants, I mean. Like at the cottage. Cooking, cleaning. Singing me to sleep."

Junna looked as though she were thinking of something entirely different. Finally she said, "Yes, you would . . . now." Again she was silent. After a minute or so, she got to her feet. She extended her hand to Marcia. "Come, we must go to your home." Marcia hesitated, then reached out.

Being suddenly surrounded by falling snow startled Marcia and made her slightly dizzy. One second ago she had taken Junna's hand in the garden. Now they were standing on the sidewalk in front of her building in a snowstorm. She turned to her companion.

It had been over half a year since Marcia had seen Elyssa. In that period, her memory of the dazzling aura had dimmed. Now it was before her again. Junna's aura was the same—like a blazing fire.

Three older women chatting by the mailboxes stopped to stare at Marcia and her companion as they came in from the storm wearing no coats or outdoor clothing of any kind. Marcia, at least, had on a light sweater. Junna was wearing only a thin dress that was not, in the harsh light of the lobby, completely opaque. They were standing in front of the elevators before Marcia noticed that she was also barefoot.

When they reached her door, she tapped on it very lightly. How would she introduce Junna to Mrs. Ingram? *Strange as it may seem, Mrs. Ingram, this half-naked black woman is my cousin Junna.*

It was Borphis who answered the door. Judging from his horrified stare, he regretted it. As they entered the room, Suzy got up from the couch.

"Lady," she said, inclining her head in a way that looked both perfunctory and formal.

Borphis had positioned himself partly behind a chair. He imitated Suzy's bow and murmured something brief and inaudible.

Junna nodded, letting her eyes rest on Suzy for a moment, then Borphis. She turned to Marcia.

"Where were you when you heard the chime?"

In the bedroom, Junna went to the rocking chair. "Yes," she said, "it was here that I saw you, seated in this chair." She waited for Marcia to close the door to the living room.

"The dreen and the demon have been of service to you. You must see them rewarded."

"Rewarded? What can I give them?"

"For the little demon, if you think he is worthy, it is simple. How many names has he?"

"Four, I think he said. No, it was three. He was supposed to have four, he said, but something happened."

"Well, then, you must give him his fourth name, or more, if you wish."

"You mean I just make up a name for him?"

Junna laughed. "No, not by any means. He will know the names proper to his status and his clan. Once he tells you the names that call him now, you may give him more. Usually names are added one or three at a time. If he now has but three, and yet has served you as you related, he has outdistanced his rank. You might triple that number, or even quadruple it, but no more. More than a dozen would exceed a proper balance, for now. And, of course, you must remember them all."

"Oh, no; I'm impossible with names."

Junna smiled at her. "You will find your capacities . . . augmented, I think." She went to the window and pulled the drapes back to look out at the snow. "As for the dreen," she said, "that is more complicated. Her form, does it please her?"

Marcia thought back to snatches of conversations with Suzy. "She said it's graceful. And deceptive. But she told me it was her true form now."

"So it is, but only at the whim of the mistress of Uldum." Junna let the drapes fall back into place. "So, breaking that link might be a gift she would value."

Marcia began to wonder if she had been mistaken for someone else. When she had to choose a gift, her thoughts usually turned to boxes of overpriced chocolates. If bestowing names and breaking spells were among her talents, she was not aware of it.

"You do understand," Junna said, "that you are responsible for your companions? And," she went on, "that they must remain in your care until they are returned to the Lower Regions?"

"By me?"

"Yes. When you choose, of course."

Marcia said, "You mean I will still be on my own?"

"Yes. As always."

"But I don't know what I'm supposed to be doing. Father—the old man—no one ever *told* me to follow him, exactly. It just happened."

"I see," Junna said. "Chance."

Marcia was still trying to think of something to say when Junna went on.

"You do seem to have a habit of doing more than might be expected. Evidently that is your path. You did well to follow the old man. Were you to find him again, follow him further, it would not be amiss."

Marcia felt positively elated. Finally, some answers. She began to think of all the questions she had been wanting to ask. Now these mysteries would be solved. At least some of them. She tried to organize her thoughts. Regions. She definitely wanted to know about Regions. And should she dare to ask Junna who (or what) she and Elyssa were? There were so many questions. Where to start? She lifted her hand.

"This ring I wear," she began shyly, "I hardly know the powers it has. I'm only starting to learn how to use them."

Junna walked around the bed and joined her. She took Marcia's hand in hers. "Well, that, at least, will not be a problem for you now." She slipped the ring from Marcia's finger and onto hers. She put her hands on Marcia's shoulders.

"Good-bye, little sister," she said in an intimate whisper. She leaned forward to brush Marcia's cheek with her lips, and then was gone.

CHAPTER
·18·

The first thing Breksin noticed upon entering the residence of Black Jack Flanders was the wine stains on the carpets. The foyer was lavishly—too lavishly—laid with carpets from the looms of Baralun, with the inimitable greens and golds characteristic of products of that metropolitan confluence of herdsmen and weavers.

The wine stains looked almost like the result of purposeful destructiveness, as though the rugs had been marred for pleasure. It was said to be one of the beauties of these carpets that even in their errors they achieved a kind of superiority—a species of lofty imperfection. The person who had scattered wine in droplets and poured it by the glass on this worked wool was susceptible to no such rarefied aesthetic.

The pirate chieftain kept them waiting at the bottom of his staircase until Count Reffex was nearly beside himself with the sheer vexation of the thing.

"This is scandalous, I tell you," he hissed to Breksin. "This is *not* the way negotiations are conducted. I am the envoy. I bear messages of importance. We could conclude this business at once if everything weren't so damnably strange."

The pirate's descent on the stair of polished wood might have been silent but for his noisy breathing, for his feet were bare. He loitered down the stairs in a dressing gown that gapped open with each step. His face was lined, but curiously youthful. He might have been a twenty-five-year-old actor made up to play a man of fifty. His long gray hair looked as if it had not been combed for days.

He reached the bottom step before he acknowledged his visitors. His eyes slid across Reffex and stopped at the giant. He looked him up and down and nodded.

"Lances and hammers," he croaked, fixing Breksin with his stare. His eyes were small and black, and seemed to reflect every bit of light from the windows.

"That's right, Captain."

Reffex took a step forward and began to speak, but was interrupted by the pirate.

"But no swords?" He made a number of surprisingly quick and graceful motions in the air with his fist, like a man wielding a rapier.

"No. Not in the hills and forests. Heavy two-handed swords sometimes, but usually only for games."

"Aye, games. What games they must be!"

Breksin nodded solemnly. "They are rough," he agreed, "and hard."

Reffex waved his hand at Breksin. "This is my—"

Jack Flanders ignored him. "Did you bring your spices?" he said to Breksin, who told him he had. "Then do me a kindness, Doctor, and come to the kitchen to make up your potion. I have heard news of this remedy."

They filed down the hallway to the kitchen. As Breksin broke eggs and heated wine, Reffex attempted to engage the captain in conversation, but the man stood in the middle of the room, unmindful of the grease and dirt under his bare feet, and stared at the window like a priest in a holy trance.

"Gods, that's vile," said the captain mildly after he had drained the steaming cup. He looked past Reffex, who was attempting again to introduce his assistant, and addressed Breksin. "How is it you come to be with Baron Riffle, here?"

Reffex spoke hastily. "My assistant, Captain Breksin," he said with a hurried wave at the giant.

Captain Flanders turned his gaze slowly to Reffex. "He's no captain of an Ambermere guard, Your Worship. That, I will not believe."

"Well, it's an honorary title, you see," Reffex said. "For the purposes of, uh, protocol," he added lamely.

Breksin said, "I am a merchant of Ambermere. A trader in wines."

Jack Flanders looked at the giant with a sidewise glance. "But you did not arrive with the Earl of"—he squinted at Reffex—"Piffik, or on any ship, from what I've heard."

"No. I am passing through Devlin on foot. But when Count Reffex told me of his embassy, I offered to help. I am worried about your prisoners."

"Well," the pirate drawled with a sour grin, "you say 'prisoners.' The duke here calls them 'guests.' "

"Ah," Reffex began suavely, "what Breksin means of course is—"

"He means prisoners," the pirate said in a monotone. He stared into his empty glass. "Are you sure this isn't a poison?" he asked the giant.

Jack Flanders declined to discuss the ransom or the release of the hostages, but did, upon Breksin's urging the point, allow a visit. They were taken to the top floor of the house, where Breksin spoke with the princess and her party as Reffex fluttered at his elbow chattering about how vitally important it was, in delicate negotiations of this sort, to have the services of not just a nobleman, but a nobleman of the right sort. He himself, he reminded them, was the cousin of a duke, *thrice* removed.

By the time they left, Breksin had satisfied himself that the prisoners were being denied nothing required for their well-being but liberty. Reffex had told them of Rogan, and they spoke much of the magician, to the great puzzlement of the count, who had more important things to discuss. On the subject of Rogan, though, there was the matter of the fool of a seaman who said it had been he, Reffex (an aristocrat), who untied the boat. This was an absurd libel, and one that threatened to be compounded by the captain's confusion about who had been dragging whom when he caught a glimpse of the count and the magician on deck during the height of the storm.

Daniel managed to mollify Reffex by pointing out that his reputation was absolutely secure. "Believe me, no one who knows you is going to change his opinion of you," he said, and the others all agreed. They agreed, too, that lamentations were prema-

ture. "Rogan knows more than fireworks magic," Daniel said. "If
he had a boat, I'll bet he found a way to stay alive."

That afternoon, Breksin walked the city again, talking to merchants and whores, fishermen and pirates. Now that he had seen
the prisoners, he had less reason to cultivate acquaintances, but
there was always a chance that he might hear something of interest.

As he strolled, he turned over in his mind every scheme that
occurred to him, none of which offered the slightest hope. Even
if there were a way, somehow, to get the prisoners out of the captain's house, there was no way to get them out of Devlin. The
matter was in the hands of the diplomats. Hebbick and the spies
certain to be stationed in Felshalfen would get to the bottom of
what was doubtless an intrigue concerning the royal succession.
In due course, Hebbick would arrive to acquaint Captain
Flanders with the latest news from Felshalfen, and to secure the
release of the royal party.

It was only if things went badly awry that a giant with a battle
hammer might be of use. Breksin decided to keep a night watch
for ships from Felshalfen. He could pay a boy to stand a turn in
the afternoons while he napped. If Hebbick arrived, he wanted to
join his embassy to the pirate king. If any other came to call on
Black Jack Flanders, he would have to deal with Breksin on the
way.

CHAPTER
·19·

After Junna left, Marcia stayed in her bedroom. For a while she lay on her bed staring at the ceiling. Then she stood at the window watching the snow fill up the fading afternoon. Finally, she sat in Great-grandmother Mibsey's rocking chair for over an hour concentrating on nothing more complicated than the gradual withdrawal of the day and the subtle advance of the early winter dusk.

At last she sighed, looked down at the empty spot on her finger and got up. She stood by the window again and examined her aura in the waning light. It was unchanged. She looked again at the scars on her arm, probed at them with her fingertips. There was no trace of the soreness she had felt before Junna had put her hand on the bruises. The marks on her arm looked no more recent now than the scar next to her eye.

She began to worry her way through the things Junna had said to her, the instructions she had left. One of the things she had said, unnoticed at the time but now significant, was, "You were of the Sisterhood." Past tense. And yet she had called Marcia "little sister" when she had greeted her *and* when she had said good-bye.

And Marcia was responsible for Borphis and Suzy—for returning them to the Lower Regions when the time came. *When you choose.* And she was to reward them. Marcia began walking

179

slowly toward the living room door. Father again. She felt like a metaphysical bounty hunter. It must be that her ring was to be returned to her. Maybe it had to be purified or something. A feeling of relief washed over her. In the morning, she would awaken to find the ring on her finger again.

Except that was not the impression Junna had left when she took it from her finger. What had she said? Not understanding the ring wouldn't be a problem anymore. What did that mean? Obviously, if Marcia didn't have the ring, her inability to control it would not be a problem. But it might mean, as well, that Marcia was to receive instruction of some sort. Just because Junna had been enigmatic didn't mean she wasn't coming back. After all, with the exception of her friend Breksin the giant, everyone she had talked to lately had been enigmatic.

She paused with her hand on the doorknob. Actually, it was quite clear. She would just have to wait and see what developed. Junna had told her to do things, like visiting the Lower Regions, that she didn't think she could manage without the ring. She had no choice but to wait for the situation to sort itself out.

She glanced at the clock. Almost five. It would probably make sense for her to worry about things she could be expected to do something about. Dinner, for instance. There would be no pizza delivery in this weather; she would have to figure something else out. She had plenty of wine on hand, so that was not a problem, but Borphis would, have to do without his beloved cognac; the bottle was down to a sniff and a swallow, as someone in one of her old movies had said. Of course, there were the sprites, but despite the fact that they had provided breakfast and lunch, she didn't expect them to whip up a dinner—not while her magic ring was out for repairs.

"It's so hard to get reliable help these days," she said to herself. She started to open the door, then closed it quietly and went to the highboy. She slid her fingers under the molding and found the small wooden button that released the hidden drawer. She had never forgotten the dramatic moment when Great-grandmother Mibsey had revealed this marvel to her, though the old lady had done it in a most undramatic, matter-of-fact fashion.

"Here, child. This piece is coming to you, and I don't like to think of you using it for fifty or sixty years and never finding the little drawer."

The ring was in a box and wrapped in tissue paper. It was old, and had been worn thin on the fingers of two bona fide Mibsey women before coming to Marcia's mother by way of circumstance and marriage.

"Mind, that's not to be buried with your mother, girl." Great-grandmother Mibsey had evidently thought it undignified to address a child by her name. She alternated between calling Marcia "child" and "girl," and was so consistent as to refer to her as "the child" or "the girl" on those rare instances when Marcia was, briefly, the topic of conversation. So in awe was Marcia of the old lady, that when she heard herself spoken of as though she weren't present, she felt flattered and slightly uneasy, as though some honor far beyond her merits had been bestowed upon her.

As Marcia slipped the ring onto her finger, she thought of her last view of her father's grandmother. At that moment, in the hushed and empty funeral parlor amid the scents of dying flowers, she had learned the dead do not have auras.

By then she had been old enough to resent the fact that beyond a few massive antiques, little had come to her mother. Her mother's explanation that there had been little to leave had seemed incredible to her. Five years later, she had been incredulous again to learn that the financing of her undergraduate education at the state university had been "seen to" in the old lady's will.

Marcia closed the little drawer and crossed the room lost in a cloud of memories. In the living room she found herself brought back to the present via one of her old movies.

"This is the one that plays the harp. Watch what he does." Borphis was seated on the edge of the love seat with the remote control of the VCR clutched in his hands. Next to him, Suzy was squinting at the television like someone trying to make sense of a piece of abstract sculpture. Neither of her guests seemed to notice Marcia's presence. She watched the antics on the screen for a moment, then strolled in toward the kitchen to see if she had enough spaghetti to feed the three of them.

On the counter were three steaming mugs on a glazed ceramic tray that she didn't recognize. Marcia had smelled the spirits and spices before she entered the kitchen. This was the same hot punch that she and Annie had found waiting for them that first evening at the cottage. She remembered asking Annie if it took long to get used to having invisible servants. Marcia smiled as she lifted the tray from the counter and repeated Annie's prompt and cheerful reply.

" 'No,' what?" said Borphis, freezing the movie with a stab of his thumb. He slid from the love seat. "That smells good," he said. He bounced toward her on tiptoes trying to see into the mugs, and then followed her to the table like a pet cat at suppertime. Suzy got up lazily from the couch and joined them.

After Borphis had emptied half his drink, he looked at Marcia earnestly and asked, "Do we have any cigars around here?"

Marcia set her cup down and stared at him. "Cigars? No, we do not," she said, wondering if on her next trip to the kitchen she would find a cedar box fastened with a little brass hasp and a silk ribbon. It was, she supposed, all that Borphis lacked to make his life perfect. She looked at him indulgently. Well, some new clothes wouldn't hurt, she thought. Her glance strayed to Suzy. At least she could do something about her.

Suzy's reaction to the offer of a bath and a change of clothes was one of placid indifference. "We didn't get wet enough yesterday?" Nonetheless she consented to be introduced to the fixtures and soap and shampoo. "Okay. Then what?" she said.

"I'll leave some fresh things for you on my bed," Marcia said, and was hurried from the room by the sight of Suzy unconcernedly stepping out of her dress.

Borphis had turned off the television and was looking out the window at the snow. Marcia joined him. The afternoon had turned abruptly to night, the "chance of flurries in the city and western suburbs" had become a blizzard. They watched the weather in silence. Marcia sipped at the remains of her punch and thought about winter storms of her childhood.

Before long, Suzy emerged from the bedroom, scrubbed and brushed and dressed in clothes provided by her hostess. Marcia's first thought was that she had never realized how drab that outfit was. Suzy looked like a flower wrapped in burlap. All traces of her makeup were gone, but she was just as stunning as before.

Marcia discovered another tray of drinks, but Suzy turned down a refill. She settled herself on the love seat and lapsed into the passive state that made it look as if she had stopped breathing. Marcia dithered, then took another mug of punch, promising herself not to finish it.

She took a comforting sip, then said, "Dinner at seven, please," as she left the kitchen. She shrugged and giggled. No harm in trying, she thought. She offered to draw a bath for Borphis, who declined politely. Time enough for that, she thought. For all she knew, they might be here for weeks. She supposed new clothes for the little demon would have to come from the boys' department. She giggled again and gazed deeply into her drink.

When she finished it, she decided that perhaps a shower would be just the thing for her. She lost herself in the steam and beating water and stood in a timeless daze.

Finally she turned off the water and dried herself. Now she was freshly scrubbed, just like Suzy, but instead of bouncing, honey blond curls, a pretty face, and natural color that made makeup superfluous, Marcia came out of her shower with straight brown hair, features regular to the point of being dull, and a complexion that was both unblemished and unremarkable.

She looked at herself in her bedroom mirror. She did look younger, though. And she had put on weight. She turned in front of the mirror, looking over her shoulder to see herself from the side and back. She was no Suzy, but she was no stick figure, either.

And her face, she thought as she began to dress, had definitely been improved by the tiny scar next to her eye. It drew attention from the dull symmetry of her features. She continued to peer at herself under knit brows, then rolled her eyes and let her shoulders slump in a posture of exaggerated despair. Her body could be conceded to be okay, her face, passable. But her hair. . . .

The living room was filled with the aroma of spices. Marcia realized she was very hungry. Her kitchen counter was crowded with platters and covered dishes. She was about to recruit Suzy to help set the table and carry in the food, but stopped in midsentence. Instead, she took her guests into the bedroom and closed the door.

They came back a few minutes later to find that dinner was on the table. When Marcia saw the mountain of golden rice and the platters of meats and vegetables, she knew that even Borphis would finally have to give up and stop eating while there was still food on the table.

The wine was heavy and dark, and served in a pitcher. When they had emptied it, rather sooner, Marcia thought, than they should have, Borphis took it to the kitchen. He went back a few minutes later and found it was full again.

Marcia tried to remember where she and Breksin and Father had been served a wine similar to this one. She took a long, re-

flective swallow. It had not been as good as this, of that she was
certain. She sipped from her glass and held the wine in her
mouth. She wished Breksin were here to enjoy this feast. She
could almost see him, looming across the table, his alarming size
offset by his warm smile, his sympathetic glance. What would he
say about this most excellent wine? Marcia emptied her glass
slowly, then watched with a smile as Borphis stood in his chair
to pour for her.

After dinner, they found a bowl of macerated fruit in the
kitchen. To accompany it were three small glasses of a heavy,
sweet pale wine. Marcia found the fruit refreshing. The wine was
at first cloying, but upon reflection she thought it a perfect drink
with dessert.

Faced with dirty dishes and the remains of dinner, Marcia and
her guests retired again to her bedroom. Borphis immediately
flopped backwards onto her bed and closed his eyes. Marcia and
Suzy went to the window. Marcia listened, but could hear nothing from the living room. She hoped the sprites wouldn't quit
now; she was not in the mood for housework. Besides, she
thought with a small surge of indignation, the dishes didn't even
belong to her. She dropped into her chair, then got back up and
started for the living room.

The dishes were gone. She checked the kitchen. There was no
evidence of the meal. Nor was there anything else. Not even coffee. Marcia felt suddenly discouraged. How sad it would be if
her sprites deserted her. She closed her eyes. She pictured herself
standing there in her kitchen, all alone. It was really overwhelming, if you stopped to think about it.

". . . the kindness of others," she murmured. Her melancholy
musings were interrupted by the sound of Borphis talking in the
living room.

"This looks promising," he said in a loud and enthusiastic
voice. Marcia opened her eyes and looked around the kitchen as
though surprised to find herself there. She rubbed her eyes and
shook her head, then stepped through the door into the living
room.

On the coffee table in front of the love seat were brandy
snifters—her own, she was pretty sure—and a misshapen bottle
of heavy brown glass that did not look particularly clean.
Borphis watched her as she crossed the room.

"May I pour?" he said.

Marcia nodded and sank to the couch. She wondered if she had eaten too much. Probably, she thought. Some brandy would be good for her.

Borphis pulled the cork gently with his fingertips. Marcia was sort of pleased to note that the bouquet didn't leap from the bottle as it did with her fifty-dollar cognac. She watched the little demon pour, then took the snifter and warmed it in her hands. The liquor was a pale amber in color. She thought she could detect a faint aroma. It occurred to her that there was such a thing as too much subtlety.

The bouquet was stronger as she raised the glass to her lips. An intense perfume, too heavy to rise, seemed to cling to the surface of the liquor. She breathed it in as she sipped.

"Jesus Christ," she whispered reverently, unmindful of her sin.

"Who?" said Borphis.

Marcia was staring into her glass. "Never mind." She began to giggle.

It wasn't until Borphis was performing the chore of refilling everyone's snifter that Marcia chanced to think of the chores she had been given. Junna had not, she reasoned, given her any cause to think she should put off her duties, and if the sprites were any indication, she retained the powers of her ring. Besides which, it would be fun. She buried her nose in her glass. Anyway, she was feeling guilty about Borphis's cigars.

The little demon looked astonished when she brought up the subject of names. "Uh, that's right." He lowered his voice and sent a quick glance in Suzy's direction. "Three." After he had whispered them to her, rather reluctantly, she thought, she sat back and closed her eyes. She was obligated to remember all of his names. Maybe it would be better to just give him one, or three. She opened her eyes. Suzy was watching from her chair. Borphis looked like a child at a surprise party.

Marcia straightened up and put her drink on the table. "Give me the next . . . nine," she said solemnly.

Borphis reeled off polysyllables so fast that they seemed to combine into one outrageous name. This was impossible, she thought. Perhaps she shouldn't have tried this after all the food and drink. She got up and walked to the other side of the room. She thought she would see if she could remember the first three names, but when she closed her eyes, all twelve were there, as familiar as the names of the months. She smiled and pronounced them to herself slowly, feeling their weight and cadence. Names, she realized suddenly, were real things. She went back to Borphis and looked down at him.

"They are yours," she said.

Borphis looked stunned. He made an awkward bow and gestured aimlessly. When Suzy stood and raised her glass, he looked relieved. They drank to his twelve names. Borphis looked pleased but terribly conscious of the new weight of dignity that had been thrust upon him.

When they had said everything that could be said on the topic, and then a little more, Marcia's thoughts turned to Suzy. What was Suzy's real name? she wondered. She seemed to know instinctively that the dreen would have only one, and that it would be a private name known only to herself.

She gazed across the table at her. Without thinking about it consciously, Marcia shifted her view, tilted it so that forms flattened and auras fragmented, colors turned upon themselves and were rendered into shades of gray.

There was no ogre hidden inside Suzy. The form she bore was her true form, but it was . . . entailed somehow. It carried a piece of Ulda's darkness, bore the imprint of her hand. But it could be turned. It could be seized and handled, just as boundaries could, just as Regions could. It seemed to Marcia that if she would only look a little deeper, shift the spectrum yet a little further, that she would touch . . . She shrank away from the vision and focused her attention on the dreen. The form was true, but she could see the force within it as well. Suzy's strength was not like that possessed by Borphis. Borphis was weight and muscle and leverage. Suzy's strength was more abstract—and much greater.

When Marcia spoke, she heard her voice as fleshy noises and had to think to make the words. "True but not fixed. Shall I make it yours?"

She disregarded the noises that came back; took the meaning from the thought. Assent. And as she began to think how to fix the form, remove the shadow, she did it. She turned it in her mind and it was done—without thought, like blinking.

"Thank you." Suzy was standing in front of the chair. Marcia rose and looked around the room, restored now to the shapes and planes of the everyday. Colors and opacities, she thought, blinking in the light. She felt tired and even a little dizzy. What had she been thinking of? She was undeniably tipsy—little wonder!—and had been blithely performing the metaphysical equivalent of open-heart surgery on her friends.

"You are most welcome," Marcia said with exaggerated care. "But I think the party is over." She peered at Suzy uncertainly, then shifted her gaze to Borphis. She wondered what chance there was that she would remember his names in the morning. Or her own.

CHAPTER

◆ 20 ◆

Each time Marcia woke up, there was a fresh glass of water on her nightstand. She raised herself unsteadily and drank. Why, she asked herself, would she ever drink anything but water? The perfect wine she had drunk with dinner became in her memory a syrupy beverage that left a salty residue in her throat. Even the angelic distillation from the brown bottle had been nothing more than another snare, if one of insidious subtlety.

She glanced down at the little singer propped against his pillow. She smiled, then blinked and scrambled to a sitting position, but he was no longer there. Marcia stared blankly at the pillow propped against the footboard. When she leaned forward to peer through the darkness, she could feel the beginnings of the headache she knew she deserved.

Having gone so far toward getting up, she took herself into the bathroom. On the way back to the bed she considered pulling the drapes to see if the snow had stopped, but didn't bother. She walked stiffly across the chilly room and rolled back into bed. As she settled her head on the pillow, she heard the singer brush the strings of his guitar and take up his high, clear song again.

She dreamed of Borphis and his names, then of Suzy transformed from the waist down into an amphibious mermaid, hopping alluringly on green legs with tight skin and prominent tendons. Marcia was aware off and on of the pain that spread from the back of her neck to encircle her forehead. For a long while her dreams were random and close to the surface and kept her sleep from being restful, but finally she was visited by the vivid dream of last night.

She was huddled in a cramped room, dressed as before in colorful clothing that glowed against the dun bricks and floor of mud. The dream ground on, troublous images crowding her sleep in a jumble of causeless effects and formless fears. Even when she became conscious of the dream as a dream, she was powerless either to leave it or to force it into a pattern that could be deciphered.

She was awakened, finally, by a cool touch on her cheek. Junna, she thought, and opened her eyes. She sat up, ignoring the ache in her head. She was alone in the room. Even the little singer was absent, his pillow back at the headboard. Marcia raised her hands to massage the back of her neck and tried to recall just how much she had drunk last night.

In the bathroom, she considered taking a therapeutic shower, but settled for cold water on the face and back of the neck. She remembered her college remedy for the effects of late nights and cheap wine in the dorm. She wondered what the chances were that the sprites would be able to serve a breakfast of Texas chili and root beer.

It was only a little after five. She got back into bed. She wondered if her musician would come back. He didn't, but the dream did. She had barely closed her eyes when the images returned. But now she was not trapped in restless sleep; she was awake. As if to verify it, she opened her eyes and sat up.

This would not do. She got out of bed and put on a warm robe and slippers. She seated herself in the rocking chair. If there was to be no rest in sleep, she might as well indulge her passion for trying to sort out her situation. Just figuring out where she was and where she had been were challenge enough. Then there were her former companions. For instance, what was Breksin doing now?

She counted backward through the recent days. Just eight had passed since she had last seen him. According to what he had told her, he should have easily reached Devlin by now. She could not help feeling that she should be helping him. Not that he was by any means alone. Not only did he have the help of Little Egri, who could certainly be a powerful ally, but Alexander was with him as well. Marcia was not exactly sure what a necromancer was, but she knew the old man had powers. She smiled to herself as she remembered his whispery voice, his eccentric outfit of pastel silks.

Alexander! Her smile disappeared. A cloud of darkness seemed to fall on her. Marcia felt ill as she recalled disconnected fragments of her dream: the feeling of dread, the looming threat. The huddling figure beleaguered by encroaching darkness she had taken to be herself, attired for the dream in strange garments of muted pastel hues. She closed her eyes and pushed her way into her memory. She saw again the person hemmed in by darkness. As it had been in the original dream the night before, the scene was distant. She moved closer, pushing as though against an opposing force. As she slowly drew near, she could see a wall of warding magic that seemed to bleed from the little figure. He was surrounded by the web of his own spells and then, beyond that, a menacing power not expressed in spells, but as a weight of dark malice that Marcia recognized at once.

She pushed the terror away from her, stepped back from her own emotions. She forced herself to gaze into the reality of the vision. It required only a small adjustment, a slight shift of view. Now she felt divorced from what she saw, removed—an abstraction. What was all this anger, all this fear? Why these clashing emotions, when it amounted, finally, to nothing more than one illusion vying with another? She wanted to move her hand and sweep it all away—the strife, the cunning, the play of forces. And the players, too. Their strivings were an annoying irrelevancy, an inky thumbprint on the vellum of the Law.

The figure stirred. The bowed head rose. Alexander was scarcely to be recognized through the hurt and strain written on his features. Still Marcia looked on coldly. The necromancer looked up, gazed at the spot she occupied. He raised one hand a few inches. A weak smile passed across his face and then was gone as though it had never been. He stared a moment longer, then shook his head slowly and closed his eyes.

When Marcia got up, she staggered and gasped for air. She had been holding her breath, and felt as though she had been trying to lift an impossible load. She looked around her bedroom, surprised at the surfaces, the predictability of the corners and angles, the way one form impinged upon another. The heirloom rocking chair rocked, nodding at the heirloom highboy by the window.

So this was the other prisoner Suzy had mentioned. It was old Alexander they had left there to be assaulted by Ulda's malice. She thought of herself, armed with power that could bend time and twist space in ribbons, tamely following Suzy, hiding in alleyways, sheltering with the weak and timid, thinking no thoughts but of escape. She narrowed her eyes.

If Alexander was trapped in Ulda's magic, what of Breksin? Was her friend in some trap of Ulda's devising? Marcia ignored the pain in her head. She felt the tingle of the demon's scar on her cheek, a twinge from the marks Ulda had left on her arm. Did the hag want her? She would not have long to wait or far to look. She would need no snares or sorcery.

Marcia glanced down at her ring with a thin smile. Here was no circle of power, only an antique wedding band, but if the great ring was gone, much of its potency remained, of that she was certain. She could see it in her aura, feel it animating her quiet anger. Junna had taken her ring, but not her powers. How else had Borphis got his names, or Suzy's form been fixed and closed?

As the first heat of her anger lessened, she noticed her aching head again. In a reflex of exasperation, she turned her attention inward and willed the pain to cease. It took less than one second for her headache to obediently expire.

"No ring required," she said aloud. She slipped into her robe and headed for the living room with a determined step.

Suzy looked up from her chair when Marcia turned on the lights. Borphis was curled up on the love seat amid a tangle of bedclothes. He appeared to be dressed except for his shoes, which were on the floor. He looked confused.

"Did I miss breakfast?" he said as he more or less tumbled from the love seat.

"Breakfast has been canceled," Marcia said. She swept the room with her glance, then started back toward the bedroom. "We're leaving as soon as I'm dressed."

"Is something wrong?" Borphis called after her retreating figure. Marcia turned.

"You bet there is," she said, and disappeared through the door.

They were ready in less than ten minutes. They stood at the table and drank the coffee that had miraculously appeared. Borphis alternated between taking desperate swigs and stuffing biscuits into his pockets. Suzy put on the shoes Marcia had brought her from the bedroom and then waited calmly with a little smile on her face.

When she had drunk half her coffee, Marcia put the cup down. "Okay, let's go." As she took the little demon's hand, Suzy came around the table to stand beside them. Marcia reached out for her hand and pulled her to her side. Borphis looked up at her.

"Where are we going?"

Marcia caught Suzy's eye before answering. "*I* am going to Uldum," she said. Suzy's expression hardened. At that moment, Marcia had no difficulty imagining the troll-woman's hammer falling harmlessly on the dreen's face.

"What's Uldum?" Borphis asked in a worried voice.

Suzy said, "The Dark Land," before Marcia could answer.

"That's a real place? I thought it was a story."

"It's real," Suzy said grimly.

Marcia forced a smile. "Fortunately, you don't have to go with me," she told Borphis. "I'm just taking you—"

"Actually, he does," said Suzy. "The names." Borphis straightened up—seemed to stand a little taller. Marcia almost jumped. In her anger and hurry, she had forgotten about the names. She consulted her memory. They were at the front of her mind, as clear and ready as if she had known them always. She turned to the dreen, looked into her startling eyes.

Suzy nodded. "Neither am I permitted to accept your gift at night and quit you in the morning."

Marcia thought of Alexander as she had seen him in the vision. She had no time to argue about the etiquette of obligation. "All right," she said. "No more talk, then." She closed her eyes for a moment, then opened them and drew her attention inward.

It was so simple. The boundary lay just where it had to. It was unmissable when you turned your view toward it. A little shift was all it took. Then you entered. Chose your path. It required nothing more than concentration. She considered the refuge of the little mage, but saw no reason to burden him. He was clever, and had his powers, but he could do nothing to help her now.

Marcia studied Ulda's web, the structure of forces that lay over her domain. There was no difficulty identifying the place where Alexander was under attack. There were two concentrations of force. The greater lay at the verge of the rising sea where

Ulda exerted herself to contend with the will of the elements, as though she thought she could stem a rising tide.

But at another place, removed from the waters, was another gathering of shadows, and beneath it, pulses of flickering light. It was there that Marcia turned. She allowed the mists to embrace them, then stepped forward to pass from the boundary and into the heavier fog that veiled Uldum. Marcia released her companions' hands and led them forward until they were free of the mist.

Borphis did not look pleased. "We got up early to come here?" He looked up at Marcia, then at Suzy. In neither face did he find cause for cheer.

They were standing in an open field on a hill that overlooked the city. Although Marcia had hiked through miles of its lanes and alleys, this was the first time she had formed a clear idea of its size or layout. She was surprised to see that among the dark expanses were areas that appeared to be well lighted. She scanned the scene below but found it impossible in the general darkness to find the castle or the community of shacks where Ulda had put her.

Just below them on the hill was a shanty. But for being isolated, it was like the one Ulda had put Marcia in three nights ago. The hill was dark and quiet; no sound came from the little building. With an ease that she found surprising, Marcia shifted the spectrum enough to perceive the cords of Ulda's magic.

And Alexander's. He was there, and holding Ulda's force at bay, a thing he should not have been able to do. Ulda had spoken as though her power were equal to Elyssa's. Marcia didn't think that was true, but neither did she believe that Alexander, a necromancer, meaning some sort of spell worker of the Middle Regions, had strength enough to resist her.

Marcia looked around. This was going to be easy. If she could get to Alexander without attracting Ulda's attention, the four of them could be back in her apartment in time for breakfast. She started down the hill.

As they got close to the shanty, Suzy said, "There are wardings here."

Marcia told her about Alexander. Suzy looked confused. "Ulda can overwhelm any mage or necromancer with ease," she said. "I myself can breach these wardings, though only with great destruction, but his other workings might cause us harm."

Once again Marcia shifted herself to an altered plane. She studied the vision of lines and force for a moment, then dropped the view. She turned back to Suzy. "I can pass through this magic," she said. "Wait here, and I will get the necromancer."

"No," Suzy replied at once. "It is only standing with you that we have any security at all." She looked down at her feet. "You do not know how very long I was here," she said, "or what Ulda will do if I come under her power again. You must not leave us unprotected." She raised her eyes. "To me, perhaps, you have no obligation, but to one who bears names by your gift, you do."

Moving past the magic was simple. It was like traveling between Regions, but with fewer dimensional complications to keep track of. Marcia took her companions' hands and ushered them through the wardings and around the projections of force. When they reached the shanty, Suzy pushed the flimsy door open. They entered, still hand in hand, and Marcia guided them until they were safely inside the magic of the necromancer.

Alexander was huddled against a wall, exactly as he had been in Marcia's dream. He at first appeared not to notice them. He stared straight ahead, his lips moving soundlessly, his fingers working in spasms of tiny movements. Just as Marcia was about to speak, he raised his eyes and caught her in his febrile gaze.

"My girl," he whispered, "I could see you. I tried to warn you not to come." His eyes strayed to her companions. "What's this? A dreen? A demon of the dry lands? You have wandered far, my dear. Very far." He squinted up at Marcia. "But have you such power? A dreen." His eyes appeared to lose their focus. "I have always wanted to talk to a dreen." For a moment he was silent, then he shook his head.

"I don't understand," he croaked. "How do you come to be in such a place? You had no such force when I saw you last." He nodded to himself. "The vampires. You were overcome. Now you transcend Regions; travel in the company of a dreen." He looked at Suzy, then turned his glance to Borphis. "And a demon, of course," he added apologetically. Alexander shifted his position, then leaned away from the wall and pulled himself to his feet with the help of the arm Borphis extended.

He breathed as though with great effort. "And," he said after a few moments, "my spells, I see, cause you no difficulty."

Marcia felt uncomfortable, as though she had been guilty of

some breach of protocol. "It's just that I was able to avoid them," she said.

Alexander whispered, "That is what I just said." He smiled weakly. "I don't know why I'm bothering with them, really. Habit, I suppose. This witch, or whatever she is, is much too strong for me. I tricked her at first. Got away long enough to cause some trouble with the weather." His laughter was silent. "It took her quite a while to deal with the rain." He looked around the shanty as though he were seeing it for the first time. "I don't know why she has let me continue. I don't even know who, or what, she is. Or what this dark place is."

Suzy said, "This is Uldum. She is Ulda."

Alexander was silent for a moment. He looked very tired. "Then this is all hopeless," he said.

"It is not hopeless," said Marcia. "I left here with Suzy—"

"Suzy?"

"The dreen. We left here two days ago. This time we will take you with us." She smiled at Borphis. "If we leave now, we'll be back in time for breakfast," she added. She wondered if the sprites would make doughnuts. "Why don't we go outside?" she said. "Then we won't be cramped."

Alexander said, "I must make the adjustment. I had resigned myself. . . . It will take just a few minutes to dismantle the spells."

Marcia watched him as he stood muttering and making small motions with his hands. He looked pale and drawn. She decided she would put him in her bed as soon as they got back. No doubt the sprites would cook him up something nourishing to help him regain his strength. Perhaps a medicine.

"All right," he said. "I've closed down the show."

Marcia noted that although Alexander was making an effort to sound cheerful, he looked worried. She could tell that when she had time to ponder the matter, it was going to bother her greatly that she had not rescued him sooner. After the necromancer had taken one last look around, they left the shanty. Suzy and Borphis led the way through the door, with Marcia and Alexander following.

Marcia had taken Alexander's arm, and felt him stiffen at the unexpected scene that greeted them. The door of the shanty opened, not onto the lonely hill, but a large empty room. Marcia recognized the dance hall immediately. As before, the source of the room's illumination could not be detected. There was an ambient glow like that of the Lower Regions outside of Ulda's mask of darkness.

The door they had passed through was the one she had used before, but now there was no music or dancers. A few rough tables and chairs were pushed against the near wall. The ceiling was high, lost in shadows, but the room actually looked smaller empty than it had when it seemed crowded and full of life.

A single table, draped in a ragged cloth, stood in the center of the room. Ulda was seated behind it. Standing next to her chair was the wizened midget Marcia had seen in her brief vision. The rat people and the crones were not present.

"My, you *are* foolish," Ulda said in the weary voice of one whose patience has been not only exhausted, but forgotten. She put her hands on the table and leaned forward. "But I see you have returned my dreen. And what's this? A sturdy little demon." Her smile was quick and ugly. "You do well to bring gifts, little witch."

"I have brought no gifts, old woman. I have come for the necromancer."

Ulda glowered at Marcia and her companions. She turned her eyes to Suzy. "Dreen! I give you this one chance, for the sake of our long ... association. Come stand with me against these fools. And bring the little desert thing with you. Then I will deal with the stupid witch and her doddering mage."

Suzy did not answer. Borphis was as still as a ceramic garden gnome. Ulda waited in silence, then turned slowly to her single companion. The little man looked at her. Marcia noticed an almost imperceptible darkening in the air around him. It came to her that this was a summoning, a calling of some sort. Without conscious thought, she shifted the plane of her perspective so that she could view the workings of Ulda's power and see what was gathering there.

She watched with fascination as the little man—Victor, clearly—was indued with energies of Ulda's summoning, a distillation of lines of force that seemed to enter the room from all directions and converge on the hag. The forming shadow congealed and settled over him, an immense black fog that hid him from sight.

Marcia turned her view further, shifting until her gaze could pierce the cloud and see the midget wrapped in Ulda's cloaking spell. Was this some trick? she wondered. Was Ulda hiding Victor so that he could do some mischief? Marcia's arm was still linked with Alexander's. She felt his urgent grip, heard him say her name. She adjusted her view—let the spectrum settle into its habitual mode.

The thing was immense. It towered over Ulda; the floor seemed to sink beneath its weight. It would have looked like a bear, if bears had horns and long, protruding fangs and stood twelve feet tall. Its tiny yellow eyes glared down on Marcia and her friends.

Ulda ignored the horror by her side. All her attention was on the companions. "So," she said. "My dreen?" Her mouth turned into a cruel parody of a smile. "Suzy?" she called in a mocking, drawn-out whine.

The beast was forty feet away, but Marcia could hear its breathing. An unwholesome odor slowly filled the room. She thought of rotting flesh and drying blood. She seized the fear that began to shake her and thrust it away. In its place she felt the now-familiar icy touch of deadly anger. Hate, she thought in a strangely detached way, would be a better, more honest word. Without taking her eyes from Ulda, she removed Alexander's hand from her arm.

Suzy said no word. She turned to Marcia with a somber expression, then returned Ulda's stare.

"You know to keep your pet away from me," she said quietly.

Ulda looked down at the table. "Now where," she said quietly, as though talking to herself, "shall I find another dreen?" she raised her eyes to meet Suzy's. "I have not forgotten your strength," she said patiently. "Surely you have not forgotten mine." She got up from her chair and stood beside the looming horror. "I will see that you do not interfere. None of you. You will be crushed by this 'pet' of mine. Crushed and chewed and swallowed."

With its first step, the monster seemed to move much closer. Marcia felt Ulda's eyes on her, felt the cold stare seize her and hold her where she stood. The gigantic thing took another step, then another. Its breath fell on her like a foul wind.

Marcia thought of Elyssa, of Junna, and finally, of her stolen ring. Then her mind seemed to wander, to pursue irrelevancies. Odd, she thought calmly, how the floor sagged and splintered when struck by the advancing foot of the beast.

The scar on her cheek was like a tiny glowing coal. On her arm, the marks that Ulda had made there throbbed and ached. The forward step she took was involuntary. From somewhere she heard a shout, followed closely by a roar that shook the air. With a violent motion of her consciousness, she swept herself across views, dimensions, with a giddy haste. She plunged ahead into a curtain of black fog like a hound in pursuit of a hare.

The shrunken little man stared up at her in astonished terror. Marcia bore down on him in an irresistible rush until he stumbled and fell to the floor. He lay before her screaming and hiding his face behind his flailing arms. His legs kicked spasmodically a few times, then began to tremble. As Marcia stretched out her hand against him, he seemed to shrink beneath her, to wither like a dying leaf.

Marcia felt a force gather inside her. One that she could hurl at the hateful creature to destroy it. She could feel it, knew that she need only release it with a thought, a gesture, to see it smash him where he lay.

It was not out of pity that she refrained, but out of malice. She was too cruel to release him, and she knew it, and it gave her a deep and satisfying pleasure. She turned from him coldly. She pulled at the fabric of time and stepped across the dimensions she had rushed past in pursuit of the beast. She noted them as she made the passage, seeing them with greater clarity than ever she had before. Finally, she took a breath—her first since she had willed her force to rise—and let her eyes fall shut momentarily as she exhaled.

All eyes were fixed on her, but for those of the midget, who lay unmoving on the floor. Marcia looked at her friends without feeling, almost without recognition, then turned to Ulda. The hag stood gripping her chair.

The stench of the beast lingered in the room. Marcia took one step toward Ulda. When she spoke, it was in a flat voice almost too soft to hear. "If you try to touch me again—try to grip my mind—I will bring everything down, though it destroy us all."

There was a long silence. Finally Ulda spoke. "I concede your strength. I marvel at it, as it is unlooked for." She dropped her hands from the chair and walked around the table. Marcia did not move. "And," continued the old woman, waving her hand in the direction of the midget, "I am willing to grant your cruelty; it is something I can understand, something I can trust. But do not," she went on, "do not think you comprehend my power." The hag lowered her voice to an intimate whisper. "You know not, little sister. And know not that you know not."

Marcia kept her attention focused, not so much on the witch as on herself. She took a step back, glanced at her companions. *Little sister?* "We are leaving," she said. "If you try to interfere, I will use against you all the power I can find."

"And when it is done," said Ulda, "I alone will stand. But we need not contend in this way. I have no use for this worker of spells and callings. I give you leave to take him and go in peace. Only leave these others. The dreen is mine in any event. The little one"—she peered at Borphis, then glanced in the direction of the fallen midget—"you owe me for the hurt you have done my servant."

Marcia shook her head. "I will leave no one," she said quietly.

Ulda took a slow step toward Marcia, then a second. "You are strong, but ignorant. Ask the dreen. Ask the old mage. To overcome my *things* is not to overcome me. I tell you, this is a lesson you must learn now, at this moment, for without it, you will never learn another. My power is not like yours; it is not derived." Ulda drew herself up, seemed to become taller, to amplify. "I am—" She stopped and bared her teeth again, whether to smile or to sneer, Marcia could not tell.

"The demon is nothing," she said with a wave of her hand. "I present him to you as a gift. I forgive you the injury—make you free of it. Only return my property. Little Suzy—her I will not forgo."

Marcia forced her mind into cold logic. Now it was necessary that she see clearly. Not all that Ulda said was false. Her aura alone showed that the force she could call on was great beyond Marcia's ability to reckon. She gazed at the old woman, then slowly, imperceptibly, forced herself to look beyond the strange aura, beyond the rags and wrinkles.

Was everything always a trick? There were other faces there, other forms. Was there one that was more real, more true than others? No matter. Ulda would let her see none of them clearly. But what she could see was force. And force to bolster force. And then more force, half-seen, behind the force in view.

Marcia pulled her vision back to herself, pulled her own strength to a focus, gathered it, as she had seen Ulda's gathered within her. She was strong. Stronger than she would have imagined. This was something she had not known she could do. With her eyes still on Ulda, she polled the precincts of her power; glimpsed, however imperfectly, the force she could bring to bear on her enemy.

It was not enough. She was not the equal of the hag. She looked around at her companions. Old Alexander looked drawn and weary. He belonged to the Middle Regions and would be returned there. Borphis. Marcia almost smiled. The devotee of doughnuts and of pizza. The connoisseur of cognac. He was to be returned to the Lower Regions, but at a time of her choosing. And Suzy. She was to be returned as well. But returned where? What was a dreen? Marcia still did not know. Suzy stood in Marcia's casual clothes and sensible shoes. Though she was with the others, she looked isolated. A faint bleak smile played at the corners of her mouth.

Marcia turned away from her and approached the old woman. "Very well," she said. Ulda's lips turned into a tight grin as she began to walk toward Suzy. Marcia stopped and held up her hand. "As the price of leaving without interference"—she paused and Ulda nodded curtly—"I will give you my ring."

Ulda had stopped walking when Marcia did. Her eyes shifted from Marcia to the others and then back. "I am content to have the dreen. I have no need to rob you." She flashed her teeth unpleasantly at Marcia. "You know, my dear, that we shall meet again, you and I."

Marcia said, "I will not give up the dreen. I offer you this ring."

"You will give me your ring?"

Marcia heard the rustle of silk as Alexander stepped to her side. The necromancer regarded the hag, perhaps a dozen feet away, with a glance both calm and curious. When he spoke, his whispery voice rustled like his clothing. "Marcia," he began.

"You must not interfere," she replied, cutting him off. She turned to Ulda.

"I will give you my ring; you will not hinder us in any way."

Ulda sighed like a used car salesman. "Very well," she said, and held out her hand.

Marcia was closing her fingers on her ring when she was interrupted by Suzy's voice. The dreen passed behind her. She went to the midget and nudged him with her foot. The little man stirred, then gave a shriek and sat up on the floor.

"Wine," Suzy said. He stared at her for a minute, then got up and limped into the shadows. When he brought the wine, Suzy filled two glasses. One she handed to Marcia, the other to Ulda. The old woman took it without moving her eyes from the dreen's face. Suzy did not meet her gaze. She stepped away with her eyes lowered.

"Repeat your offer," she said to Marcia. Marcia said the words again.

Ulda said, "I accept." The two women sipped. Suzy took their glasses, looked at them for a moment, then tossed them away without watching where they fell. Ulda glared at Suzy, who simply nodded to Marcia and went to stand next to Borphis.

Marcia removed her ring and held it out to Ulda. The old woman approached and extended her hand, keeping her eyes locked on Marcia's.

Marcia looked down at the ring. How long would it take Ulda to discover she had been tricked? Surely she could sense already that this was not the ring she had so coveted. If not, then when she took it she would know that this was no ring of power, no talisman with a lengthy pedigree of enchantment. Marcia hesitated before putting it in the witch's hand. What would her reaction be when she saw she had been cheated? She raised her eyes to meet Ulda's, then handed her the ring.

The old woman kept her eyes on Marcia for a moment. When she glanced down at the ring, it was seemingly with scant interest. Marcia realized she was holding her breath. She exhaled slowly as Ulda slipped the ring onto a bony finger and then let her hand drop to her side. Her eyes sought Marcia's once more and then she went back to the table and sat down.

Marcia joined her friends in a state of mild confusion mixed with relief. She had expected Ulda to fly into a rage. Instead, she had acted exactly as though the ring she got was the ring she expected. Still, Marcia would not be completely comfortable until the four of them were sitting around her table having breakfast. She reached down to pull Borphis close to her.

"Just one more thing," said Ulda. Though she was in the middle of the room, she did not raise her voice. Marcia turned to face her.

Ulda sent a hard stare at Suzy and continued, "The matter of your form, O treacherous one."

Suzy took a half dozen paces in the direction of the table. She turned herself slowly, like a model, Marcia thought, except that models were rarely seen in the fashions from her closet. Ulda narrowed her eyes and leaned forward. For perhaps a full minute, she was silent and still, then she sat back and began to laugh, at the same time waving her hand at Suzy in a gesture of dismissal.

Marcia found herself wishing that Ulda would not be so good-natured about her reverses. Again she began to reach out, shepherding Borphis and Suzy into position next to Alexander, who stood a few feet away watching the hag attentively.

"How," called Ulda, "did you know to do that? To close her form? Who has coached you, touched you since you were here before?" Her gaze seemed to knife into Marcia's eyes. "Taken your ring?"

Marcia was too impatient to be coy. She felt she was aware not only of her weaknesses but of her strengths.

She said simply, "Junna," and turned again to her friends.

"Ah, Dunai," said Ulda, nodding. "Your acquaintance widens. You know Tziann and Dunai." She raised her hand to her throat. Marcia could see the glint of gold from her ring. "And, of course, Ulda." She paused for a moment. "Not to mention—"

Marcia had turned to face her again. She waited to hear what Ulda had to say. As she did she took Suzy's hand.

"And you have been so clever"—Ulda began again to laugh softly—"with your travels, your allies, your rings. . . . But here is a conundrum for you, a riddle: Which of your companions will you leave behind? Which abandon to my attentions?"

Before Marcia could answer, Suzy spoke up. "You have pledged the glass, old one. Even you—"

Ulda's howl of glee cut off her words. "Pledged the glass. Why, yes; so I did. You have always been so quick, Suzy. For a dreen."

Marcia said, "I will leave no one behind. We will all leave, as you agreed."

"I did not. Our agreement is that I will not hinder your departure. And so I shan't. But you will not take three companions with you." Marcia began to protest, but Ulda went on. "I could allow you to depart in ignorance, but like you, I am cruel. I want to see you make the painful decision."

Marcia said, "I am listening."

"Little fool! You have but two hands; you will make your crossing with but two companions. If you had the great ring, the one you were *so* clever about, you might do more. Might—I am not certain. As you are now, with everything you can muster, you will perforce leave one of your precious friends behind. I will be . . . interested to see which one it is to be."

Alexander continued to watch Ulda, his eyes narrowed as though he searched his memory.

Marcia leaned close to him to whisper. "You believe this—what Ulda says?"

The old necromancer nodded sadly. "It sounds quite plausible to me, I'm afraid. It fits all the patterns."

Marcia looked at Borphis and Suzy, then turned back to Alexander. "I will leave no one," she said softly.

"I fear you have no choice," he replied. "I think—"

"How strong are you?"

Alexander shook his head. "We cannot overcome her. You may cause her some hurt, some injury—even some loss—but she will prevail. It is as she said, in the end only she will stand."

"No," said Marcia, "physically. How far can you walk?"

"I don't know. Some way. I am not yet spent."

"Good." Marcia turned once more to face the sorceress. "We are leaving," she said. "We will walk for a while before we decide."

"Very well," said Ulda carelessly. "Protract your misery, if that is to your taste. I will even offer a suggestion: If you walk the mage to death, that will end your dilemma. I care not how you seek your pain; only that you find it. And I will know. I will watch and I will know when you leave the Lower Regions."

Marcia did not expect to find the hillside when she opened the door, and she did not. She led her troop down the stairs and through the hallways she had walked less than one week before. Alexander faltered on the stairs, and had to rely on Borphis's shoulder to make the descent. Even so, in less than two minutes, they were on the broad avenue in front of Ulda's castle. Marcia had vivid memories of standing there, of being pursued by the rat people, of her bizarre evening in the dance hall.

She brought her mind to the present. Her companions were looking at her expectantly.

Borphis rubbed his hands and looked up at Marcia with an expression that was almost shy. "That," he said, "what you did— that was even better than the gorgle. When you started toward that thing, I thought it was real—"

Suzy broke in. "It was real; as real as you, or I, or Lulu here."

Alexander looked puzzled. "Lulu?" he whispered.

"My alter ego," said Marcia. "You'll probably meet her. If we live long enough."

"Ah," said Alexander, "that brings up my next question. What are we to do?"

Marcia shifted her eyes to Suzy. "I hoped we might go far enough that we could make two trips."

Suzy shook her head.

Alexander said, "But, a portal? Might we reach a portal?"

Suzy's response was the same. "I know this place, and all the lands around."

"And the little mage?" said Marcia softly.

"Not now," Suzy said. "You would only lead her to him."

For a moment everyone was silent. Borphis looked up at Marcia.

"What about your friend, the great lord?"

Marcia looked at him with no sign of comprehension.

Borphis sighed. "You know. Rhastopheris. You told the gorgle you were looking for him."

"Oh, that was just a name I heard." Marcia looked at the necromancer. "From Alexander." She glanced down at her bare hand. *Divorced.* "You told me I should meet him."

Alexander looked around at the empty darkness that enveloped them. Finally, he turned and smiled at Marcia. "Yes. That was before. It seems like a long time ago. You are much changed. Such a meeting would now be ... more difficult. Still, Rhastopheris is ancient. There is much to be learned from him, if only he will teach it." The mage seemed to sag. He put his hand on Borphis as though to steady himself. "But Rhastopheris is far from this place, I think. Farther, surely, than I shall ever travel."

Suzy said, "Not so far, necromaunt. Not with this rising sea. We might reach him. But can he be a friend of yours?"

Alexander smiled at Suzy, and peered at her through the gloom. "A dreen," he said wonderingly, then seemed to recollect himself. "Your pardon," he said. "No, not a friend, of course. But so old an enemy that the difference blurs, sometimes. Still, I would not dare face him unprotected."

Suzy replied impatiently. "I know you are of the Middle Regions, but you are not blind. You saw Marcia with the beast. Why did Ulda not crush her, as surely she could? Because the price would be so great." Suzy reached out and touched Marcia's arm. "Show the necromancer your scratches," she suggested. Marcia turned her arm to expose her scars.

"Ulda herself made those marks, meaning to do much worse," Suzy said. "I think we need not fear Rhastopheris."

"Yes," said Marcia, "but what can he offer us?"

"Refuge?" said Alexander. "Respite?"

"At least that," Suzy replied. "The greatest lords are sovereign by long usage. Ulda will not insult him with a trespass."

"And you know where to find him?" said Marcia.

Suzy nodded.

Marcia turned to the necromancer. "Then we must leave it to you."

Alexander said, "I see no other hope at all. This, I believe is best. It even follows Ulda's logic, for if we do not reach him, you may walk me to death, though I do not—"

Suzy interrupted. "We will not walk," she said.

CHAPTER

·21·

They walked down the hill to the water, which seemed to Marcia to have risen in the days since she had first come to Uldum. Suzy led them on a pathless trek among the huts until they came to a boat drawn up just above the debris-choked water. She ignored the knot of men nearby and started to push the craft from the bank.

The boatmen were profoundly unhappy until they got a good look at Suzy. Then they were profoundly afraid. They moved away, casting worried glances over their shoulders. One, bolder than the rest, or more stupid, called out. "You'll bring her back, then?"

Suzy stood beside the craft. "No," she replied matter-of-factly. "You must build another. This one is lost."

It seemed to Marcia that there should be some sort of preparation, a discussion of water safety, at least, before setting out in a vessel that was little more than an oversize rowboat. But as soon as Borphis took water and food from supplies piled nearby, Suzy dragged the surprisingly heavy craft off the shore and held it while first Marcia, then Alexander, supported by Borphis, stepped in. Suzy gave a push, then leapt lightly across the stern and settled herself by the tiller.

In the darkness, they were out of sight of land in no time at all. Marcia looked up at the crude piece of canvas attached to the even cruder mast. She knew nothing at all about sailing, but had the impression that sails, to be effective, had to be numerous, and used in association with complicated arrangements of ropes and pulleys, all operated by swarms of shouting men wearing eye patches and cutlasses. This nautical venture seemed to be more along the lines of the one undertaken by the owl and the pussy-cat.

"How," she said after they had been at sea for less than five minutes, "do we know where to go?"

Suzy answered. "All we need to do," she said, "is get out from under Ulda's darkness. By then we will be able to see the mountain peaks in the distance. I know them all." She was silent for a moment. "It is from the mountains that I come."

"There's not much of a breeze," Borphis said.

Marcia had thought Alexander might be asleep. His eyes were closed and he was slumped against the mast. But he answered Borphis in a whisper. "Just give me a minute. Weather is a hobby of mine. We shall have a breeze. Or a gale, if you prefer."

"No, thanks," said the little demon. He was huddled in the absolute center of the boat. "I'm from the desert. I'm already having enough fun."

Alexander's breeze materialized as promised. It was no more than an hour, Marcia was certain, before the little craft slipped from under the cloud of darkness and into the eerie light of the Lower Regions. Having nothing better to do, Marcia tried to figure out what time it was in her apartment. She had completely accepted the curious idea that time here meant, if anything at all, something different from what it did at home.

She thought they had probably left the apartment no more than three hours ago. It was when she got that far in her reckoning that she remembered how Borphis had stuffed his pockets with biscuits. It hadn't seemed appetizing at the time, but now, compared with the greasy packet he had tossed next to the ewer of water, she found that the biscuits had become much more palatable.

The sea had the placidity of a stagnant pond. Nothing disturbed the surface of the yellow water but the passage of their boat and the edges of the necromancer's breeze. Far in the distance, the mountains were visible. They seemed to hang in the indistinguishable merging of the yellow sea, the yellow light, and the pervasive yellow mists. And as the sea was, to Marcia's eye, more properly a lake, so the mountains were hills; low, dark masses at the edge of visibility.

It was difficult, with no sun overhead, to mark the passage of the hours, but the biscuits Borphis had smuggled had been eaten, and Marcia was casting increasingly less skeptical glances in the direction of the other food that he had brought on board, and still the mountains seemed to be no closer. Despite Marcia's urgings, Alexander had eaten very little—part of a biscuit, a morsel of the oily cheese in the packet, and a mouthful or two of water. He sat motionless against the mast with his eyes closed.

After they had been sailing for what Marcia estimated at very close to four hours, the breeze failed. Marcia waited, reluctant to disturb the necromancer, but finally she called his name. His response was no more than a fluttering of the eyelids. Marcia moved to his side and tried to wake him, but without success. At last she leaned away from him and examined him from an altered perspective. She stared for more than a minute, then turned to the others.

"He is wandering," she said. "I am afraid he is slipping away. In any event, he is very weak." She looked at the limp sail. "I will try to raise a wind." She shrugged. "I've never done anything like that, but—"

"Wait," said Suzy urgently. "A wind at sea is no small matter. You may call upon a zephyr and summon a howling gale. You must let Borphis and me deal with this matter."

Borphis said, "Huh? My last good idea was the biscuits. All I know about boats and water is that I don't care for either of them."

Suzy stood up and walked lightly past them to pick up a pair of heavy oars that were wedged behind the ewer. She dragged them back and gave one to the little demon. "It gets fastened to that groove with the pin," she said, demonstrating with her oar.

Borphis remained where he was. "You don't mean I'm supposed to sit right next to the water there? What if I fall in?"

"So you want Marcia to row?"

Borphis moved himself with infinite care into an ultraconservative rowing position. He fitted his oar into the lock with the deftness of a salt. Marcia wondered if all demons shared his talent for things mechanical.

Suzy pointed out politely that it would be necessary for Marcia to man the tiller.

"Me? What do you do?"

"Steer," said the dreen. "Not in circles. Just keep us pointed at the second-tallest mountain." They consulted briefly to be sure they agreed which hill was the second tallest, then Suzy and Borphis began to row. Borphis was clumsy for two strokes, tentative for half a dozen more, and then settled smoothly into the work as though he had never been ashore. Marcia found the tiller to be more rebellious than she would have expected, but was able to hold the course and keep a worried eye on Alexander as well.

The rowers did not tire. Little Borphis rowed with an easy swinging motion of his upper body, moving the oar in its path with the inevitability of a machine that happened to be dressed in badly cut clothing and a battered hat. Suzy moved only her arms, and seemed to be expending approximately the amount of energy required for a good strenuous session with an emery board.

By the time they stopped so Borphis could have a drink, the hills on the horizon had moved noticeably closer. Marcia was able to waken Alexander just enough to get him to swallow some water. At one point he opened his eyes for half a second and whispered something she could not hear, then fell back into a state that was more like a trance than a slumber.

Before long they came to a place where the water seemed to clear to a less murky yellow. It was possible, in the depths below, occasionally to see a passing shadow, the bulk of some swimming thing. Soon afterward, the sea became less calm; the boat rocked a bit and tipped gently from side to side. At the same time, the temperature began to drop, first to a zone of comfort, and then quickly to temperatures that made Marcia wish she had packed a sweater.

They paused again, this time for Borphis to give up his jacket to cover Alexander. It was when Marcia was about to call another halt so that she and Suzy could contribute their blouses to the mage's coverings that they ran into the wall of heat and moisture. One moment Marcia was shivering lightly and beginning to envy her companions their warm work, the next she felt as if they had entered a hothouse or a tropical garden.

And as suddenly as the atmosphere had changed, so had their

distance from the mountains. Marcia was shocked when she looked up to find them filling her view. Even through the heavy air, she thought she could see a distant shoreline, catch the occasional vagrant whiff of vegetation.

Marcia had begun to think they would never land. They had been afloat for hours. By now the streetlights were probably on at home. She wondered what the sprites did when she was away. Would they make themselves hot rum punches and lounge around watching Marx Brothers movies? She herself did not find the thought of hot punch appealing at the moment, but she did think she could eat a couple of hamburgers and a quart or so of french fries. Even the cheese Borphis had commandeered would have made an acceptable snack. Unfortunately, it had all been eaten.

When she stepped ashore, Marcia felt wobbly. Her body had grown accustomed to the rocking of the boat, and solid ground seemed positively treacherous at first. Suzy had pulled the boat well up onto the shore. They had landed at a place where bare cliff descended to the water. Marcia had steered according to Suzy's directions, wondering how they were to land on a wall of sheer rock. When they got close enough, however, she could see the vertical seam that ran from far up the rock wall and plunged into the water.

It turned out, when they reached it, to be wide enough to admit a larger vessel than theirs. Marcia felt a twinge of fear as they drifted into the embrace of the mountain, but before she had much time to worry, the bow was scraping a shelf of rock. Suzy sprang from the boat and pulled it completely out of the water as Borphis sat gripping his shipped oar with an expression of profound relief on his face.

Marcia went to Alexander and was surprised to find his eyes open. "I must apologize," he said, speaking almost too softly to be heard. "I could not hold the breeze." With Marcia's help, he got unsteadily to his feet.

"This is excellent," he said. "I am only sorry I was not present for most of the journey. To think we have sailed a birthing sea. And these," he asked Suzy as she and Marcia helped him from the boat, "these are the cliffs where Rhastopheris makes his home?" He looked around. "He has told me often that we have chosen similar surroundings for our refuges."

Alexander sat down with his back to the rock wall. "How far is it, then, to my enemy's castle?" he asked Suzy. "I fear I cannot walk any great distance in my current state."

"It is high above us, necromaunt, but you need do no climbing." She pointed to the boat. Borphis had climbed the mast and was tearing the sail from the spar. When he left the boat, he brought the sail and the oars with him, as well as a length of waxed twine from the locker in the bow.

It seemed to Marcia that they had traveled so far from Ulda's darkness that they might now traverse Regions safely, even if they could not all travel at once.

Suzy began to answer, but Alexander spoke sooner. His voice, though barely audible, was earnest. "Only imagine your feelings when you come back here and find the one you left has been lost irretrievably. Dare you take such a risk?"

"The mage is right," Suzy said. "Except that where he speaks of risk, I would speak of certainty. We dare do nothing except from a place of refuge."

As they talked, Borphis sat apart working with the things he had brought from the boat. When he finished, he had a serviceable stretcher. Alexander was persuaded to lie in it—"lacking the power of flight, I suppose I must," was his comment—and the four began to make their way up a rocky slope strewn with pebbles and gravel that rolled alarmingly underfoot in the case of Marcia, and seemed to trouble Suzy and Borphis not at all.

A quarter of an hour brought them to a narrow opening in the rear wall, where a broad stair hewn of stone climbed until it passed from sight.

"Have you heard, necromancer, of the place where the magic failed?"

Alexander turned his head on the stretcher to look at Suzy. He nodded once.

Suzy shifted her position so that he could see the stairs. "This is the place," she said solemnly. "Here on this last step those ancient ones gave up their sea—found they could pursue the falling waters no farther, could cut into the rock no more." The dreen turned her head to look back over the round they had crossed. "Now it seems the sea pursues the stairs. Who will stand here when next the waters drop?"

Alexander waved his hand at Marcia. "Let me up," he said when she bent near. "Help me to my feet so that I might stand

on that final step, that I might walk this ancient ground." Borphis
joined him to serve as a crutch and support as the mage shuffled
to the step, then turned to gaze across the land that had once
been ocean in another age, and now would be again.

After a few minutes, Alexander lay again on the stretcher. At
Suzy's direction, Borphis took his end and climbed the first few
stairs. As he did, Suzy kept the stretcher level by raising her end
until the oars lay across her shoulders.

"Okay," said the dreen, "now Lulu steadies the oars on my
shoulders."

Marcia stared at Suzy. "Isn't that going to be a bit awkward?
I'll be tripping on your heels." She thought about it for a moment. "Anyway, what are you going to be doing with your
hands?"

"Holding you on my back."

"What? You're going to carry me? That's impossible."

Suzy faced her with a smile. "You don't know how far these
stairs go. What's impossible is that you could climb them, especially as fast as we are going to go." She nodded toward the little
demon. "Even Borphis may have to stop for a rest before we
reach the top."

Borphis spoke without turning around. "I'll be all right," he
said brusquely. "You just tell me when you're ready."

As Marcia climbed onto Suzy's back, she tried to remember if
she had ever felt this ridiculous. She clasped her arms around the
oars and tried to rid her mind of the picture of a skinny woman
whose hair was a mess being carried piggyback by a gorgeous
cover girl.

"Go ahead," Suzy called to Borphis.

Borphis stared up the steps. "How fast?" he said.

"As fast as you can manage, little one."

From time to time in her adult life, Marcia had flirted with the
idea of taking up horseback riding. By the time Borphis and
Suzy settled into their stride, she had banished the thought forever.

It turned out to be no small trick to manage a pair of oars
while riding on the back of a 120-pound girl who was running up
an endless flight of stairs. Keeping track of time was out of the
question, but it was not long before Marcia was panting with ex-
ertion and feeling the strain in her arms and her legs.

Borphis looked exhausted but smug when they reached the top

without having stopped for rest. Suzy was breathing deeply and her skin showed a ladylike film of perspiration, rather as though she had just carried six loads of groceries in from the station wagon. "You surprise me," she said to Borphis when they had put the stretcher down. "You are stronger than I thought." Borphis smiled, and breathed, but did not speak. Suzy looked closely at Marcia.

"You are all right?" she asked.

Although Marcia was in fact trying to figure out why she felt as if she had just run up the stairway with Suzy on her back, she didn't say so. "I'm fine," she replied in a breezy, if somewhat breathless voice. She paused, then cleared her throat with a dainty cough. "How much farther to the castle?" she asked casually.

Instead of answering, Suzy raised her arm and pointed across Marcia's left shoulder. Marcia peered off into the mist. Still there was the damnable yellow mist, she thought. Even on the top of a mountain.

She had been searching the distance for the castle. When she saw it she started, for it was much closer than she had expected. The squat, featureless building that Suzy referred to as Ulda's castle had all the charm of an abandoned penitentiary. The castle of Lord Rhastopheris resembled an illustration from a nineteenth-century book of fairy tales. It lay less than a mile away and stood like a black hand raised in the yellow mist. Marcia could make out towers and spires and turrets in the changeless ambient glow. She tried to guess how many stories high it was, which led her to thoughts of how exalted its proprietor might be. And how powerful.

Marcia was tired. She did not feel strong enough to drink a cup of tea, let alone vie with some supernatural heavyweight. "How much do we have to fear from this Rhastopheris?"

Suzy glanced at her, and said simply, "You are stronger." Marcia wanted to ask more, but found she was too tired.

Borphis had helped Alexander to sit up; the mage was gazing in the direction of the castle. Marcia went and sat next to him on the stretcher. After a long look at the castle, the necromancer turned and spoke to her.

"How strange that I should come here thus," he whispered. "It was only to be at my uttermost moment that I was to visit this place, if even then. Yet, here I am. Weak, perhaps, but not yet

fled the body, and perhaps not soon to fly. I expect yet in this life
to show you the roses that climb my garden wall."

Suzy said, "This may be the garden of Lord Rhastopheris, but
I would rather see his wine cellar." Marcia looked up at this un-
precedented interest in food or drink. She remembered Alexander
at tables she had shared with him. He and Suzy would be a good
pair, sipping and nibbling, and handling their napkins more than
their forks.

Borphis scrambled to his feet. "It's not me holding you up,"
he told Suzy. "You're no more interested in this lord's cellar than
I am."

Alexander reached out for Borphis's arm. "Let me but stand
and stretch my legs," he said, "and I will be ready."

A few minutes later, the procession was in motion again. Now
Borphis held the oars on his shoulders. At Suzy's direction,
Marcia walked in front with the demon. "This is not a place that
is free of dangers," the dreen said. "You must go first now."

As they advanced, the character of the landscape changed rap-
idly. They had been traversing bare rock, but as they drew closer
to the castle, they began to find weeds, shrubs, and small trees.
The air was now heavy with the smell of overripe vegetation.
The ground became softer, until they were walking on a carpet
of moss interspersed with tenacious little grasses. When Marcia
came upon a flowering vine snaking around a spindly tree trunk,
she was so surprised she brought them to a halt. The heavy,
drooping flowers looked overbred and decadent. Even inde-
cent, she thought, feeling foolish. The petals were burdened with
a deep red that might have tinted the emblem of one of the
fleshly sins.

Marcia led her party forward, wondering if moral reactions to
vegetation were as uncommon as she suspected. The flowers became more plentiful. Some were delicate little innocents with
fragile blue petals, others were sultry and looked as though they
were the product of some unspeakable excess. As they neared
the castle itself, Alexander insisted on walking.

"I will not be carried to his door. I will manage myself well
enough, I think."

Borphis rolled the stretcher neatly around the oars and pushed
them beneath a bush of thorns and dark red flowers that were almost black. They continued, Alexander supported by Borphis
and soon reached the castle.

Marcia realized she had expected a moat. There was none. A path with a look of long disuse led directly to a tall and narrow door of dark wood.

Suzy glanced at Marcia, then raised the clapper that dangled from a cord of braided leather and struck the bell three times. Alexander straightened his back and walked, still leaning heavily on Borphis, to station himself in front of the door.

When it opened, Marcia was surprised. She wasn't able to say what she had expected, but it wasn't this dapper man in black, no larger than Alexander, with pale skin and, except for his heavy jaw, delicate features. And yet this was no demonic butler, she was certain. This could only be Lord Rhastopheris.

The demon stared at Alexander, his eye straying to no one else. When he finally spoke, it was in a voice that, though soft, clawed at the ear.

"I see no spells of sealing, no workings, yet you stand at my door. How can you put yourself here? You have presumed much, old one, on our long . . . association. How can you know—" Rhastopheris was silent for ten seconds. Still he stared at the mage. His eye moved to Borphis, who bowed as well as he could without toppling Alexander.

Rhastopheris frowned. "A demon of the plains." He turned his eye to Suzy. "A dreen?" He nodded in her direction. "Most impressive," he said, turning back to Alexander. "But still, how can you, knowing me, come to the seat of all my power in this way?"

Marcia stepped forward to stand between Suzy and Alexander. Rhastopheris held her eye for one second, then bowed before turning again to the necromancer.

"I withdraw my question," he said slowly. "What trouble have you brought to my keep?"

Suzy said, "Only uninvited guests, Lord Rhastopheris, nothing more."

Rhastopheris stood in his doorway for a few seconds longer, then stepped back and waved them in. He conducted them through gloomy hallways to a cavernous room. The walls were covered with tapestries, the floor was black stone polished to a gloss. Alexander settled himself carefully onto a divan piled with cushions. He looked up at his host with a weak smile and whispered, *"Eh bien, mon prince,"* then began to cough.

Marcia wondered if her life was to be measured out in obscure rituals. It seemed to her that there were a number of really quite

pressing questions to be addressed, but the aristocratic demeanor
was absorbed in the niceties of hospitality, and most particularly
in the minute details of the serving of a welcoming drink.

It was, it seemed, to be a ceremony. Rhastopheris took a slender bottle from a cabinet and carried it to the divan, where he
displayed it to Alexander.

"We were to break this seal," he said, "on that ultimate day—
the day when every dire fury is to be released. Now we drink on
a quiet occasion."

Alexander looked at the bottle, then at his host. "But the sea,"
he said, "this is a momentous time, the turning of an age."

Rhastopheris nodded. "Indeed. But not the turning I had
looked for, though I had not looked for that one so soon, nor for
this one at all." He returned to the cabinet and took five tiny
crystal glasses like stemmed phials from a shelf. These he filled
from the bottle with a clear liquid, each precisely to the brim. He
served them from a silver tray, the first to Marcia, then Suzy,
Borphis, who was rigid with formality, like a plowman at a genteel tea, Alexander, and himself.

Marcia was prepared to sit through a lengthy toast, but
Rastopheris merely nodded and raised his glass to his guests.
The drink was strong and initially bitter, but resolved itself into
an appealing complexity that lingered on the palate most agree-
ably, and in a way that Marcia was sure even Breksin would
have trouble putting words to.

Rhastopheris remained silent while Suzy explained the reason
for their sudden appearance. The mention of Ulda made no
change in his expression that Marcia could detect. When she finished her recitation, he turned to Marcia.

"You are fortunate; you defy Ulda when she is distracted—
perhaps unhinged. The rising waters eat at her domain. They
threaten to engulf all that she has exerted herself to build and to
perpetuate. She has invested Uldum with a great network of
force—made it the seat of her power. She cannot bear to see it
lost."

"She would lose her power?"

"She would have to remove herself and everything she has in
place. She would lose, if not force, at least much labor, and for
a time she would not be the power she was." Rhastopheris
moved to a window that looked out toward the cliffs. "If the wa-

ter rises to its former limits, Uldum will be nothing but another crumbling city crushed beneath the weight of the sea."

Marcia said, "She told me her power was not derived. Can you tell me what that means?"

The demon glanced in Alexander's direction before answering. "That, I fear, is a question you must ask of one who gives himself to the study of the old books." He left the window and returned to the center of the room. "Or we may perhaps speak of these things together in the necromancer's house, which rests above another ocean, one that is more stable than ours—or thought to be. It will be . . . easier there than here to have such a discussion."

When Marcia spoke, it was in the manner of one who thinks aloud. "She called me 'little sister.' " Rhastopheris caught her eye for an instant, then turned again to the necromancer.

"You are tired, old one, and this is no place for you to rest, to recover your strength, not when you might be so easily in your own home."

"You are right, of course," said Alexander. "We must all go." He started to get up, but fell back against the cushions. "We will have a party," he whispered, and began to cough.

"The lady should not go," Rhastopheris said. "Ulda's promise to watch her is one she will keep, at least while Marcia has more companions than she can protect, and you do not want Ulda to know where you make your home. I can return you to your keep with no help. I have trod that path a hundred times by your invitation. Invite me again, now, and we shall tread it together."

Alexander nodded. Rhastopheris helped him to his feet. "Who else?" he asked. "The mage lives in solitude, as I do. I think he must have a companion for a time."

Marcia pulled her thoughts from the multitude of unanswered questions she was accumulating, and concentrated instead on Alexander's problem. When she asked him, Borphis agreed to go with the necromancer and stay until she found her way to him.

"In that, you will have no difficulty," said Rhastopheris, "for you hold his names."

Alexander said, "But you, dear girl, where will you go from here?"

"Home, I suppose," said Marcia. "And then I have to find—"

"That would be not be wise," Rhastopheris said. "If Ulda watches you still, you should not lead her to your home."

I just rent. Marcia smiled. "Too late, I'm afraid. It was in my home that she first found me."

Suzy shook her head. "No. I was with her. You were wandering and the ring caught her attention."

Rhastopheris smiled. Marcia wished he wouldn't; his heavy, sharp teeth matched his air of refinement very poorly. "And this, old one," he said to Alexander, "you will describe as chance, I suppose?"

Alexander gave a tired smile. "Lacking deeper understanding, yes, but I am willing to concede your point." He brought his gaze back to Marcia. "Better somewhere else, dear girl. . . . I suppose I should not be so informal, now. Might you not rejoin the giant? Perhaps Father has turned up."

"I had thought of that, but I don't even know if I can find Breksin. I've never been to—what is it?—Devlin."

Again Rhastopheris smiled his disquieting smile. "I don't have a deep understanding of your methods."

"That's the problem," Marcia said. "Neither do I."

"Still," the demon went on, "I believe if you focus your concentration on the one you seek, you will find him. One caution: Do not travel to another place within the Lower Regions. Once you do, Ulda may then say that the bargain has been satisfied, leaving her free to harry you if she wishes."

"I understand. But what about Suzy?" She turned to the necromancer. "Can she stay with you as well?"

Alexander looked as delighted as his condition would permit. "A dreen? Of course. I have always—"

Suzy broke in on his enthusiastic whisper to address Marcia. "You might have left me to Ulda. Should have, I would say. You closed my form; that was ample recompense for my small service to you, which in any event I performed to effect my own release. Now I will stay with you until you no longer wish it." She looked at the others one by one. "This I say in the presence of the mage of the Middle Regions and the little one of twelve names, and in the presence of the great lord of names unnumbered."

"In any event," Rhastopheris said to Marcia, "like you, I can travel with no more than two others."

That left little else to be said, and in a few minutes, having made their good-byes, Marcia and Suzy were alone in the castle of Rhastopheris.

Suzy was silent briefly, then said, "Lulu, let's *do* something. This place is dull."

"Creepy, too," said Marcia.

She took Suzy's hand and began to allow the shift to occur. Together they moved forward into the gathering mist. She saw the path that the others had taken, and saw as well that they had traveled on a different level than she used. When Rhastopheris had spoken of treading the path across the boundary, he had been speaking literally. They had walked an unearthly terrain, traversing the same realm in which, somewhere, the little mage of Uldum had his secret refuge.

Marcia found that when she focused her thoughts on Breksin, the path they traveled brought her closer to him. She could not see him, but only knew that he was nearby. When it seemed right to do so, she stepped forward, leading Suzy from the mist that surrounded them. Now she was in a . . . *place* from which she could survey her destination, just as she had when she had gone in search of Alexander.

But here there was no network of magical powers, no cage of force. Only in one area, at the edge of her view, were there workings to be seen—small flickerings of a lively, darting spell. Marcia moved closer. This was a strange, naïve magic. She thought of witches, perhaps one of no great powers, like the woman who had treated her after the adventure with the little bloodsuckers.

But even that did not seem right. This magic was being deployed. The spells fluttered to and fro like cavorting wrens. Marcia moved closer yet, still with Suzy's hand firmly in hers. She looked at her companion, then stepped forward through the final barrier of fog.

The boy was nearly hidden in the evening shadows. He was sitting by a large tree and staring intently in the direction of the nearest house. Marcia could just catch the sound of his boyish voice droning on as though he were singing the rhythm of a song but not the melody. With one hand he seemed to be keeping time with the tuneless music.

When he heard the sound of their approach, the boy jumped to his feet, snatching something from the ground beside him and holding it behind his back. He watched the two women take another step, then turned and started to run.

It took Suzy three strides to catch him. She snatched him off the ground. The boy didn't make a sound as she carried him. Suzy put him down in front of Marcia.

Marcia peered at him in the darkness. "What are you doing?" she said.

"Nothing," the boy whispered. "Just playing. Who are you?"

Marcia told him their names and asked his.

"Rickey. Chardric, really, but—"

"Well, Chardric the magician, what spells were you working?"

Rickey looked at the ground. "Just practicing," he muttered.

"Oh? And what do you have in your hand?"

"Nothing." He knit his brows in concentration, then smiled up at Marcia.

The magic was transparent. It involved a slight manipulation of the same fabric that Marcia passed through when she traveled between Regions, except that what the boy did seemed need-lessly complicated to achieve such a trivial result. Marcia reached out her hand and pulled the coins from where he had hidden them. It looked like a stage magician's trick, snatching things out of the air. Rickey stared at her with his mouth open.

"How did you do that?" he demanded. "Anyway, that's my money."

"I doubt that," said Marcia. "I think it came from that house."

"Are you a magician?"

Marcia thought for a moment. "I'm a witch," she said.

"I thought witches did things with potions or something."

"That's not the kind of witch I am. Why are you stealing money?"

"I'm not! That's my father's house, except he's dead, and now my uncle is going to make me work on the fishing boats, so I took some money to pay Jicker when he comes to get me in the morning, and that'll make up for the money he has to give my uncle for me."

Marcia looked down at Rickey. "Where is your mother?"

"With my father." He wiped at his eyes with his sleeve. "I'm not going to stay here," he said defiantly. "I'm going to be an ap-prentice to a great magician. He's staying with my aunt and me. I found him on the beach."

"A magician?"

"He was washed overboard in a storm. I found him and I'm going to get him to teach me magic. He already showed me this one spell."

"A spell for stealing money?"

"No, no. It's for *hiding*. He wrote—indited it for me and I learned it. Then I just changed it around a little. When I get it better, I'm going to show him." He paused for a moment. "He says *whilst*."

Marcia said, "Ah."

"He's from a great city and he lives in a palace and he works for a king. He's real fat."

"The magician?"

Rickey laughed. "No, the king. Rogan is kind of skinny. He doesn't like food."

"Rogan? Rogan the Obscure?"

"You know him? I told Aunt Edorra he was famous. Just like he said."

The house was by itself, beyond the village in the direction of the sea. The woman who got up when they entered was a head taller than Suzy. Rickey introduced Marcia and Suzy and went skipping through an inner door before his aunt could stop him.

"Well," said Edorra as she put water on for tea, "this is an odd place for travelers, miss. I don't have much room, but I'll work out some bedding for you here in the parlor. There's grander houses in the village, but it's a sour sort of place and I wouldn't like to send you on." She looked over her shoulder at them. "Have you eaten?" she asked.

"Not that you'd notice," said Marcia earnestly, before she remembered herself. "Oh, but we don't want to inconvenience you." She noticed Suzy looking at her strangely.

At that moment, Rogan entered the room, shepherded by Rickey.

"Greetings, ladies," he said guardedly. "Chardric tells me we are acquainted."

"We haven't met," said Marcia. "But you know my friend Hannah, I believe?"

Rogan looked surprised and glanced down at Rickey. "Why, ah, yes. We are, that is, she—"

"And Daniel," Marcia went on. "He and I are from the same city."

"Felshalfen?" said Rogan hopefully.

"No. The other place."

"Ah. I see."

Marcia was distracted by Edorra, who was putting bread and cheese on the table. From the expression on Suzy's face, Marcia doubted she would see much dabbing and nibbling from her friend tonight.

As they ate, Rogan told the story of how he came to be lost at sea.

"It was that idiot, Reffex," Rogan said. "Completely lost his head. I can hardly wait to see him; I'm going to turn him into a frog."

"Really?" said Rickey with a wide-eyed stare.

"What? No. That's a joke." Rogan looked at the ceiling. "I wish I could, though."

Edorra said, "And I wish you could turn Dilmur into a frog." She began to clear the table. "Or a man with a conscience. You might as well say he's selling the boy, his own brother's son."

"He's unpleasant, I admit," said Rogan. "But if he would put Rickey out at a better trade than fishing, that would not be so bad."

"I'm going to be a magician," Rickey said in a fervent voice.

"Now, lad, I've tried to explain to you the matter of aptitude—talent."

"He seems pretty talented to me," said Marcia. She took the coins from her pocket. Rickey turned away from his aunt and kept his eyes on the floor as Marcia described the magic he had wielded.

"But that's impossible," said Rogan indignantly.

Marcia felt a surge of impatience, almost anger. "I saw it, magician," she said evenly. She raised one of the coins, holding it lightly by the tips of her fingers. She tilted the spectrum just enough to catch the fabric and dropped the coin out of sight.

Rogan stared at her. "Witches don't do that," he protested.

Marcia reached out and opened her hand. The coin dropped into her palm.

There ensued a lengthy discussion of just exactly what it was Rickey had done, followed by some demonstrations.

Rogan was flabbergasted. "My boy, you have learned seven years' magic in a few days," he said in a shaky voice. "It's unheard of."

"This is going to mean trouble," Edorra said.

"No. Not at all," said Rogan. "The only danger is if the talent isn't disciplined." He sent a stern look in Rickey's direction. "The stronger the talent, the more volatile it is."

"What's that?"

Rogan said, "It means if your talent isn't controlled, it could burn up. Just because you can do something, doesn't mean it isn't beyond you. You must master all the details, all the simple things."

"That is not what I meant," Edorra said. "I'm talking about the money. Dilmur is a great one for keeping up his books—counts his money every night before he goes to bed, he does. And don't think he doesn't know every penny that's there."

"But why," asked Rogan, "should that be trouble for you?"

"Because Dilmur keeps his money well tucked away. But Rickey grew up in that house, and knows the hiding places, that's one thing. The other is, it would take a magician to get at those coins, and we," she said with a level gaze at Rogan, "have the only magician in the village."

"Surely," said Rogan, "a few coins—"

From outside came the sound of a distant shout. Edorra looked up. "He's bringing Jicker and the men with him," she said. In a moment, voices could be heard approaching.

"I can hide the coins," Rickey said. "They'll never find them."

"They won't care, Rickey. Their minds are made up. Remember Wincie and those nets and lines. Look how he was punished for that, and punished harshly, when they all knew he didn't do it. It makes them feel important to shout and rumble around." Edorra looked at Rogan. He was making gestures and mumbling. "By the Daughters, man, what are you up to?"

"Rebuffs," he said, looking startled. "They won't just come striding in here."

Marcia said, "Don't bother." She glanced at the lines of the spell and dismantled them with a thought.

"Hey!" Rogan looked helplessly down at his hands.

Moments later the door burst open. The first man through was tall with unruly dark hair, like Rickey's, Marcia noticed, as Edorra swept the boy behind her.

"Dilmur!" she shouted. "What do—"

Dilmur's face was dark with anger. Four or five men piled into the room behind him. "All right, boys. We know what we're looking for. If anyone gets in your way, just give them a kick." His eye fell on Suzy. "Except for this one, of course." The men's

laughter rattled against the walls. Dilmur pointed at Rickey.
"And Jicker, there's your prentice. You'll take him tonight and
we'll settle in the morning."

Marcia stood up. She felt oddly removed, as one might who
was observing events rather than participating in them.

"Don't get in the way, girlie," Dilmur shouted.

*How simple to stop his heart. How his mouth would work, his
eyes go wide with stupid terror.*

"How far is it to Devlin?" she asked in a quiet voice.

Dilmur flashed an ugly grin. "Well, boys, I think we have a
pair of Devlin whores come to visit. We'll have to make them
welcome."

He would expire in a flood of pain and fear.

"But how far is it?" Marcia asked again.

The man called Jicker spoke up. "Even with the poor winds,
less than a full day." He looked around at his companions with
a foolish smile. "If you want to arrange a passage, I'll be glad
to oblige."

Marcia looked at him calmly. "You will be taking us tonight."
She turned to the magician. "You are accepting the boy as an apprentice?"

Dilmur had been looking on with a befuddled grin. At this, he
and the others began shouting angrily. Rogan was able to quiet
them with a gesture. "Gentlemen," he said, "I believe you are
in the process of making a profound error."

"Well, let's see your magic, then, Granddad," Dilmur shouted,
then laughed as the others raised a din.

Marcia leaned toward Suzy and whispered something, pointing
at Dilmur and Jicker. Suzy nodded. She walked around the two
men. There were four others behind them. With a sudden motion,
Suzy reached out, bundled them together, and dragged them
roughly through the door.

Dilmur and Jicker stared after them, then turned to face
Marcia.

She said, "Let's arrange that passage now, shall we?"

CHAPTER
·22·

It was not much after dawn when Jicker's boat arrived at Devlin and put its passengers down on a beach of broken shells. Edorra protested when Suzy shouldered their hastily prepared bundles of clothing and other belongings. She seemed determined to pretend she had not seen the pretty young woman handle four angry ruffians as though they had been unruly children.

"I can manage," was Suzy's reply.

They scuffed their way across the shells and sand. As Rickey came fully awake and stopped stumbling, his excitement mounted. He had never been to a city and had listened with awe to Edorra's tales of the paved streets and grand buildings. Now he gazed at them in wonder.

It was just as they reached the first street beyond the salt shops that they heard a booming voice hail them.

"Rogan!" Marcia saw Breksin emerge from the door of an inn. He came toward them at a lumbering trot, his eyes fixed on the magician, an expression of pure delight on his face. It wasn't until he was near that he noticed Marcia. He stopped. "Marcia?" he said. "How, I mean, Rogan is ..."

They sorted it out, more or less, over breakfast. Rogan told the tale of his nautical mishap without drama or embellishment, noting only that he and the giant had been right about ships all along.

"So, Rogan was washed ashore near the village," Breksin said. "But how on earth," he asked, turning to Marcia, "did *you* come to be there?"

"She's a great witch," Rickey piped up. He shifted his gaze to the dreen. "And Suzy lifted four men right up off their feet and carried them out our cottage door." He giggled merrily. "Binnick got knocked silly on the post. His eyes went—" Rickey rolled his eyes, then crossed them and let his tongue hang from the corner of his mouth. Edorra began to scold him, then gave up and joined the laughter.

Though he laughed with the others, Breksin looked troubled as he glanced from Suzy to Marcia, but he did not pursue the topics of witchcraft or magic. Instead, he described his visits to the royal prisoners and explained what he knew or had guessed of the politics surrounding their abduction, as well as his hopes for their release. Then he inquired after Alexander, and looked relieved when he learned that the mage, at least, was safe at home.

Rogan looked up from his breakfast with a startled expression. "Alexander?" he said. "The nec——that is, the gentleman who dresses in rich clothing? Pale blue jacket, scarf knotted under his chin? Talks in a whisper?"

"That's the one," said Breksin.

"That's odd. He visited me, let's see, eleven days ago, looking for the shrine of the goddess, what's-her-name, Elyssana."

Marcia began to ask for details, but she was interrupted by the arrival of Egri. Suzy noticed him first. "Here is your Free One," she whispered to Marcia.

"My what?" Marcia said, but was drowned out by Breksin's shout.

"Egri," he boomed. He sounded like the Breksin she had first met, the giant who shouted his way through quiet chats imagining he was speaking just above a whisper.

Egri walked toward them slowly. He kept his eyes fixed on Suzy as he sat down next to Breksin. Marcia put her hand on the dreen's shoulder. "Egri, this is Suzy. She is with me."

Suzy said, "Little Egri," and accompanied the words with a slight nod and a mocking smile.

Marcia introduced Edorra and Rickey.

"Little Rickey," the boy said with a grin. It occurred to Marcia that Egri's answering smile was perhaps the first she had ever seen on his lips. Of all the unusual acquaintances she had made, Egri was in some ways the strangest of all.

After breakfast, Breksin went off with Edorra and Rickey to find quiet lodgings for them, and to look in on Count Reffex. Rogan, unused to rising so early, retired to Breksin's room for a restorative nap.

As soon as he was alone with Marcia and Suzy, Egri began speaking without preface or pleasantries.

"When we were together before," he said to Marcia, "you could not prevail against the little monsters, despite your ring. Now the ring is gone and you travel with . . . Suzy."

Marcia thought back to the vampires. How had they overcome her? They could be brushed aside with a thought. She looked across the table at Egri and thought of their days traveling with Breksin. They seemed to inhabit some realm of distant memories, those days of little more than a week ago. But since then, she had changed. Her ring had been stolen, returned, then taken from her again. She looked down at her hand. When she thought of the family wedding band she had given to Ulda, a sense of disquiet passed over her.

"What did Rogan say about a shrine?" she asked. "Did he mean in Ambermere?"

"Yes. Just outside the city is a small chapel dedicated to the goddess."

"Elyssana? You are certain?"

"I am certain," Egri replied. "The one who cares for the altar is a friend of my mistress."

Marcia looked surprised. "Your mistress? You live in Ambermere?"

When Egri nodded, Marcia began to say something, then paused. After a moment, she said, "Hannah. You were sent by Hannah."

"Of course."

"But, I know her. I was her adept."

"Yes," Egri said. "She has spoken of you."

"Spoken of me? You mean you knew who I was? All this time?"

"Certainly. Your name, the ring—there was no doubt."

Marcia stared at the young man. "Why didn't . . . oh, never mind." She shook her head as if to clear it. "Is Hannah in Ambermere now?"

Instead of answering her, Egri was staring through the window. Marcia turned and followed his gaze. Out beyond the Devlin reefs, a dark schooner had come to anchor and was lowering a boat.

"This is what Breksin has been watching for," Egri said. "He is afraid that those who plot against the heirs will come to do mischief before the diplomats can complete their work." He narrowed his eyes and peered across the water. "The longboat holds armed men wearing the colors of Felshalfen. There are eight of them. Hebbick is not with them."

Marcia squinted in the morning light. The longboat was no more than a tilting spot of darkness against the water. "Hebbick is the diplomat Breksin is waiting for?"

"Yes. And a boat from Felshalfen without Hebbick is what he fears."

"I see," Marcia said. For a while she was silent, then she lay her hand on Egri's arm. "Take me to this Black Jack Flanders who is causing so much trouble for my friends."

"I cannot," said Egri. "I must guard the giant. If he comes upon this company of soldiers—"

"Can you do more than the dreen?"

"No, by no means, but—"

"Suzy, I want you to see that Breksin comes to no harm. If he does not return before the soldiers come ashore, follow them. If he comes upon them, do whatever you must to keep the giant safe."

Egri looked at the dreen. "You are sure she will do your bidding?"

Suzy said, "I am bound to her, Little Egri. Sworn before a great lord. You need have no fear for your charge."

"What lord?"

"You will not know his name, Free One. He is of the Lower Regions."

"It is Rhastopheris," said Marcia impatiently. "Are you satisfied?"

Egri looked at the two women. "It seems I must be."

According to Marcia's guess, it took twenty minutes to reach the great house at the base of the cliff. Behind them, the city stretched to the harbor. Egri gazed across the rooftops.

"Soon they will be ashore," he remarked.

Marcia looked, but could not make out the longboat against the water.

There were armed men outside the pirate's door. As they approached, one bawled at them, "Too skinny." The others laughed.

Marcia walked up to the noisy one. "Take us to Jack Flanders."

"Naw, he likes 'em with more meat. Bounce, he calls it." The man bared his teeth at her and winked. "She'll do better in the town," he said to Egri.

"Thank you for your kind advice," Marcia said, speaking in a lilting voice. When the man leered at her, she trapped his gaze in hers. "Now," she said in a voice greatly altered, "take us to Jack Flanders."

The man turned meekly and began to lead them to the door. His comrades raised a laughing protest, but fell silent under Marcia's stare.

"The cap'n? He's asleep," said the disheveled man who opened the door. "Hell, I'm asleep. Come back in the afternoon." He began to close the door, but Egri held it open. The man gave him a kindly look and rested his hand on the knife at his belt.

"Laddie," he said in a voice of mild affability, "trifle with me and I'll slit you crotch to crown." He gazed at Egri with the air of a master craftsman appraising a piece of material. "Open you right up," he said.

The man jumped when Marcia put her hand on his shoulder. He stepped back from the door and watched with a look of dumb shock as she and Egri entered and closed the door behind them. On Marcia's command, he led them to a room at the end of a hallway on the second floor.

Their knock at the pirate's bedroom door was greeted at first with silence, then with a shouted profanity, and finally with the impact of something heavy and breakable striking the other side of the doorframe.

Marcia waited, then knocked again. After a moment, the door was opened by a rather fleshy naked woman who stood blinking at them stupidly. Behind her in the darkened room, the pirate was sitting up in his bed glaring at the open door.

The woman began, "Jackie says—"

Marcia interrupted her. "Go with him," she said, pointing to the man who had brought them to the room. The woman stepped obediently into the hall and joined the staring man. Marcia looked at him for a moment, then at the naked woman that filled his eyes.

"Go to bed with him," she said, waving them away.

"And they say women aren't good tippers," she said to Egri. He answered her with an expressionless gaze. *Like a cat,* she thought. "The truth is, Little One, all this begins to weary me." From the bedroom came a querulous shout.

Egri said, "What do you mean to do?"

"I mean to have a discussion with the pirate king. He is going to follow my suggestions, or he is going to"—she paused and peered into the bedroom—"drown in the air he breathes. In other words," she laughed, "I am going to make *Jackie* an offer he can't refuse."

When Breksin saw the ship in the harbor, he hurried back to the inn.

"Nay, Master Breksin," said the innkeeper. "You've missed them. Half a dozen or more Felshalfen soldiers went right up the avenue, they did."

"And was there an older man, gray, a bit stooped, with them?"

"Nup. Just soldiers. And led by the nobleman with the scarred cheek. I know him from seeing him pass this way before."

On his way out, Breksin called, "Did Egri—the dark-haired boy—did he follow them?"

The innkeeper's answer stopped him. "He went off with the one girlie, he did. Then the other, the little beauty, she took off behind the troop."

Breksin took the stairs to his chamber two at a time. When he clumped back down seconds later, his hammer was at his belt.

After covering four blocks at his longest stride, Breksin was relieved to see the men just at the next crossing. As he drew near, he counted eight in the squad. He might manage them all, he thought, but the important thing was the nobleman. That enemy dispatched, he could think about the luxury of survival.

When he got near enough, he hailed the troop with a shout. At that moment, he saw Suzy standing in the shadow of a building. A pleasant enough last sight, he thought in a quiet corner of his mind.

When the men turned and saw a giant with a battle hammer, they unsheathed their swords without waiting for an order.

"Where do you go?" he called.

The leader stepped forward. "Where we will," he spat. "Must we cut you down on our way? They say hill men bleed a long time."

"I only ask where you go."

The man with the scar looked toward the harbor. "We have no time to chat," he said. "There are meddlers enough behind us without you. Move away or die."

Breksin put his hand on his hammer. "I protect the heirs of Ambermere and Felshalfen," he said.

Again the man glanced to the harbor. "Heirs?" he laughed. "You are mistaken. I serve the heir to both those crowns. If you serve the pretenders, you are my enemy. On my command!" he called over his shoulder.

As Breksin snatched his hammer from his belt, he noticed Suzy from the corner of his eye.

"Keep back!" he called to her without taking his eyes from the soldiers. The nobleman was stepping out of the way. Breksin noted the arrangement of the other men, plotting out the shortest path of corpses by which he could be reached.

"Strike!" came the call from behind the squad.

As the men surged forward, Suzy skipped into their path. They hesitated for an instant as the pretty girl came toward them. When Breksin thought about it later, he remembered the moment as sad and almost touching.

Suzy struck them like an avalanche, driving the troop to the ground with crushing force. By the time Breksin had taken two strides, the street was littered with battered, groaning men.

Breksin was still trying to conquer his astonishment and confusion when he was surprised by the arrival of a squad of the Felshalfen Royal Guard. He raised his hammer and shouted a warning to Suzy, then heaved an oceanic sigh when he recognized Hebbick.

The diplomat greeted Breksin and surveyed the scene. "My, my," he said with a calm smile. "My, my."

Breksin, Suzy, and Hebbick left the nobleman and his troop in the care of the royal guard and followed the avenue to the cliffs. Outside the mansion of Black Jack Flanders, men were beginning to load a wagon with trunks. Just inside the door they found

the pirate king bidding farewell to his royal guests in a tremulou
whisper.

Hebbick surveyed the scene. "It seems I was not needed," h
remarked. He bowed to the prince and princess, then looke
more closely at Jack Flanders. "Captain," he said, stepping to hi
side, "I hope we do not find you ill. You are pale as death."

The pirate turned to him slowly. "I have had a difficult morn
ing," he whispered.

"Oh, dear," murmured the diplomat. "How unsatisfactory fc
you. Perhaps we should have our little talk later when you ar
more yourself."

When the royal party and the others left his house, strollin
beside the squeaking wagon, Black Jack Flanders watched ther
from the open door like a host reluctant to see his guests depar

"What did you *do* to him?" Daniel asked Marcia the first tim
he got a chance to talk to her alone. They had all gathered in
quiet tavern.

Marcia's expression was somber. "More than I should have,
she said as they were joined by Modesty.

"Breksin will not come with us," Modesty reported to Danie
"He says he is satisfied that the Felshalfen troops that guard ▪
are *real* soldiers." She turned to Marcia. "And you," she sai
"the mysterious friend from my husband's mysterious home, ha
he changed your mind?"

"He has made it most attractive," Marcia replied, "but I hav
other duties that will not wait."

When Modesty left Breksin, he made his way to where Suz
stood alone by a window. "I must thank you properly," he rum
bled, "for saving my life."

Suzy smiled up at him. "I think the lives I saved were tho:
of your enemies. There were no such battlers among them ▪
you."

"Or you," Breksin replied with a troubled frown. He hesitate
then went on as though with reluctance. "I saw a sword stril
you," he said in a voice just above a whisper. "Square and heav
there." He pointed to her shoulder.

"It troubles you, then," said Suzy, "that I am not what
seem."

He looked down at her. "You are a girl. Pretty. Soft. And then you . . ."

"And you, giant, are known as the royal cellarer. The sampler of wines, turner of cheeses. Guardian of sausages." Suzy stepped closer to Breksin. "And yet," she went on in a soft voice, "I saw in you a warrior, a killer. I saw your eyes change as you turned your mind to murder. If you had crushed those men today, their blood would not have been the first to stain your conscience."

Breksin looked relieved when his conversation was interrupted by the arrival of Edorra and Rickey, and just behind them, Rogan the Obscure.

When they were presented to Iris and Hilbert, Edorra was calm and dignified, but it dazzled Rickey to be introduced to a real prince and princess. A few moments later, he looked up at Rogan as if he had never seen him before.

That afternoon the royal party set sail for Felshalfen. Rogan had declined the invitation to accompany them. Hearing of this, Count Reffex decided that his "duties" included a trip to Felshalfen. He managed to avoid the magician entirely by boarding the ship several hours in advance of its departure.

Rogan declined as well a cabin on the ship that would return Hebbick to Ambermere in a few days. "Breksin and I shall walk," he said, adding that he didn't care if it took a hundred years. Rickey was determined not to leave the side of his new master, and Edorra was willing to permit it as long as she went with them. Breksin began to tell her of the hardships they might meet, but she cut him off. "I can walk, sir," she said. At that, Breksin said no more, but watched her stride off as though he had just noticed her for the first time.

To avoid worrying her friends with an inexplicable disappearance, Marcia delayed her departure until Breksin and his company set out for Ambermere in the morning. She and Suzy walked with them to the mountain road at the edge of the city, then watched them until they passed from view over the crest of the first hill.

When they were alone, the two women joined hands, and were gone.

CRAIG SHAW GARDNER'S
FUNNY FANTASIES!

"A lot of fun!"-Christopher Stasheff

The Ebenezum Trilogy

On a road fraught with peril and dark magic, the mighty wizard Ebenezum and his hapless apprentice, Wuntvor, search for the City of Forbidden Delights.

__A MALADY OF MAGICKS 0-441-51662-9/$3.50
__A MULTITUDE OF MONSTERS 0-441-54523-8/$3.95
__A NIGHT IN THE NETHERHELLS 0-441-02314-2/$3.50

"A fun romp!"-Robert Asprin

The Ballad of Wuntvor Trilogy

With Ebenezum still suffering from his allergy to magic, Wuntvor sets off on his own to seek a cure. But before he does, he'll have to outsmart the dread rhyming demon Guxx Unfufadoo and Mother Duck herself!

__A DIFFICULTY WITH DWARVES 0-441-14779-8/$3.95
__AN EXCESS OF ENCHANTMENTS 0-441-22363-X/$3.50
__A DISAGREEMENT WITH DEATH 0-441-14924-3/$3.50